ENTANGLED

The Duel, Book 1

Mary Lancaster

Text by Mary Lancaster
Cover by Dar Albert

Dragonblade Publishing, Inc. is an imprint of Kathryn Le Veque Novels, Inc.
P.O. Box 23
Moreno Valley, CA 92556
ceo@dragonbladepublishing.com

Produced in the United States of America

First Edition March 2023
Trade Paperback Edition

ARE YOU SIGNED UP FOR DRAGONBLADE'S BLOG?

You'll get the latest news and information on exclusive giveaways, exclusive excerpts, coming releases, sales, free books, cover reveals and more.

Check out our complete list of authors, too!

No spam, no junk. That's a promise!

Sign Up Here

www.dragonbladepublishing.com

Dearest Reader;

Thank you for your support of a small press. At Dragonblade Publishing, we strive to bring you the highest quality Historical Romance from some of the best authors in the business. Without your support, there is no 'us', so we sincerely hope you adore these stories and find some new favorite authors along the way.

Happy Reading!

CEO, Dragonblade Publishing

Additional Dragonblade books by Author Mary Lancaster

The Duel Series
Entangled (Book 1)

Last Flame of Alba Series
Rebellion's Fire (Book 1)
A Constant Blaze (Book 2)
Burning Embers (Book 3)

Gentlemen of Pleasure Series
The Devil and the Viscount (Book 1)
Temptation and the Artist (Book 2)
Sin and the Soldier (Book 3)
Debauchery and the Earl (Book 4)
Blue Skies (Novella)

Pleasure Garden Series
Unmasking the Hero (Book 1)
Unmasking Deception (Book 2)
Unmasking Sin (Book 3)
Unmasking the Duke (Book 4)
Unmasking the Thief (Book 5)

Crime & Passion Series
Mysterious Lover (Book 1)
Letters to a Lover (Book 2)
Dangerous Lover (Book 3)
Merry Lover (Novella)

The Husband Dilemma Series
How to Fool a Duke

Season of Scandal Series

Pursued by the Rake
Abandoned to the Prodigal
Married to the Rogue
Unmasked by her Lover
Her Star from the East (Novella)

Imperial Season Series

Vienna Waltz
Vienna Woods
Vienna Dawn

Blackhaven Brides Series

The Wicked Baron
The Wicked Lady
The Wicked Rebel
The Wicked Husband
The Wicked Marquis
The Wicked Governess
The Wicked Spy
The Wicked Gypsy
The Wicked Wife
Wicked Christmas (A Novella)
The Wicked Waif
The Wicked Heir
The Wicked Captain
The Wicked Sister

Unmarriageable Series

The Deserted Heart
The Sinister Heart
The Vulgar Heart
The Broken Heart
The Weary Heart
The Secret Heart
Christmas Heart

The Lyon's Den Series

Fed to the Lyon

De Wolfe Pack: The Series
The Wicked Wolfe
Vienna Wolfe

Also from Mary Lancaster
Madeleine
The Others of Ochil

CHAPTER ONE

"I HAVE NO time for the Landons. They would be nobodies if they were not so deliberately eccentric. And as for *Michael* Landon, the fellow was promoted over better men and a coward to boot."

The duke's sharp voice cut through the genial conversation like a sword.

In the George Inn's parlor, chatter died away to uneasy silence.

The two parties of gentlemen—the duke's and the group of army officers—had amiably agreed to share the inn's only private room and had enjoyed a simple, pleasant supper and a few card games. They had also shared a fair amount of postprandial brandy and cigarillos. As a result, the room was thick with smoke and the smell of spirits.

Major Giles Butler, whose head was harder than most, but who, up until now, had been enthusiastically enjoying the company, set down his glass with deliberation. His friends clearly recognized the sudden change in his manner, for their own outrage suddenly drowned in anxiety. Butler sought and found the direct gaze of the duke.

His Grace, the Duke of Cuttyngham, was a distinguished looking man in his forties. His dark brown hair might have been graying, his face growing a little pouchy, and a paunch developing at his middle, but no one would ever have mistaken him for other than a top-notch aristocrat.

One of the duke's sycophants let out an annoying, nervous titter. Others glanced uneasily at the military men, particularly at Butler.

"I assume you do not refer to Colonel Michael Landon of the 148th," Butler said mildly.

Now was the moment for the duke to back down, to say of course not and turn the subject, but somehow Butler knew he would do no such thing. It was not in the duke's supercilious nature to back down, to change his mind, or even to placate.

"That's the fellow," he said. He even smiled. "I hope he was nothing to do with you fine officers."

Butler stared. "He was my colonel." *My comrade and my friend.*

"My commiserations."

It could have meant anything.

"The duke is nothing to us," Mac breathed in Butler's ear. "Let it go."

But Butler could not. Simmering with rage, he stood and snatched up his glass. "To Colonel Landon of the 148th. A great man, a fine officer."

His comrades stood with him. "Colonel Landon!"

They all drank. Most of the duke's party were happy enough to drink to a dead man they had never met and did so.

Butler sat down again.

"Sadly," the duke said into the silence, "I cannot drink to a coward who let down his king, his country, and his own men."

The titled fellow beside the duke—a Lord Frostbrook—closed his eyes. Someone groaned.

Butler felt a pulse begin to beat in his temple. Very carefully he said, "Perhaps Your Grace would explain to us, who knew him well, how you reached such an erroneous opinion?"

"The man was an upstart," the duke said contemptuously, "of no great family or distinction, promoted over the heads of better men of my acquaintance. But blood will out. When tested in battle, he ran."

The utter untruth took Butler's breath away. It was so wrong that for an instant, his grief and rising fury stood aside for simple curiosity. "What the devil makes you believe such arrant nonsense?"

The duke stared at him, clearly stunned by having his opinion contradicted. "The French bullet in his back, sir. A man is not shot in the back if running *toward* his enemy."

The sheer injustice of that, to Landon, to his widow and children, to his regiment, slammed into the rising, reckless rage that had carried Butler safely through several forlorn hopes.

"Your Grace is mistaken," Butler uttered, his voice barely controlled. "No doubt from lack of experience. Colonel Landon was no raw recruit. He rose through the officers' ranks with distinction. As for the rest, do you really imagine the chaos of battle to be two lines rigidly facing front and taking the odd, gentlemanly poke at each other? Never turning any way but forward to fight, or to see one's men, or to give orders or encouragement? One is spun in all directions, whether by an enemy or a blundering or dying man, by a weapon or a shot. One receives and acts on orders to move position."

The blood sang in Butler's ears as he shook off whoever was trying to drag him away by the arms. Nothing could have stopped his rising voice. "I take leave to tell Your Grace that not only have you slandered a man of unimpeachable courage, you display the crass ignorance of a pampered imbecile!"

Again, silence filled the smoky room.

The duke blinked several times. A muscle twitched at the corner of his aristocratic mouth. "Since you are an officer, I suppose you must be a gentleman. Name your friends, and mine will call upon them."

"MacDonald, Elton," Butler snapped and marched out of the room. He barely noticed that all the officers came with him.

IT TOOK A long time for his temper to calm. He seethed alone in the room he was sharing with his friends, until those same friends walked in quietly and closed the door. They looked serious and rueful.

"I hope you haven't bound me to go to London a week today," Giles said. "I have a ship to catch, and so do you."

"Which is why we arranged it for this morning," Mac said with a hint of grimness. "The duke's seconds want discretion, as well, though for his sake rather than the Landons. None of us want a killing affair, Lune."

Giles didn't even smile at the nickname—Lune, short for Lunatic—which had been bestowed upon him years ago after a spectacularly reckless single-handed rescue. "I won't kill him," he said impatiently.

Elton scowled at him. "You know it's conceivable he might kill you? He shoots at Manton's and is considered a fine shot. Moreover, he's used to handling delicate dueling pistols. You're more of a rifle man."

"I am," Giles acknowledged.

His seconds exchanged glances, then Mac said, "An apology would end this. His Grace of Cuttyngham is clearly ignorant and just plain wrong about the colonel, but you shooting at each other won't change that. According to Frostbrook—his second—he will never apologize. But if *you* were to apologize—" He flung up his hand to ward off Butler's furious objection and continued, "If you were to apologize for rudeness—and you *were* rude, you know. You can't go around calling a duke of the realm a crassly ignorant, pampered imbecile to his face, even when he is. So, apologize for that. His Grace will very probably accept that apology and all is well."

Giles stared at him.

"You wouldn't be admitting he is right," Elton pointed out,

"just that you were rude. And then you come off to Brussels with the rest of us, healthy and whole to fight Boney."

"And he goes off on his own way," Giles said furiously, "telling whomever will listen that Michael Landon was a coward and a bad officer! I won't have that. It isn't fair on his memory or on his poor widow."

"No, it isn't," Mac agreed. "But Frostbrook assures us his friends will make sure the subject never comes up again. The duke's seen how strong the feeling is among Landon's fellow officers. Frostbrook thinks he'll leave it alone. If you do. Besides, Wellington will be furious if you're fighting duels rather than battles."

Giles sprang to his feet, pacing relentlessly. Then he tugged once at his tousled hair. "I can't," he said abruptly. "We'll get it over with quickly and quietly, and I'll make damned sure not to kill him. Or even hit him."

"And if he kills you?" Mac demanded. "Or even injures you?"

"I've been injured before. I'll just have to take that chance." He paused in his pacing, glancing from one to the other. "I can't leave it," he said with difficulty. "I can't."

Elton, who knew how deeply he felt the loss of Landon, gripped his shoulder and sighed. "We know. But we had to try."

GILES BUTLER LEFT the inn and faced his fate in the cold, wet dawn. Hardly the first time he had done so but confronting the general enmity of the French seemed very different from this much more personal affair.

"You can still stop this," Mac murmured as he arrived at the little huddle within the woods. "The duke is still willing to accept your apology."

"For what?" Butler asked flatly. "Defending my friend who died for his country?"

"You know for what," Elton growled. "Then we all live to fight another day in a cause that matters. You do recall that Bonaparte has escaped from Elba and is back in Paris, just waiting for you to trounce him?"

"Boney must wait in line," Butler said implacably. Although the rage of last night had vanished, he could no more withdraw from this fight than he could any other. To do so would dishonor Landon, his colonel and his friend whom the duke had so casually impugned.

"Then let's get it over with," Mac said briskly. "Ten paces each, turn and fire, and for God's sake, stay focused."

Giles followed him to where the Duke of Cuttyngham and his seconds were gathered in the middle of the clearing. Lord Frostbrook, expressionless, held open the case containing the dueling pistols, which the seconds had already agreed to. Without looking at each other, the duelists lifted one each.

"Your seconds will have told you they have hair triggers," Frostbrook warned.

Giles nodded curtly. He met the glare of the army surgeon, Justin Rivers, who was scowling at him from the side.

"No wonder they call you Lune," Rivers had snarled at him five minutes earlier. "As if there aren't enough ways to die in war. Couldn't you wait?"

If Giles apologized to anyone, it would be to Rivers, who would patch him up if the duke hit him.

"Ready, gentlemen?" Frostbrook murmured.

Giles and the duke stood back-to-back, and the count began. Giles cleared his mind of all but the count and the necessity of staying alive and not killing his idiot opponent. Walking forward, he held the beautiful pistol loosely in his right hand at his side.

Something moved within the trees, some yards ahead of him. Someone watching—a female figure he had no time to consider. On the count of twenty, he turned, presenting his right side to the duke, and raised his pistol in his steady hand.

Cuttyngham's posture mirrored his own. Giles took aim at a

point well to the left of the duke's shoulder and touched the trigger.

The duke staggered to the left as twin explosions rent the air, and then crumpled slowly to the ground.

Dear God, how in hell did I hit him?

Without conscious volition, Giles dropped the pistol and ran toward his opponent. Somewhere he registered that *he* had not been hit, although the duke had definitely fired.

Dr. Rivers pushed the duke's seconds out of the way and dropped beside his patient.

Even the birds seemed to have stopped singing. Mac grasped Butler's arm.

"He moved," Giles said, his voice sounding as dazed as his brain. "He moved to the left..."

The duke lay unmoving on the ground. Rivers had already cut away the coat and the shirt covering the man's shoulder. There was hardly any blood, which gave Giles a moment of hope before Rivers raised his head and looked directly at Butler. "He's dead."

The world tilted.

"He can't be. I aimed well to the left..."

"You killed him," exclaimed the other second, who wasn't Lord Frostbrook. He sounded hysterical. "I'll see you hang for murder if it's the last thing I do!"

"He knew the risks, Severne," Frostbrook said briskly. "We all did. I'll need your help, gentlemen, to get his body to the coach."

Mac tugged Butler's arm. "We need to go. Now."

"Go where?" Giles asked. His voice seemed to come from very far away. He had just killed a man, a civilian.

"Out of the country. Brussels. Wellington might support you, at least until after Boney's dealt with."

Giles shook him off and addressed the duke's seconds. His face felt cold. "My condolences on your loss. Does he have family?"

"A wife and two children, fully grown," Frostbrook said briefly. He indicated the other, grief-stricken second who was bent over the body. "And a cousin."

A wife and two children. Just like Landon. Giles had not even the excuse of war to have deprived them of their husband and father. And how in God's name did what he had done help Mrs. Landon?

He dragged his shaking hand through his hair.

"I will have to tell them," Severne mourned. "The duchess will be devastated… And Hera. Christ, poor Victor is now the Duke of Cuttyngham, God help him!"

Giles turned and strode away. The watcher he had glimpsed earlier vanished in a flurry of skirts. It didn't matter now that someone had seen. The Duke of Cuttyngham had just died of a bullet wound to the shoulder. There was no way the duel could now be kept from the rest of the world.

THE DUCHESS OF Cuttyngham had planned her escape with care. The anonymous lease of a cottage, the saving of pin-money, the arrangements for her journey. The duke, her husband, was on his way to Cuttyngs, so it was time to go.

Having dismissed Perry, her very superior dresser, she threw the few things she needed into a carpet bag and the saddlebags she had hidden beside it. She called in at the duke's rooms to leave her letter among his other nonurgent correspondence.

As she made her way down the grand staircase, she wondered if she would find herself missing anything about this fine, gracious house. It was almost a palace, and yet it had never been home. Changes were frowned upon by her husband and greeted with indifference by his children. His children who were, respectively, three years older and one year younger than she. Hera was in the midst of her second Season in London. Victor was, as usual, buried in the library.

Once, she had foolishly imagined her stepchildren might be her friends and allies. But Hera had only ever wanted to escape her father and Cuttyngs, and had even chosen an aunt rather than her stepmother to sponsor her in London. His Grace, the duke, had merely shrugged. Victor barely spoke to her, although he was never actually rude. He lived in his own world of academia, and the only time he had actually smiled at her–a quick, rueful grin of understanding–was when she had suggested to His Grace that Victor go up to Oxford as he wished. He had known, of course, that his father would refuse.

"He won't cope," Cuttyngham had snapped. "The place is full of stairs and well-bred louts who can barely conjugate a verb. And all several years younger than him."

It was this memory that caused the duchess to detour to the library now. She propped her bags against the wall and stuck her head around the door. Victor, the Marquis of Dean, heir to the Duke of Cuttyngham, was walking with one stick, his gait uneven and ungainly, as he carried several books to his already heaped desk.

"I'm going for a ride, Victor," she said when his gaze clashed with hers.

He nodded curtly. As always, his angelically beautiful face was scowling, though whether with pain or mere annoyance at life, she had never discovered. And now never would.

"Goodbye, Victor," she said lightly and whisked herself out again. If he would take her advice, he would simply go to Oxford and to the devil with his father's objections.

It was a pleasant May morning, perfect for a long ride to freedom. With her saddlebag over one arm, artfully hidden by the scooped-up train of her riding habit and her carpetbag gripped in her other hand, she felt like singing.

Until she got to the stables.

She had chosen her time carefully, for when she knew the grooms and stable boys joined the house staff for a mid-morning break in the servants' hall. She could then saddle her own mare and leave quietly without the servants seeing exactly how much baggage she was taking on her ride. She wanted to leave no clues that she had taken a longer ride than to the village and back. If anyone noticed she was missing, they would waste time combing the countryside nearby rather than following her.

However, before she set foot in the stables, she knew from the horses' restless behavior that someone else was in there, presumably a relative stranger.

Drat! Laying down her bags once more, she crept into the building, wondering if she could extract the mare unnoticed. She would still need to collect the saddle and bridle from the tack room…

A man's back came into view in one of the stalls. Gregson, His Grace's groom, who was meant to be with him. Now what the devil was he doing here before the duke? Unless… Surely Cuttyngham wasn't home already? Even if he was, why would Gregson be trying to saddle the horse Cousin Anthony stabled here?

She didn't like Gregson. She was sure he tattled and even told lies about her—and about others—to the duke. But he'd been Cuttyngham's groom forever, and His Grace would never consider dismissing him.

No, she would have to give up the idea of riding. She'd hire the gig from the village inn and pick up the mail coach in the town of Cuttyngham. The decision made, she backed out of the stables, picked up her bags, and hurried on foot down the path to the main drive. She would have to hurry to avoid the risk of being seen by the gardeners.

The gate at the foot of the drive was open, though Old Dan at the gatehouse was gossiping with someone in his little garden. Ducking down lower than the hedge, she scurried past the gatehouse, out the gates, into the road, and around to the right, away from Dan, before she straightened and became aware of several things.

Two saddled horses stood in the road. One, a large chestnut, was a stranger to her, but she recognized the other as one of the duke's. His name was General. General snorted by way of greeting, and she stepped back, looking around uneasily for signs of her husband.

Not the duke, but a tall, slightly lanky soldier stood a few yards away, watching her with interest. He wore the blue and gold uniform of an officer, though without a hat, which hung instead from the chestnut's saddle. His hair was something the same shade as his horse's, his expression curious though not unfriendly.

He was also a complete stranger, for which she had to be grateful since he had observed her sneaking past the gatehouse and peering around like a hunted deer for signs of her husband.

She tightened her grip on her carpetbag and smiled tentatively at him. A faint twinkle dawned in the stranger's eyes, which were very dark and yet extremely lively as he strolled toward her.

"I can't make up my mind," he said with clear amusement, "whether you are hiding or seeking."

"Neither can I," she admitted, although the seeking was more to aid the hiding. "I don't suppose you've seen anyone else lurking about?"

"Such as the rider of that horse? Do you suppose he has taken a fall somewhere?"

"No." She supposed, in fact, that he was currently in the Cuttyngs stables saddling another horse. Why? What the devil was Gregson up to? Leaving General in the road to fetch another horse smacked of secrecy. It must surely mean that the duke was not home, and yet Gregson could appear at any time and see her with her bags—as could Old Dan, his visitor, and any other passer-by. Such as this soldier.

She took a deep breath. "I shouldn't worry. One of the stable staff will no doubt be down directly to see to General here. And I must be on my way. Good day, sir."

He frowned as she turned away. "You have a heavy load

there if you mean to walk."

"Not really."

"Why don't you use the horse?"

She turned back in surprise. He really had the most beguiling eyes—mischievous and ready to laugh, and yet behind the constant twinkle she could almost imagine sadness.

"He does not have a ladies saddle," she pointed out.

"But he is a stout enough fellow to carry your bags."

A breath of laughter took her by surprise. She would rather like to see Gregson appear with his newly saddled horse and discover that with General gone, he would have to return and prepare yet another horse. The stables' quiet time would be over, too, and he would be seen.

General ambled toward her, as though he, too, thought it a fine joke.

Her lips twitched. "Do you know, I think I might?"

"Allow me," the officer said, lifting the saddlebag from her arm. While he slung it across General's back, she stroked the big horse's nose. The officer took the carpetbag, too. His fingers brushed hers, casual and impersonal, before he secured it to the saddle with brisk efficiency.

And then, the distant sound of a horse's hooves on the drive reached her ears.

"Oh, the devil, he's coming now," she breathed. "Quick!"

The soldier's eyebrows flew up. "You don't want to be seen? Come, then, which way?"

She had planned to go to the village, but to do so with General would be noticed. She pointed in the opposite direction and hoped Dan had gone inside. And then she could only blink as the officer leapt into action.

By some means she barely saw, he sprang into the saddle of his own horse, and reached down to her for General's reins. She gave them, in a bewildered kind of way, and realized his hand was still held down to her.

Sharing a saddle with a stranger was unthinkable, but she

could not ride General. In the soldier's saddle, he could at least stop her sliding off. And the clop of Gregson's horse drew nearer.

In desperation, she seized the soldier's hand and jumped. She landed surprisingly lightly in the saddle before him. The horse was already wheeling around and then it surged forward, causing her to gasp and grab hold of the soldier's arm and coat.

A ripple of laughter shook him. "I won't let you fall." And then they were galloping along the road, General eagerly keeping pace.

The horse sped beneath her; the wind seemed to blow a great billow of excitement against her face because she was escaping and had confounded Gregson and therefore Cuttyngham, and in such a way. A wild impulse was sweeping her into the unknown, and she was *glad*.

They hurtled around the bend in the road, and she grinned up at her savior. "He won't see us now. He'll have no idea!"

"Excellent. Neither have I." His gaze flickered down to her with a dazzling smile, and back to the road. "Do you have a name, strange lady?"

She laughed. "Rosamund." How long since anyone had actually spoken her name? Did any but her husband actually know it? She suspected even he had forgotten it, for certainly he never used it. To the world, since her marriage five years ago, she was merely Her Grace, the Duchess of Cuttyngham. But not today. From now on, she would retake her old name. "Rosamund Daryll."

He took one hand off the reins to briefly shake her hand. "Giles Butler. Where are we going?"

"Good question! Where were you going when I met you?"

"Harwich."

"We're not on the road to Harwich."

"I took a detour."

"Harwich will do perfectly," she said. "Or anywhere on the way I can acquire a lady's saddle for General. And a map."

The soldier gave a shout of laughter that sounded perfectly joyous because it echoed her new freedom.

Chapter Two

Guilt and shame had turned Major Giles Butler from the road to Harwich. He was not used to avoiding the consequences of his mistakes. He always owned up to them. In all honesty, he was a good soldier and rarely made such mistakes, but this one, this duel, had been a spectacular idiocy.

He was accounted a crack shot in the regiment. But what in the world had made him so cocksure that he could shoot exactly where he wished in such lethal circumstances, with an unfamiliar weapon? Losing Landon had undoubtedly been a deep, personal loss to him, and the duke's casual slander unbearable. But dear God, the man hadn't deserved to die, and certainly not at Butler's hand.

And so, on impulse, when he had seen the road sign for Cuttyngs, the main seat of the duke, he had taken the detour. His intention had been to throw himself at the duchess's feet, admit his crime with abject apology, and promise to pay the price when Bonaparte was once more in captivity. Only, arriving at the gates, the massive flaws in the gesture had deluged him.

Surely, her husband's killer was the last person the duchess would wish to see. His presence would cause her only more pain. And he himself was likely to be arrested, which was certainly what he deserved, but not what needed to happen just yet when Wellington was desperate for experienced officers.

The riderless horse had been an excuse to dither, to mull over the realization that he had done enough harm to the poor duchess and her family and should remove himself from the vicinity before he caused further damage. And then the girl had appeared, laden with bags and bent double, clearly sneaking past the gatehouse and into the road, where she had darted glances all around her like a stage character in hiding.

Although she had clearly come from Cuttyngs, she was just the distraction he needed. A lady by her dress, up to mischief by her actions, and thoroughly delightful by her artless beauty, she provided a reason for his presence and his departure. And a pleasantly intriguing mystery. He didn't recognize her name. Though she must be something to do with the Severne family, he had never moved in the kind of society that would know of the connection. But he did feel an obligation to help her, to atone in however small a way.

On the other hand, slowing to ease the burden on poor Chessy, he acknowledged that he rather liked holding this Rosamund Daryll before him in the saddle. Neither fragile nor plump, she was utterly feminine and fitted rather pleasantly against his own much larger body. Though it struck him she was either far too trusting of a stranger or far too frightened of what she was running from at Cuttyngs.

"So, whose is the horse?" he asked, nodding toward General, plodding along beside them.

"The Duke of Cuttyngham's," came the immediate reply. "Though my suspicion is, he was being ridden by Gregson. Gregson is His Grace's personal groom and an odious, tattling kind of fellow."

"Then we are quite right to remove his horse. Only, won't you get into trouble with the duke?"

"In absentia." She frowned. "Though I probably should send him back. Only I hadn't really bargained on buying a horse, and my money might run out. Would it be cheaper to hire a post-chaise? For I'm not sure the mail coach or the stagecoach will go very near Little Fiddleton."

"Little Where?" Giles asked, bewildered.

"Fiddleton. That is where my cottage is."

"And the duke's family would not take you home?"

"I didn't ask them. Being of an independent spirit."

"And afraid of being prevented," he said shrewdly.

"That, too," she admitted.

"I'm not assisting an elopement, am I?"

She regarded him with interest. "Would you mind if you were?"

He thought about it. "Probably not, so long as you are safe. Will he look after you?"

Her eyes gleamed for a moment, and he could almost see the stories forming in her head. Then she merely gave an embarrassed smile. "I'm not eloping. I have merely decided to forego the duke's charity and live where I please."

"Then you are connected to the family?"

"I'm afraid so."

"Don't you like them?"

She shook her head, then added quickly, "That is, I have never had much chance to know them. My—His Grace's daughter lives mostly in London with her aunt, and his son shuts himself away with books most of the day. The duke has very firm views of what his—his connections might do around the house and estate, so I am mostly bored. I have been bored for years. Do you have any idea what that is like?"

"No," Giles confessed. "I have been bored for hours on a dull watch or while waiting for battle. Even for days at a time. But never for years. And I rarely find nothing to do."

"I suppose your case is the opposite," she said with interest. "Life must be too exciting for you. Though, of course, you have the great honor of serving king and country, rather than merely appearing at the odd dinner and an autumn ball once a year. Do you like being a soldier?"

"Yes. Mostly. It's all I've ever done. And, I suspect, all I can do."

"You do great things," she said with unexpected warmth, making him blush with shame as he remembered what he had done to her connection, the duke. "I do nothing, help no one, exist for no purpose."

Taken aback by her vehemence, he said, "I'm sure that is not true. You must brighten the lives of everyone who knows you." Although he spoke to make her feel better, he realized it was true. There was something vital and appealing about her, something quite aside from her physical beauty, an inner energy that shone.

"Hardly," she said. "But I'm going to change that. I haven't been *entirely* idle at Cuttyngs. I have learned all about herbs and their use in medicine and physic, and in my own little cottage at Little Fiddleton, I shall put my learning to use."

"You are going to be a herbalist?" he said cautiously.

"I am."

"Aren't you a little young to be the village wise woman? Won't you be expected to attend child births and horrific injuries and all sorts of things a young, unmarried lady shouldn't even see?"

"I *am* married," the girl said defensively, and then blushed, which at least distracted him from his own unreasonable disappointment. "That is, I was." She looked away and mumbled, "I am a widow."

Which might explain why she was now dependent on the duke. Or at least on his successor. *Expected* to be dependent, he corrected himself with amused admiration, for she clearly had her own utterly unconventional idea of how to make her life.

"A doctor friend of mine says he would rather be treated by a wise woman than most who call themselves physicians. English physicians at any rate. I think I'll dismount and walk to give poor Chessy a rest."

"If we turn left at the crossroads, it's only a couple of miles further to Cuttyngham," Mrs. Daryll volunteered as he dismounted.

To his surprise, she slid down beside him, and he only just managed to catch her. There was a breathless moment when her body struck his, and he recognized all the delight of her curves and softness. He couldn't help holding her just a moment too long or smiling down at her with sheer pleasure. Her eyes widened, and a hint of color stained the lines of her cheekbones.

"What is there at Cuttyngham?" he asked, releasing her before he made things worse.

"A livery stable, amongst other things, so I can change saddles and possibly horses. And since it's market day, there will be enough people to hide among. If I am traced to the town, no one will find me after that. And you may go on to Harwich, too."

She took the duke's horse's reins from him and began to lead the animal left at the crossroads. He followed with Chessy and caught up with her.

"Doesn't the duke's family know of your cottage in Little Fluff town?" he asked lightly.

"Fiddleton," she said with mock severity. "And no. I acquired it only recently."

He frowned. "You haven't been there, have you? You don't even know that it is sound."

"I do! My agent told me it was. It is perfectly comfortable and has a large garden. Exactly what I want."

"Do you intend to live there alone?" he asked with growing consternation.

"Oh, yes," she said so fervently that he closed his mouth on his other doubts.

Really, it was none of his business. And if she knew what he had just done to her duke… Fortunately, she didn't appear to like His Grace very much, but even so, Butler's companionship was really an insult to her. He would make sure she was safe in this Cuttyngham, that she got her horse and saddle, and was safely on her way before he went on his. And that would be that. Another girl to remember in the long watches of the night and perhaps dream of, a little. Before someone less…untouchable distracted him.

Well, she might not have been touchable, but he could and did enjoy her company. She was interested in everything, from the stray dog who accompanied them part of the way, to the trees and hedges by the roadside, to the people returning from the market with laden carts and donkeys. In between time, she chattered artlessly about everything and nothing and asked him questions about his life in the army, about the battles he'd fought in, and whether or not he had met the national hero, the Duke of Wellington.

"I've met him," Giles admitted, "and I'm not looking forward to our next encounter."

She was beguiling. He almost blurted out what he had done, which would have been unforgivable. For one thing, one didn't talk about duels to ladies. For another, she would probably run from him screaming, and then who would make sure she got safely on her way to Little Fiddleton? There was more to her escape from Cuttyngs than met the eye, but everyone was entitled to their secrets.

"I suppose he is already furious about Bonaparte's escape from Elba," Rosamund speculated. "And according to one of Cuttyngham's letters, he isn't happy about the quality of the troops at his disposal. Will you be joining them in Brussels? Is that why you're going to Harwich?"

"It is." Originally, he had planned to travel with his men, but now he should probably get out of the country as quickly as possible and throw himself on Wellington's mercy. When Bonaparte was recaptured was time enough to return to England and face the consequences of what he had done.

"You are looking forward to it," she said with an odd mixture of wonder and accusation. "To war and battle."

He cast her a crooked smile. "In some ways. It's what I'm trained to do. I like army life. I miss it when I'm away from it."

"Are you never afraid? In battle."

"I'm always afraid in battle. Except when I'm angry."

She eyed him doubtfully. "You don't seem a very angry kind of man."

"I'm not, as a rule." Just occasionally, when he let temper lead him by the nose into scrapes, like the duel which had killed an important man. A man responsible, apparently, for this girl who had no idea what he had done.

"YOU DON'T SEEM a very angry kind of man."

"I'm not, as a rule."

The unexpected bleakness in his pleasant voice reached deep inside her, sparking compassion as well curiosity.

Rosamund liked people. Their lives and the workings of their minds and emotions fascinated her. That she should like this amiable, happy-go-lucky young officer was not surprising, but she should not be quite so intrigued by the hidden layers of the man. Nor so affected by the unhappiness she glimpsed beneath the kindness. And he *was* kind, or he would not have gone out of his way to help her.

He was handsome, too, in an unusual, angular kind of way. His ready smile was charming enough, she suspected, to draw women to him in droves. There was something intimate about it, as though drawing its recipient into the intimacy of their shared fun. It struck her now, like a blow, that she would like that intimacy with him.

She realized his focus had returned to her, and heat seeped up through her body. She had been held in his arms, more or less, for the last hour, feeling the warmth from his chest and the brush of his thighs. Yet only now did she recognize his sheer masculinity. And it almost overwhelmed her.

Even though there was more concern than threat in his eyes.

"Have I offended you?" he asked.

She forced a quick smile to her lips. "Of course not." What the devil had they been talking about? Fear. Anger. Battle. "I cannot imagine your life. It is so different from mine."

He shrugged. "We all have our own battles to fight. For instance… How far is it to Little Fiddleton?"

She grasped the topic like a lifeline. "I'm not quite sure, but I think about twenty miles from Cuttyngham."

"Then you must know you cannot ride alone, and not only for the sake of appearance. Roads are not safe for anyone, let alone for a lady on her own. If you are not afraid of that, common sense should tell you that you should be."

She scowled. "Perhaps I am angry!"

He grinned at that. "Touché. You are right to be. I have no right to dictate to you. But I advise you most strongly to hire a chaise to take you the rest of the way. On horseback, you would have to stay overnight somewhere."

She sighed. "I know. I had planned to, only I hadn't planned on having to buy a horse as well."

He blinked. "You meant to walk to Cuttyngham?"

"No, I meant to ride my own mare, but Gregson was poking around in the stables, and I didn't want him to see me."

Captain Butler's brows drew together. "Are you afraid of this man?"

She grimaced. "I don't like him. I'm afraid of what he would tell the duke. And *when* he would tell him. I want to vanish, you see."

He appeared to think about that as they walked. They were almost at the town, now, the scattered cottages set closer together along the road. "Will that not cause a lot of worry to a lot of people?" he said at last.

"No, they'll just keep it quiet, give out that I've gone to a relative in Scotland or that I'm traveling on the continent."

"You don't expect them to look for you?"

"I do. And if they find me, I shall be dragged home in disgrace and probably shut up in some discreet asylum for the insane."

He stared at her. "Seriously? Someone threatened you with such treatment?"

She slid her eyes free, with mingled shame and discomfort, even though the shame was not hers. "I overheard a conversation. Which is when I started making my own plans."

He seemed speechless for several moments. Then, "Have you no other family with whom to seek refuge?"

"No one who would not send me back to the duke."

A frown flickered briefly across his face, as though that didn't make any sense—which, of course, it didn't unless one knew she was the duchess. Which she would not reveal, even to this winning stranger.

Then, with odd grimness, he said, "You need not worry about the duke. I shall escort you to your cottage."

A shock of mingled relief and pleasure and alarm thrilled through her. "Oh, no! You are kind, but you have to go to Harwich."

"Another day will make no difference. I would rather see you safe."

She lowered her voice as another cart rumbled past them. "Sir, you have no obligation to me."

"It seems I have."

He didn't sound too pleased about it either, which caused her to blurt out haughtily, "It makes no odds. I don't want you or your obligation."

To her astonishment, he nudged her with his elbow, as though they were children, knocking the wind out of her imperious sails. "Don't be daft. It will be much more fun with two of us."

CHAPTER THREE

IN THE END, Rosamund found herself unable to part with General.

"He looked at me with such sad eyes," she told Captain Butler when she joined him in the inn's coffee room. "I just knew Gregson had been cruel to him. I can't leave the poor thing with strangers, so I just swapped his saddle instead."

Captain Butler, who had risen at her entrance, sat down when she did. "Then you decided against the post-chaise?"

She sighed. "I did. I never realized how ruinously expensive they are to hire, and I shall need all my money for the first few weeks in my new home. I will have to buy food and jars and bottles, so it will be expensive just at first. Until word spreads and I begin to earn some money. Goodness, is all this food for us?"

"You said you were hungry."

"So I did." She fell to it with enthusiasm. When she had swallowed her first mouthful, she added, "It's as well General is so big. He'll need to be to carry me after all this."

"He is huge for a lady's mount," the captain agreed. "Are you sure you can manage him?"

"Oh, yes. I used to be a great rider when I was young."

"As distinct from now when you are an old lady of what? Twenty?"

"I am two and twenty, if you must know," Rosamund replied

with dignity.

"How long have you been a widow?"

She had almost forgotten she had told him that to account for her independence. Now she felt rather ashamed of the lie, though it was really no worse than the sin of omission she committed by keeping her identity secret. That had been instinct, though now she wondered if he would actually behave any differently.

"Um, a few years. I was married at seventeen."

"You are so young to have dealt with widowhood."

"Oh, I don't regard it," she said hastily, shifting in her seat with discomfort. "He was much older than me, and we didn't get on. Though, of course, I'm sorry he's dead."

"So am I. If only so he could protect you," Captain Butler said. The grim sorrow hovered about his eyes, and then he asked abruptly, "There is a son, is there not? The academic you described. Would he not do the right thing by you?"

"He has troubles enough. His father is…not kind to him. Goodness, this is filling for a midday meal, do you not think?"

"Make the most of it," he advised. "It will be a long time before supper."

"You sound like my mother."

"Perhaps she was a soldier in a previous life."

Rosamund laughed. "You say the oddest things."

"So do you. Come, eat up and let's be on our way before someone recognizes you."

Rosamund didn't really mind being recognized in Cuttyngham, which was probably the first place anyone would look for her. It was where she went after that she wished to remain a mystery.

In the end, however, it was Major Butler who was recognized. At the inn's front door, a soldier in uniform stood politely aside to let her pass and then exclaimed behind her, "Lune! Damn it, what a grand surprise!"

Rosamund turned quickly to see the two men enthusiastically shaking hands. The stranger buffeted Butler on the shoulder at the same time, and the major's smile of pleasure in the meeting did strange things to her stomach.

"Off to join Nosey in Brussels?" the soldier inquired.

"I am indeed."

"Excellent! Do you sail from Harwich or the south coast?"

"Harwich."

"Even better. We can travel together. What of MacDonald and Elton?"

"On their way there as we speak. And I'll join you after I've escorted my cousin home."

The strange officer's gaze moved at last to Rosamund. His eyes widened. "Lucky dog. I wish I had such a cousin."

It was spoken below his breath, and Rosamund probably wasn't meant to hear, so she pretended she didn't. All the same, she was surprised by the sudden steel in Major Butler's eyes as he murmured, "Mind your manners, Goughie. Cousin, allow me to present Lieutenant Gough of some hussar regiment or other. More of a parade soldier, as you see, but we tolerate him since he learns quickly. Goughie, my cousin, Mrs. Daryll."

Lieutenant Gough bowed correctly. "Delighted to make your acquaintance, ma'am. I hope you know your cousin here is quite the hero—don't let him tell you otherwise. Good day and a pleasant journey to you. Lune, see you in Harwich! Or failing that, Brussels."

Major Butler clapped him on the back and civilly offered his arm to Rosamund. It felt oddly formal to take it, so casual had their dealings been up until now.

"Why does he call you Lune?" she murmured.

"Term of endearment," the captain replied with a grin. "Short for lunatic."

"Really? How did that come about?"

"Oh, an act of sheer stupidity on my part—the anger I mentioned before getting the better of me, though it worked out rather fortunately in the end. Friend of mine yelled at me, *You dashed lun–* and then broke off when the colonel appeared. For some reason, Lune stuck and spread."

"It's an odd name for a hero," she pointed out, not quite pleased.

"Oh, the hero bit is just Gough's nonsense, trying to raise your opinion of me."

Rosamund wasn't so sure about that, but she let it go since they had reached the stable, where their horses, freshly fed and groomed, awaited them.

General's back did indeed seem very broad and far from the ground, and there was no obvious mounting block. But without fuss, the captain bent and threaded his hands to make a step for her. She placed her foot on it and was boosted high into the saddle. She settled herself quickly and stroked General's neck while Captain Butler efficiently adjusted her stirrup length. To Rosamund, there seemed a rare, almost breathless intimacy about the courtesy, although the captain remained focused on the task in hand and seemed quite casual about shifting her foot and even patting it when he was satisfied. Then he swung himself up into Chessy's saddle, and they set off on what seemed increasingly like an adventure.

GREGSON, THE LATE Duke of Cuttyngham's favored groom, was in a towering rage by the time Mr. Anthony Severne got to the house in a self-righteous fury of his own.

Gregson had never in his life failed to carry out an instruction from his employer. Not that the late duke had ever deigned to notice. Which was one reason he now had two employers—the newly inherited young duke and Mr. Anthony Severne, his heir, who seemed to Gregson to be the up-and-coming man, and the one who would make Gregson rich. But this, his first appointed task by Mr. Severne, had been a fiasco.

As bidden, he had ridden like the wind to Cuttyngs and, conscious that he should not be the one to break the news to the household, let alone the family, he had left General outside the gates while he secretly saddled a horse to take back with him to meet his new master, Mr. Anthony Severne. He hadn't needed to ask Mr. Severne why. He knew the late duke had banned the post houses from providing his cousin Anthony with the ducal horses. And Mr. Severne had to be the one to break the news of the duke's death to his son and heir, the crippled Victor, Marquis of Dean—who was now, in fact, Victor, Duke of Cuttyngham.

It had all seemed a simple matter to Gregson, until, leading the newly saddled horse to the Cuttyngs main gate, he had discovered the reliable General gone. He had wasted a whole hour searching around the grounds and up and down the road. The deaf old fool at the gate had noticed nothing, seen no saddled horse wandering away. And inevitably, of course, the rest of the staff had seen Gregson, plaguing him with questions about His Grace that he was not allowed to answer.

So, he fumed and wriggled and fumed again until, as it grew dark, Mr. Severne finally rode up to the stables on a sorry-looking nag. This amused the stable boys and even Forman, the head groom of Cuttyngs. Without a word, Gregson rose and went to meet his new master. No one stopped him. In fact, they generally gave him a wide berth, knowing, no doubt, that he had been responsible for at least two dismissals in the past.

"Where in the fiend's name have you been?" Mr. Severne demanded. "Look at this *donkey* I'm reduced to! Hardly a mount fit for the new heir to the duchy of Cuttyngham!"

"Sorry, sir," Gregson said. "General went missing, stolen, most like, and by then, everyone had seen me, and I had to say His Grace was returning with you. Which he hasn't."

"No, I left the body with the magistrate," Mr. Severne snapped, dismounting and thrusting the reins at Gregson. "Lord Frostbrook will bring him down in the fullness of time. Here, take this beast out of my sight. I'm going to find the new duke."

The new duke, however, seemed to have found them first.

Stumping unevenly across the stable yard, he caught sight of them with apparent surprise. And not of the pleasant variety, for his black scowl grew deeper.

"Cousin," he said, staring without welcome. "What do you want?"

"I'm afraid I bring sad news, Cousin. Shall we go into the house?"

"I've just come out of the damned house," Victor said impatiently. "And my father isn't here."

"I know," Mr. Severne said sorrowfully. "It is my sad duty to report that your father the duke is dead. And that you are now Duke of Cuttyngham. *Your Grace.*"

Victor's huge dark eyes widened. His walking stick wobbled until his fingers tightened on it so hard that they shone white in the torchlight. And then, bitterly, he swore.

ROSAMUND AND MAJOR Butler arrived at their chosen inn rather later than they had intended, one of Chessy's shoes having loosened and necessitated a stop at the first blacksmith they could find. However, the journey had been fun, much more fun than it could ever have been on her own, and she had enjoyed getting to know the captain better. While they alternately galloped and walked their horses, they had talked of everything and laughed a good deal. She told him about her social disasters, which no longer seemed so tragic now that she could laugh at them. And he told her funny stories about life in army camps.

She heard a good deal about his fellow officers Mac and Elton, and the acid-tongued surgeon, Dr. Rivers, who had put them all back together several times after battles. Only occasionally did he stop himself from saying something, usually with reference to the future. And once, when she had asked suddenly what he had been doing on the Cuttyngs road, he had said shortly, "Got lost," and changed the subject.

Beside his travels and adventures, her own seemed very dull, but he appeared to be interested in her tales of childhood, and various dogs and cats and frogs. Unlike most of her male acquaintances, he did not rail against the wasted time caused by repairing Chessy's shoe. Instead, he accepted it philosophically, and while they waited, took her for a short walk to admire the village church and drink a glass of small beer at the local inn.

As a result, they were on very comfortable terms by the time they reached the Dragon's Tail in the village of Fellsworth, even calling each other by their first names, although she couldn't quite recall which of them had done so first. In any case, since they had decided she should be his sister rather than a mere cousin at the Dragon's Tail, first names were really a necessity.

As darkness fell, Giles had produced a lantern from his saddlebag and had kept a sharper eye on their surroundings. For the first time, she noticed the pistol at his belt. But if highwaymen or footpads were abroad, they clearly decided on different prey, for they reached Fellsworth unmolested.

"I hope they have rooms," Rosamund said just a little doubtfully as they approached the Dragon's Tail. "I thought it would be larger."

"It has no need to be, with the much bigger posting inn only a few miles back," Giles observed. "I thought that was why you chose this place. To avoid anyone who might know you. And since you don't actually have a brother, that is probably very sensible."

"I just wish I had written to bespeak rooms in advance."

He glanced at her as they rode into the yard. "I believe that's the first time I have ever seen you look worried."

She smiled a little ruefully. "Perhaps I'm tired. Or finally facing the reality of my escape."

Before she was ready, his hands closed on her waist and lifted her out of the saddle. Perhaps it was surprise that made her blush and brought the shock of awareness of his lean strong body, so briefly, so tantalizingly close to hers, before he turned to speak to the ostler.

When they entered the inn's main room—a cozy, tobacco-filled place with a staircase leading to an upper floor—the innkeeper himself came bustling to meet them.

"Good evening," Giles said, amiable in response to the man's greeting. "We require bedchambers for my sister and myself, a light supper, and, preferably, a private parlor?"

"Got two lovely bedchambers for your honor, and supper is no problem. But I'm afraid we've no parlors as such. The best I can do is the corner over there. Though by the time your supper is served, this lot will have mostly gone off to leave you in peace."

"I'm sure that will be fine," Rosamund said hastily, relieved simply to have a bedchamber.

"You could eat in your room if you'd rather," Giles pointed out.

She cast a quick glance around the tables, seeing only a few farmers and a shabbily dressed man asleep on a bench by himself. Perhaps it would be more comfortable alone, and yet she found herself reluctant to part with Major Butler's company before she had to.

"I'm sure it will be fine in the corner there," she said. "Thank you."

"Then my wife will show you to your rooms. Are these bags all you have?"

"Quite," Giles said pleasantly yet somehow cutting off all further questioning.

A thin, beaming woman in a mob cap bustled over and led them to the stairs. A boy followed behind with their meager bags.

"Very pleasant," Rosamund pronounced when she saw the room, which was quite large, with two shuttered windows and a fire laid in the grate.

The innkeeper's wife, who introduced herself as Mrs. Davies, smiled even more broadly at Rosamund's praise and kneeled to light the fire. "It'll be lovely and cozy by the time you've had supper. Is there anything else you need?"

"Some warm water to wash would be welcome."

"Ned here will bring it directly." Mrs. Davies fled, pushing Ned before her, and Rosamund turned to her bags to dig out a hairbrush.

"Will it do?" asked Giles from the door. Somehow, whatever he said, his strangely rich voice reached to her bones, gently, deeply thrilling. And was far more welcome than it should have been.

She turned quickly to face him. He stood in the open doorway, leaning one shoulder against the frame, tall and lean and casual, one eyebrow quizzically raised. And her stomach seemed to tumble.

This is ridiculous. I only met him this morning, and I am a married woman! It made no odds that she was fleeing her husband. Who had never made her feel remotely like this, even in the early days of their marriage when she had tried so hard to please him. But in leaving her marital duty, she had no intention of ever entangling herself with any other man. For an instant, panic overwhelmed her, until his raised eyebrow fell into the beginnings of a frown, and she realized how ridiculous she was being. She was tired, excited by her escape and the new life ahead of her, and Major Butler was the first man who had ever gone out of his way to be kind to her.

In fact, she should not trust him, although it seemed she did. She was grateful to him.

Now what had he asked her? *"Will it do?"*

"Oh! Yes, it is perfectly comfortable," she said hastily, waving her arm around the room. "Is yours?"

"Palatial compared to cold, hard ground and flee-infested barns." He moved back to allow Ned to pass with the large jug of water. "I'll leave you to your ablutions. Ten minutes?"

"Perfect," she replied, relieved that her voice sounded calm again.

Ten minutes later, she had changed out of her riding habit

and into one of the simple and somewhat crushed everyday gowns she had brought with her. The fastenings were a challenge she had heroically overcome by wriggling and twisting both herself and the dress. Then, somewhat cleaner and with her hair brushed and re-pinned in the simplest of knots, it was her turn to tap at Major Butler's half-open door.

She was touched to see that he had shaved and brushed the dirt of the road from his uniform. He had donned a clean cravat, possibly even a clean shirt. When he emerged and offered her his arm, he smelled of soap and something elusive she already associated with him, like the hot earth and warm sunshine of foreign countries, with a hint of the exotic plants that thrived there.

She blinked away the fantasy as they descended the stairs. The room below was already quieter. Only a couple of men remained chatting, while another was shaking awake the sleeper on the bench.

Mrs. Davies, still smiling, showed them to the corner table, where the smell of tobacco and ale was fortunately less. Davies materialized with a dusty bottle of wine, of which he appeared to be inordinately proud, and Ned brought in two bowls of hearty soup.

In the flurry of tasting and eating, Rosamund was glad to lose the last of the discomfort that had lingered since her earlier, confusing thoughts about her companion. Now, she found that simply accepting him and the situation in which they found themselves was the way forward. And God knew it felt good to have a friend at last.

Finally, they sat back, replete after a surprisingly tasty meal, and Rosamund breathed a sigh of contentment, not just in her company but in her sense of freedom. Here, she was merely Mrs. Daryll, not Her Grace of Cuttyngham, despised, neglected, and barren wife of a duke. It was delightfully liberating to be on this journey, to be neither at Cuttyngs nor yet at her new abode, just an anonymous traveler under the protection of her soldierly "brother."

"Will you ever go home?" he asked into the silence.

"Little Fiddleton will be my home. If you mean Cuttyngs, then no."

"What if circumstances changed? If the danger of the duke's threats no longer hung over you?"

She shrugged. "There is no point in thinking that way any longer. I have chosen a new life and providing there is no scandal over my disappearance—I trust His Grace to ensure that much—then everyone will be relieved by my departure."

"And the proprieties—will you have someone live with you?"

She laughed. "At the moment, I am contemplating the joys of being quite alone!"

"Thank you," he said politely.

She nudged his elbow, an unthinkable intimacy in the world she had just left. "You know I except the present company, for which I am most grateful. I just feel as if I have woken after a year-long sleep or broken out of prison."

"You really felt that trapped?"

She nodded, picking up her wine glass more for something to do with her suddenly restless hands. The urge to confide in her new friend was strong. "Trapped and lonely," she confessed, settling for generalities. "Unhappy and fearful, latterly. Hopeless." She tried to smile. "It is not in my nature to be hopeless. But after five years of...of being under His Grace's thumb, I knew there was no hope of anything better, not unless I *did* something. So I did. And now I am determined to make a difference to somebody."

She met his gaze defiantly but could not read his expression.

At last, he said, "I understand about following one's heart and about freedom. But freedom is always tempered by something and not just for women. For example, I chose to join the army but am compelled by discipline and rules and orders, some of which are foolish beyond belief. But it is the road I chose to follow."

"You mean I have made my bed and must lie in it?"

He shifted as though uncomfortable. "By what you say, you had no choice but to join the duke's household. Now, however, you are making your own choice, but there will *still* be rules. And a lady living quite alone among strangers might face not only disapproval and gossip but more physical harms. I'm not trying to frighten you," he added, raising one hand as though he read her immediate defense in her eyes, "or even to talk you out of your goal. I just want you to be *sure*, because some steps are irrevocable."

To her horror, her eyes began to sting. He was saying very little she had not a least considered, but the euphoria of her new freedom was suddenly evaporating. Nothing would keep her from her course, and yet the thought of his disapproval undoubtedly hurt.

"If you knew the courage it cost me to take this step," she said, appalled by the sudden unsteadiness of her voice, "you would not even try to talk me out of it."

His eyes changed, and his hand clasped her fingers, which were twisting themselves together in her lap. "I'm not, Rosie, I'm not trying to talk you out of it, and I *admire* your courage."

No one had called her Rosie for years, not since her mother had died. Her throat tightened unbearably, and she struggled with her filling eyes.

"Just not my common sense?" she managed.

"Your planning is impeccable," he said seriously. "You even adjusted to the situation on the ground. You would make a great general. Only—forgive me—you seem a little…distant from the reality of your situation. What if your family found you? Either with me or alone? Look, I'll help you all I can, to be safe and comfortable, but my time is limited by having to leave the country as fast as possible. And besides, I am precisely the wrong person to be helping you."

She tugged her hand, but he hung on to it, and she stared at their tangled fingers, holding on to the warmth, the comforting strength of his grip while she prayed the tear at the corner of her eye would not betray her. His voice was soft, appealing, and utterly devastating.

"Will you let me suggest something?" he asked.

She nodded desperately.

"Let me take you to your cottage via a friend of mine. Hopefully, she will be able to stay with you for a few days while you settle in."

This was so unexpected that her face jerked up, and the wretched tear trickled from the corner of her eye. She ignored it and willed that he would too.

"What friend?"

"Her name is Sophia, and I have known her forever." With his free hand, he produced a clean handkerchief from his pocket, and instead of handing it to her, he gently wiped her cheek with it. He smiled, completing her downfall. "She is kind and fun and sensible, and I think you will like her. Besides, she is in something of the same situation as you."

"In what way?" she managed.

"Well, she is not widowed, but when her parents died, she was obliged to go and live with family she barely knew, and so she resides quite near here now, in a village called Dorwich. I imagine she was more fortunate in her family than you. Certainly, her letters are cheerful, and both her parents were delightful people."

Dear God, was that jealousy trying to force its way through her already confused emotions? "How are you connected to this lady?"

"Our mothers betrothed us in the cradle," he said with a quick, crooked grin.

Glaring, she pushed his hand and handkerchief away from her face. "And you think *I* am naive? How do you imagine your betrothed will react to you appearing on her doorstep with another woman? One, moreover, with whom you have been traveling unchaperoned?"

"Oh, Sophia will understand," he said comfortably. "And of course, we are not really betrothed. Even as children we agreed we had no intention of marrying. We are like brother and sister, and I know she will be happy to help."

Rosamund doubted it, but before she could say so, a thunderous knocking, compelling Davies to shout indignantly, "I'm coming, keep your hair on!" as he lumbered toward the now locked front door.

Giles released Rosamund's hand and stuffed the handkerchief back in his pocket. To her surprise, he looked tense, alarmed, and positively grim. Then the inn door was flung open, and two people exploded into the room in a gust of wind and rain.

CHAPTER FOUR

At the furious knocking on the door, Giles did indeed feel grim. Also desperate and dismayed because this was one situation he could not and would not try to fight his way out of. If the law had come for him and he had to answer now for the death of the duke, he could do nothing but hope his friends would send a plea to Wellington.

Beyond that, he didn't want to leave Rosamund alone in this world full of risks he had just tried to bring to her notice without daunting her. And he had made her cry. For that alone, he should be horsewhipped. He found himself hoping savagely that if he was taken up by the law, they would indeed thrash him. Though, of course, that would help no one.

He moved on the bench, putting a modicum of distance between him and Rosamund. No more, in case he had to defend her. If the threat was to him, he would merely move further away and pray the Davies would not turn her out for her connection to him.

And then two young strangers all but catapulted into the inn, and Davies slammed the door shut behind them.

Giles blinked at a dripping wet couple, neither of whom looked to be older than seventeen summers at the most. Clearly not the law, then. Relaxing with relief, he turned back to Rosamund and found her gazing at him with curiosity.

"Who did you expect?" she asked. "The headless horseman?"

A breath of laughter escaped him. "The equivalent from my recent and reprehensible past. I told you I was the worst person to be helping you."

She opened her mouth, clearly about to ask several other difficult questions, and he could only be glad she no longer seemed to want to cry. But then, distracted by the new arrivals, she looked toward the door instead.

"I can give you a cold supper," Davies was saying to them grudgingly, "but I've no rooms for you."

"Nonsense," the girl burst out. "I know for a fact you have two very decent rooms upstairs, for I stayed in one of them when I was a child!"

"They're taken," Davies said with some satisfaction. Clearly, he was suspicious of the young couple and didn't want them in his house. "But you'll find a post house about four miles along the road."

"In this weather?" the young man said, incensed. "You can't possibly send this lady out into the rain again! She needs to be warm and dry, or she will be ill."

"Then maybe you should have thought about that before you set off," Mrs. Davies said, joining the fray. "And you should know very well that *ladies* do not jaunt about the country alone with men not of their family! This has always been a respectable house and always will be."

Rosamund and Giles exchanged surreptitious gleams of silent amusement.

The girl drew herself up to her full, not very impressive height, causing rain to run off her hat and cloak onto the floor. "My good woman," she began haughtily.

"Don't you good woman me!" Mrs. Davies exclaimed. "When it's quite clear to all that you're no better than—"

"Perhaps we might be of assistance," Rosamund interrupted, rising to her feet. Giles rose with her and ambled casually behind her toward the door, watchful and wary lest anyone tried to take advantage of her. "What exactly is the problem? Apart from the fact that both these young people appear to be soaked to the skin."

The girl gave a dripping curtsey that betrayed her ladylike origins. The young man scowled and bowed and glanced nervously from Rosamund to Giles.

"Well, they'll have to be soaked somewhere else," Mrs. Davies said staunchly, "for there's no room for them here. You don't need to be troubling yourself with the likes of them—"

"Actually, I don't think you need to be rushing to judgment," Rosamund said, "until you have heard what accident has brought either of them here. Perhaps a glass of brandy by the fire, Mr. Davies, while we discover the problem."

Giles found himself blinking at her effortless authority. Without raising her voice, she had swept the young people past both the innkeeper and his wife and was installing them on the settle before the fire. Mrs. Davies, tight-lipped, glared at her husband, who shrugged and went to obtain the brandy.

"They arrived on horseback," Mrs. Davies said indignantly to Giles. "With nothing but a bandbox between them." She appeared to see no similarity to his own arrival with Rosamund two hours ago. "Mark my words, Captain, they're up to no good. If you ask me, they're eloping, and I won't have it."

"I have every faith in my sister to discover the truth of the matter," Giles murmured, and strolled after Davies to see about a brandy of his own. In the end, he brought four glasses to the group by the fire.

By then, the girl had removed her soaked cloak and bonnet to reveal a riot of damp, golden curls, and had spread the skirts of her riding habit before the fire. Her companion, a scowling dark youth looked nothing like her. They obviously knew there was no point in even pretending to be related.

"For medicinal purposes," Giles said as he gave one glass to the girl. "To help you feel warmer. Sip it."

"Giles, this is Miss Merton and Mr. Yates," Rosamund said.

"From Hertfordshire. Their aim was to hire a post-chaise at the Dog and Duck, but the weather has turned too foul for them to reach tonight. And they are soaked, poor things. This is Major Butler, my brother."

"I see nothing for it," Miss Merton said dramatically, "but that we throw ourselves upon your mercy! I hate to impose, but the horrid innkeeper will do nothing for us. I would happily sleep in a stable, or even here in the public room, so long as I am warm and can set off again tomorrow."

"And why," Giles inquired, "is there need of our mercy?"

"Hold your tongue, Izzy," Mr. Yates warned.

"Well, I won't lie," Miss Merton flung at him, "and I daresay they have guessed the truth in any case. Mr. Yates and I have been forced into elopement."

"Forced?" Giles repeated.

"By the actions of others," Miss Merton explained. She wrinkled her very pretty little nose. "Namely my parents, who will make me go to Bath."

"That is certainly very bad of them," Rosamund said gravely. "I don't care for the place myself."

"On the other hand," Giles offered, "a dose or two of the waters can't be worse than several days in a carriage to Scotland. You do understand that even married, you will be ruined to polite society?"

"I told you it was hairbrained," Mr. Yates muttered.

"No, you didn't," Miss Merton retorted. "You said my father was a monster."

"Well, he is." Mr. Yates glared at her and dragged his fingers through his wild, black hair. "Doesn't mean you're not a hairbrained chit. I should never have gone along with this."

"No, you shouldn't," Giles said frankly. "Why did you?"

"I love her," the boy said helplessly. "God knows why because she's dashed annoying, but there it is."

His love smiled mistily at this accolade.

"If you love her," Rosamund pursued, "why would you subject her to ruin rather than a few weeks in Bath?"

"Because *he* is in Bath," Miss Merton said with loathing. "Lord Redhyde."

Giles and Rosamund exchanged glances. "Very well, I'll bite," Giles said flippantly. "Who is Lord Redhyde?"

"A rich old man who lives in Bath. He wants to marry me."

"How fiendish of him," Giles observed.

"You don't understand. He has gout and nasty hot eyes, and my parents keep taking me there so he'll come up to scratch!"

"Merton's pockets-to-let," Mr. Yates contributed. "More or less. But that's not Izzy's fault, and it's infamous of him to sacrifice her to old Redhyde."

"Yes, it is," Rosamund said unexpectedly.

"Especially when I love Tom," Miss Yates added. "I have *always* loved Tom, and they know it."

"You do know that you could just refuse his lordship?" Giles said.

"It isn't as simple as that," Rosamund said without looking at him. "It never is."

Giles blinked at her. "Then you think we should *help* them elope?"

"I don't know about that." Rosamund frowned at the hopeful young couple. "When did you leave home?"

"This morning," Miss Merton replied with pride. "I rode over to visit Mrs. Yates, Tom's mother. I often do because she's the squire's wife. And Tom is often there. So, I told him I was to go to Bath the very next day, and he was furious, and so was I. Instead of escorting me home, we rode here to throw our parents off the scent."

"Sound tactic," Giles observed. "Especially when Miss Merton had the forethought to bring her bandbox."

Miss Merton flushed and lifted her chin. "Well, I was determined not to go to Bath, and you do understand that eloping to Scotland is the only solution?"

"Not the only solution," Rosamund said sadly. "But I can see why you might think so. It won't serve, you know, not if you want to be comfortable afterward."

"We could live abroad," Miss Merton said brightly.

"Not with Boney running loose about the continent again," Giles said. "Besides, most of the *ton* appears to have removed there, so anonymity might be difficult."

"I'm not tonish," Tom Yates muttered. "I'm the son of a country squire, and the world knows Izzy could do better."

"I couldn't," Izzy said stoutly.

"Not with Lord Redhyde," Rosamund agreed.

"In any case, it doesn't matter," Tom declared. "We've burned our boats now and must find some way to live with it. The first thing is to be married."

"Actually," Rosamund said, "your boats are not burned. You left home this morning, and now I am your chaperone."

Giles almost choked. He caught her eye, and she held his gaze defiantly. He leaned closer to speak under his breath. "Since you are fleeing from your own family to live in a cottage as the wise woman of Little Fiddlesticks?"

"Since I am a member of a duke's family," she retorted, "and a married lady."

"Widowed lady."

She shrugged impatiently.

Their asides seemed to have passed their whispering companions by, for they had both brightened.

"Of course!" Tom exclaimed. "We fell in with you on the road! That would work. Only you're bound to feel the rough end of Merton's tongue, ma'am."

"You think he'll follow us to Scotland?" Izzy said anxiously.

"I think we should rule out Scotland," Rosamund said emphatically. "I can't travel at the moment, and Giles is on his way to Brussels."

"Oh." Izzy looked crestfallen.

Giles, relieved, waited with some fascination for Rosamund's solution.

"You should both write to your parents first thing in the morning," she said at last. "They are probably sick with worry." She appeared to see no correlation with her own flight from the duke's household, all her concentration being on the younger people's problems. "Tell them you are taking a few delightful days with friends who enjoy painting the beauties of the countryside. One of those friends is the cousin of a duke."

"Who is the other?" Giles inquired with interest.

"Your friend, of course. Sophia? We can decide later whether we all stay with her or remove to my cottage."

"How big *is* this cottage?" Giles murmured.

Rosamund ignored him. "We can either banish Mr. Yates to the local inn or send him home. When Mr. Merton does appear, I will speak to him most reasonably on *my* territory and persuade him to postpone any marriage until his daughter is at least eighteen."

Izzy, idling combing her fingers through her tumbled tresses, paused and stared at Rosamund. "Wait. Then I won't be able to marry Tom either."

"Tom is, what, eighteen years old?"

"Next month," Izzy said proudly.

Giles groaned.

"How did you plan to keep your wife?" Rosamund asked Tom affably. "Do you have access to funds?"

Tom flushed. "No, but I am prepared to work, to earn—"

"How? What skills do you have?"

"Farming. Stewarding of the land."

"In effect, you will succeed your father as squire?"

"I will, but he's not exactly at death's door." Tom flushed deeper and glared. "Nor would I wish him to be."

"Perhaps your father is more sympathetic to your marriage to Miss Merton?" Giles asked.

Tom shifted uncomfortably. "Not *exactly*."

"He thinks I'm too flighty and impractical," Izzy said. "And he believes we are much too young to marry. But he does like me."

"He sounds an eminently sensible man," Giles observed, and for some reason, received a dazzling smile from Miss Merton. She would break hearts and lead poor Tom Yates a terrible dance.

"To own the truth," Tom said determinedly, "I'm not so keen to get leg-shackled before I've done anything else."

"Tom!" exclaimed his betrothed, clearly incensed.

Tom ignored her. "But I can't have them marrying her off to some gouty old roué just for his money. Or marrying her off to anyone, really, because then my chances are blown, aren't they?"

"Until she's a widow, certainly," Giles replied. "The gouty old roué *might* be obliging in this manner but—"

"Giles!" Rosamund uttered. "You aren't taking this seriously."

"I am," he assured her. "I just don't see how this is any of our business."

"Am I any of yours?" she shot back.

He closed his mouth, because of course she was quite right. As far as she knew, he had no reason to interfere in her affairs, no motive beyond kindness to help her. Guilt gnawed at him, keeping him silent while Izzy emitted a peel of laughter.

"Of course you are," she said to Rosamund. "You're his sister. As for Tom and me, I don't really see the point of waiting to marry, though if it's what Tom prefers, I don't mind, so long as we can see each other. But I won't marry anyone else, even if they're likely to die."

"Quite right," Giles said breathlessly.

Rosamund frowned at him. "Then that's settled. You may share our rooms for tonight, and tomorrow, we shall ride together to visit Giles's friend."

It gave Giles a moment's unease. Although they had exchanged letters occasionally, he hadn't actually laid eyes on Sophia in four years. He didn't know her precise circumstances or how, indeed, she would regard his arrival with three friends fleeing their families. Come to that, he was fleeing the law and really had no right to go anywhere near her.

Nor was he happy about Rosamund sharing a bedchamber

with a complete stranger, but he had to allow that to be her choice. He would certainly be keeping his eye on young Tom Yates.

GIVING IZZY MERTON a few moments' privacy in the bedchamber they now shared, Rosamund pretended to have left her reticule downstairs. In reality, she hoped to find Giles there and exchange a few words in private about their new friends. However, the whole inn was in darkness, so she only walked downstairs for form's sake, shielding her single candle so that it wouldn't blow out in a draught and leave her blundering about in the darkness. Even the fire no longer glowed in the hearth.

Reaching the bottom of the stairs, she caught a glimpse of movement, and her heart dived in alarm.

"You shouldn't creep about in the dark, you know," said Major Butler's quiet voice as a light flared at their table in the corner. "I thought you were one of our lovebirds escaping."

"Why would they do that?" Rosamund murmured, moving toward the figure in the lamp's glow. "They got a night's shelter just as they wanted."

"Well, he's not that keen on marriage, is he? And now he trusts us to look after her…" He pushed a chair toward her with his foot.

She sank down on it. "But you don't trust him?"

"I trust him to behave like a lad of seventeen."

"Were you entirely irresponsible at seventeen?"

His lips stretched. "Mostly. But then I joined the army, and I was responsible for more than just myself." His fingers, long and strong, closed around the glass in front of him and swirled the brandy before shoving it across the table to her. "Have a drink. It will help you sleep."

"I always sleep like a baby."

By some trick of the light, his dark eyes seemed to glitter. They flickered downward, to her lips, and he smiled. Heat curled around her heart and dived into her belly.

"Don't make me think of that," he said obscurely.

Of her sleeping. Frowning at him, she made a discovery. "Are you foxed, Giles?"

"Not even a trifle disguised," he replied with apparent regret. "Although I confess, I have downed a little brandy since you all retired."

"Why?"

He shrugged. "I had this idea it might make living with myself easier, but it doesn't." He reached for the glass, then let his hand fall on the table instead and curled his fingers into a fist.

Impulsively, she covered his hand with hers. "You have been very kind to me, but I don't need your escort, Giles. Or the help of your friend. Go to Harwich, and I will take these children with me to Little Fiddleton, where I shall talk to their parents."

Curiosity entered his eyes, along with a faint, beguiling smile that sent butterflies soaring in her stomach. "You will, too, won't you? You are quite authoritative when you wish to be. Did you learn that in the duke's house?"

"Yes." She glanced at her fingers on his unmoving fist, then raised her gaze to his once more. He wasn't quick enough to hide the pain he normally concealed, some secret sorrow or deep-seated guilt that made her *hurt* for him. Then his lashes swept down, and she knew he would not tell her. And yet she had to ask.

Her heart beat erratically fast. "Do you wish to confide in me, Giles?"

"Yes. But I won't." He withdrew his hand, which hurt her all over again. But he only lifted her fingers from the table and touched them to his cheek before brushing them against his lips. He rose, drawing her to her feet at the same time so that they stood so close together she could smell him—brandy and Giles and a faint echo of horse. And those liquid dark eyes, not smiling but consuming her anyway. "I'm sorry," he whispered.

"For what?"

"For not meeting you first, because then I would never have done it. Come, I'll light you upstairs." He released her and swiped up the lamp. She took the candle and together they walked sedately upstairs.

At her door, he merely bowed, and, baffled by his mood and his words, she slipped into her chamber.

Chapter Five

"WHERE IS THE duchess?"

Entering the breakfast parlor ridiculously early in order to speak to Her Grace, Anthony Severne was annoyed to find only Victor there. And even he had just risen from the table and was reaching for his walking stick.

"I have no idea," the new Duke of Cuttyngham growled. "Ask one of the maids."

"I have. They also claimed not to know."

"Then I imagine they don't. Good morning, Cousin." Victor stumped past him in his usual ungainly manner.

Anthony made a discovery. "You're wearing riding dress."

"There's no keeping anything from you, is there?"

"There's no need to be sarcastic. I didn't know you had taken up riding."

"Damned hard to get around the estate if I don't."

Anthony let that pass. "Perhaps I'll just step up to Her Grace's apartments and inquire for her."

"I wouldn't bother," Victor said. "She isn't there."

"I thought you said you didn't know where she was?" Anthony accused.

"I don't. But I now know where she isn't."

"Does she know about…?"

"About my father's death?" Victor said brutally. "Probably.

It's in the morning papers."

But Anthony was smart enough to pick up some unusual overtone in Victor's manner. "You *really* don't know where she is, do you? You actually sent to her apartments because you're worried. When did you see her last?"

Victor paused. "Yesterday morning, if you must know."

"Then she wasn't at dinner?" Anthony said, alarmed.

"No, but then neither was I. I usually eat in the library unless His Grace makes a fuss. Which, thank God, he won't be doing again. Excuse me."

Forgetting all about his breakfast, Anthony stood still, deep in uneasy thought. She should be here. He needed to keep an eye on all his little ducks. Hera was safely with Letitia, and Victor was here, but he needed the duchess under his wing for at least the next three months.

The slamming of the library door jolted him into action. He walked rapidly from the breakfast parlor, along the gallery to the room which Cuttyngham had called his study. Here, on the few occasions he returned to Cuttyngs, the late duke had answered his correspondence and took care, presumably, of estate and parliamentary business.

Anthony was sure any important papers would be in Cuttyngham House in London, but quite apart from the elusive duchess, he had always intended to have a thorough look though his cousin's desk.

There were only a few letters lying in a small pile on the great walnut desk, directly in front of the ornate, matching chair in which the late duke had occasionally sat. He had done so more often in the first year or so of his second marriage, before it had become plain that his young second wife was barren.

Anthony felt a rush of pleasure as he sat in his cousin's chair. He felt almost powerful as he rifled the waiting letters. It was not his place but Victor's to open them. But Anthony had been almost a secretary to His Late Grace, and Victor would not care. Hastily, one after the other, he broke the seals and unfolded two invitations from neighbors, a letter from the vicar and, finally, a note in a fine, feminine hand, signed only *Rosamund*.

Stupidly, it took him a moment to recall that Rosamund was the name of the duchess, not some lightskirt of the duke's.

> *Your Grace.*
>
> *I have decided to live elsewhere, under a different roof where I might enjoy normal freedom of movement. It will cost you nothing, and I do not flatter myself that my presence will be of any loss to you. You may be assured that I shall live quietly, perfectly incognita, and will do or say nothing to bring our names into disrepute. Nor will you be able to find me, so please don't trouble anyone to try. Account for my absence any way you wish.*
>
> *Rosamund.*

Perhaps such simple bluntness should not have surprised him, but it did. In truth, he barely knew her, for like the rest of the family, he had paid her little attention since the wedding. But perhaps this was just a childish ploy to demand her husband's attention, although in that case, would she not have sent it to the duke in London? Why leave it here, not even at the top of the nonurgent pile awaiting the duke's return? Probably because she knew he was on his way to Cuttyngs.

Stuffing the letter into his pocket, he rose and left the study, walking with growing unease to the stairs that led to the duchess's apartments. He didn't trouble to knock.

Her Grace's dresser stood, wringing her hands by the window.

"Where is your mistress?" Anthony barked.

"I've no idea, sir. She went for a ride yesterday morning and never came home. I'm so worried!"

"So worried that you told no one your mistress could be lying dead in a ditch?"

The maid wailed. "Oh, don't say that, sir, please! I know she likes to be free of all of us occasionally, and I thought it was only that. So, I went to bed until she sent for me, and she never did, and then this morning, she were gone again, and his lordship, that is His New Grace, sent to ask if she was well and—"

"Wait." Anthony cut through this stream with one word. "How do you know she went riding?"

The dresser looked at him as though he were sixpence short of a shilling. "She was wearing her riding habit."

"Which horse did she take?"

Again, the girl looked blank, and Anthony turned from her in disgust, only to spin back again. "Did she take any other clothes with her? Look now!"

Five minutes later, he strode furiously into the stables. "Which horse does the duchess usually ride?" he barked.

"The mare," Gregson replied, nodding toward the stall where a handsome gray mare shook her head over the door.

"Are any of the horses missing?"

"Only General."

General, admittedly not with a lady's saddle, and three walking dresses, an evening gown, toothbrushes and powder and hairbrushes. And a curt note left for her humiliatingly neglectful and controlling husband. The duchess had, in vulgar parlance, done a runner, had it away on her toes, and otherwise escaped her gilded cage.

"Gregson, I have a job for you," Anthony said grimly, hauling his henchman outside and away from the other grooms. "Ride as fast as you can to Cuttyngham and see if you can find any trace of Her Grace or General."

"*Her Grace* took General?"

"It rather looks that way, but I doubt she was throwing her title around, so find out if anyone resembling her bought a lady's saddle yesterday. Find out where she went. She's up to something, and I don't like it."

"She's probably bored," Gregson protested. "Can't say I blame her. Not to speak ill of the dead, but His Grace ignored her something awful and wouldn't let her do anything besides."

"His Grace, clearly, recognized a rebellious spirit," Anthony snapped, "where you and I did not. Find out where she went, Gregson, and report back to me immediately."

Gregson sighed and went to saddle a horse. Anthony returned to the house and wondered how long it would take the London newspapers to get to Cuttyngs. He decided to beard the new duke in his library and explain about the duel and Major Butler and the hue and cry out for his father's murderer.

Only when he reached the library, Victor was sprawled back in his chair, one of the scandal rags in his hand. On Anthony's entry, he threw it on the desk.

Deadly Duel Does for the Duke, proclaimed its headline.

"Of all the bloody stupid ways to keep me from Oxford," Victor said bitterly.

AS GILES WALKED downstairs the following morning to the welcome smells of coffee and frying bacon, he felt his last remaining controls on his life begin to slip away. He positively needed *not* to be entangled with any of these people, even Rosamund who, he had begun to think, held more power in the duke's household than he had imagined.

Although it had once seemed the least he could do to aid a member of the family he had wronged, his feelings were growing far too complicated and far too intense. Besides which, there was shame in deceiving her. And though she did not appear to like the duke very much—there seemed to be little in him that was likeable—her connection to him raised his guilt to screaming point.

And then there was the wretched child now tucking into breakfast. She sat alone at the corner table he and Rosamund had occupied yesterday evening. Miss Isabel Merton. He *really* did not want to be involved in this hairbrained elopement—he had to escape the country and fight one more war after all—but it seemed for Rosamund's sake, he already was.

The girl looked up at him and smiled artlessly. "Good morning, Major Butler! Is Tom awake, too?"

"Apparently, judging by all the groaning."

"Groaning!" She dropped her fork and stared at him. "Is he ill?"

"No, he's a very young gentleman being roused from his bed before eight o'clock in the morning. Did you sleep well?"

"Oh yes, as always. Do sit down, Major, Mrs. Davies is bringing you breakfast, and I have to say it's delicious."

It was, although Izzy Merton's constant chatter was like an irritating fly buzzing in his ear. The only time he responded was when she said, "Mrs. Daryll has been so kind!"

"She is a kind lady," he said austerely, reaching for his coffee. And then he was aware of three things at once.

Behind him, the inn door opened to let in a blast of cold air and some urgent personage. Above him, on the stairs, a clatter of footsteps proclaimed the impetuous descent of Tom Yates. And in front of him, Izzy's eyes dilated, and her face crumpled into a picture of dismay and fear.

"Oh, no!" she uttered in despair. "We are undone, and so *soon*!"

The footsteps on the stairs stopped dead.

A stranger exploded into pained and angry speech. "So, there you are indeed! Lost to all…!"

Seeing nothing else for it, Giles rose and dropped his napkin on the table before he turned unhurriedly to face, presumably, Mr. Merton.

The man was striding furiously toward their table. Of middle years, vigorous and stout, his raging eyes clashed with Butler's. He came to a surprised halt, his speech tailing off in bewilderment. "Who the devil are you?"

"Who the devil are *you*?" Giles responded, recognizing the

bullying tone and unprepared to stand for it, even allowing for the man's distress.

"Oh, it's my *father*," Izzy exclaimed, springing up and coming around the table to stand beside Giles. "Papa, this is Major Butler, who has been most kind to me—"

"I'll bet he has!" roared Mr. Merton, his eyes murderous.

"Major, my father, Mr. Merton," Izzy pursued desperately.

"How do you do, sir?" Giles said civilly, although he wasn't foolish enough to offer his hand since the older man looked ready to literally bite it off.

"*This* is who you ran off with?" Mr. Merton said in disgust. "Not even Tom Yates but some penniless, deceitful officer! How in God's name did you even contrive to *meet* my daughter, sir?"

Inconvenient laughter bubbled up from Giles's chest. "Thereby hangs a long and gory tale."

Merton's eyes looked ready to burst at such levity, but Tom chose that moment to make his presence felt. Clattering down the rest of the stairs, he said stiffly, "Good morning, sir. I am afraid you labor under a misapprehension. Major Butler has not eloped with Izzy. He merely happened to be here, and his sister took Izzy under her wing."

"Perhaps you'd join us for breakfast?" Giles said. "Mrs. Davies, if you would?" he added to the innkeeper's wife who was gawping open-mouthed from person to person as though she didn't know whether to be appalled or triumphant. In the end, she scuttled off to obey, while Giles poured coffee for both Mr. Merton and Tom.

Izzy gazed at him, her eyes full of both hope and fright.

"What is the matter with you people?" Merton yelled. "Have you no shame, Isabel? I find you alone with not one man but two, and you all expect me to have breakfast?"

"What better chaperone than the lady's father?" Giles said, which did not have the calming effect one might have hoped.

Mr. Merton's eyes bulged. "Chaperone! It's far too late for that! My daughter—"

"No, sir, it isn't," Giles interrupted firmly.

For the first time, a hint of doubt seemed to pierce Merton's fury. In the sudden silence, much to Butler's relief, Rosamund descended the stairs.

Dressed in her riding habit, with her hair simply dressed in a loose knot, she again carried herself with the dignity he had glimpsed before. It was almost as if there were two Rosamunds: one the vital young girl of sparkling fun and kindness; the other a lady of quelling authority. And yet, whether or not she had learned the latter, they both seemed to be natural.

She drew all eyes. Mr. Merton, thankfully, seemed to be bereft of speech.

"Oh, thank God," Izzy muttered. "Mrs. Daryll, allow me to present my father, Mr. Merton. Papa, this is Mrs. Daryll, Major Butler's sister, who has been so kind to Tom and me."

Rosamund glided across the inn floor, her hand held out with all the regal affability of an ancient dowager duchess. "How delightful to meet you, sir. You must have been worried sick. Young people can be so thoughtless. Won't you join us for breakfast? And we can discuss what is best to do."

Mr. Merton, probably without quite knowing how, found himself bowing over Rosamund's hand and handing her onto the bench beside his daughter. Giles gravely placed a chair for him at the "head" of the table and pushed Tom onto the chair beside his own.

"My brother and I are traveling to Harwich," Rosamund told Mr. Merton, *almost* truthfully, while the other breakfasts were being served. "Where he is to take ship to Ostend and rejoin the Duke of Wellington's forces at Brussels."

If she had hoped to soften the furious father's rage with this proof of Giles's patriotic duty and heroism, she was doomed to disappointment. Merton spared him a glare of contempt and disgust before turning back to Rosamund.

"He hates military men," Tom breathed. "Ever since a militia officer tried to run off with his lady wife fifteen years ago."

Again, quite inappropriate laughter threatened Giles, but fortunately Rosamund had the situation in hand.

She picked up her fork. "As you are well aware, sir, your daughter is an innocent—most charming innocent—with very little idea of the consequences of her…journey. As for Mr. Yates, it is my belief he had little alternative, his choice being to let Miss Merton flee on her own or accompany her and keep her safe."

Tom scowled and opened his mouth. Giles kicked his ankle, and he subsided, glaring at the major instead.

"My daughter has no reason to flee her own home," Merton growled.

Delicately, Rosamund swallowed her mouthful of bacon and eggs, and reached for a slice of toast. "Not in your eyes, perhaps. But in her own, she is terrified of being forced into marriage with a much older, unattractive man whom she perceives as a monster." Rosamund smiled and raised one hand in imaginary defense. "Of course, we are well aware that a gentleman of your clear breeding and understanding would never dream of visiting such distress upon his own daughter. But, sir, this is all about perception. In any case, the disaster is by no means beyond redemption."

"I wish you will tell me how!" Merton snapped.

"Easily," Rosamund said in apparent surprise. "Unless you have already shouted it abroad that your daughter has eloped with Tom Yates?"

"Of course, I have not! And Yates is as angry—and discreet!—as I!"

"Then there is no reason for anyone to suppose that Tom did not, as a family friend, escort Izzy to meet with me and accompany me on my journey. Even if anyone were to be so vulgar as to make inquiries, they would find only that Izzy spent the night in my bedchamber with me, while Tom slept under the eye of my brother. And now you have kindly joined us." Rosamund smiled and sipped her coffee with quiet confidence.

Again, Tom's indignation seemed about to erupt. This time,

Giles trod on his foot.

Apparently fascinated, Mr. Merton said, "And how is it we are acquainted with you? Because we are, are we not? I'm sure we have met before."

"I don't believe so, although it's possible. My family is in Essex."

"Mrs. Daryll's cousin is the Duke of Cuttyngham," Izzy said proudly.

Rosamund's eyelashes swept briefly down, and Giles wondered if she wasn't annoyed, although surely her connection to the duke's family could only help here.

"Perhaps that is it," Merton said.

"There remains," Giles said, mainly to distract Merton's attention from Rosamund, "the small matter of your daughter's wish to marry Mr. Yates."

"Which I take leave to tell you is none of your dashed business!" Merton snarled.

"I would agree, except that your daughter and Mr. Yates have rather made it our business," Giles said mildly. "Though of course, Miss Merton's marriage is certainly not under our control."

Mr. Merton, in the act of shoveling bacon into his mouth, paused and narrowed his eyes, presumably seeing some threat in his words. If either Giles or Rosamund were to blab about these events, Izzy could be ruined.

"My sister," Giles said, "always has sound advice."

Merton swallowed and spoke with a hint of desperation. "You must see that my Izzy is too young to marry anyone. As is Tom Yates! He is not even eighteen."

"Well, I think even Tom, in his devotion, recognizes that they are too young," Rosamund said delicately. "My suggestion would be that you allow them to become engaged and make the engagement a long one."

"A long one!" Izzy exclaimed, staring at her as though betrayed. "But Mrs. Daryll—"

"If you are engaged to Mr. Yates," Rosamund said patiently, "then you cannot marry the gouty old gentleman in Bath."

"Gout is not a character flaw," Merton growled. "And in fact, Lord Redhyde is barely forty and would make an excellent match for a flighty young girl."

"Over my dead body," Tom exclaimed.

"If necessary!" Merton retorted.

"Gentlemen, there is no need for such dramatics," Rosamund pointed out. "Were Izzy and Tom betrothed, Izzy would feel no need to flee, and Tom will always look after her. Moreover, it is quite possible that during their long engagement, they will realize they don't suit."

"Rubbish," Tom uttered.

"Never!" Izzy cried.

Her father ignored them both, instead regarding Rosamund with some admiration.

"And if," Rosamund continued, "in a year or two, they do still wish to be married, is that such a bad thing? It seems to me that Tom is a fine young man, who cares for her deeply."

"They've known each other forever," Merton muttered, frowning. "Of course, they are fond of each other."

"His father is the local squire, and of an old and respectable family, I understand." Rosamund drank her coffee and set the cup down in its saucer.

"We're not rich by the standards of Redhyde," Tom said fiercely, "but neither are we penniless. Izzy would have a good life with me."

"But, Tom, it will be ages away!" Izzy objected.

"Only a year or two," Tom said, reaching across the table to take her hand, while Merton glowered furiously. "And truly, it will be best, Izzy. Gives me time to make something of myself, to make you proud."

"Spoken like a true gentleman," Giles approved, clapping Tom on the back, if only to make him release Izzy's hand before her father had an apoplexy.

"So, we are agreed all to play our parts?" Rosamund said hastily.

Izzy took her father's hand, turning huge soulful eyes up to his face. "If it must be, Papa, I agree to wait and be good, if only we may be engaged."

Giles, who couldn't see why they didn't come up with this solution in the first place, rose to his feet. "Then, if you will excuse me, I have a few things to pack before we set off."

"Oh, Mrs. Daryll has invited us to stay with her," Izzy recalled. "May we not go, Papa?"

"No, you may not," Merton replied. "You may pack your things, too, and come with me to Sir Aubrey Fancott's house, where we will remain until at least tomorrow. Tom, you may go home and face whatever punishment your father deems appropriate."

"Who is Sir Aubrey Fancott?" Giles asked Tom five minutes later as they both packed up their few belongings in the bedchamber.

"An old friend of Merton's. Local magistrate, I think. He'll be kind enough to Izzy, and I suppose it's best if I go home. Though I don't mind telling you it sets my back up to be ordered around like a child. Do you mean to accompany them there?"

"Lord, no," Giles said hastily. He had no intention of going near any magistrates until Boney was defeated once and for all. "I need to get to Harwich."

DOWNSTAIRS, MR. MERTON had been left alone to brood while everyone else packed up their gear. His thoughts were not altogether happy. Relief at discovering his daughter unharmed was tempered by the feeling that he had been manipulated into agreeing to something he did not want. Although he supposed the solution to Izzy's disobedience was sensible. Tom was young and would fall in love with someone else—several someones!—before he was ready to settle down. And Izzy's flighty little heart would not break for long.

He hoped his wife would approve, too. It was she, after all, who had been so set on the Redhyde match. But then, she had wanted her daughter to be a baroness.

His pacing was interrupted by a coach that barely slowed. A bag of post was hurled into the inn yard, and a boy trotted out to fetch it. Most of it appeared to be newspapers. A few, clearly specially ordered, he stashed behind the counter with a few letters. The rest, he abandoned on the table beside Mr. Merton.

There were copies of the *Gazette* and *The Morning Post* from London, which the inn clearly took for its customers, along with a couple of less reputable scandal rags. Merton cast the latter aside to get at the *Post*, until a headline caught his eye and he frowned.

Deadly Duel Does for Duke. Even despising it, Merton couldn't help reading it. His eyes widened and his mouth fell slowly open. "Major Butler!" he said aloud. Damn it, he'd known there was something fishy about the swaggering soldier!

"I'm ready, Papa," Izzy said, appearing with her bandbox and a very uncharacteristic expression of submission.

"Good. We're leaving now. I have something very interesting to tell Sir Aubrey!"

CHAPTER SIX

ROSAMUND WAS SLIGHTLY piqued to discover that Izzy and her father had gone without even a farewell.

"I shouldn't worry about it," Tom said philosophically. "Old Merton hates to be beholden and will have rushed off before anyone expected him to acknowledge his debt to you." He grinned. "And especially to you, Major, since you have the misfortune to be in uniform."

"Did Mrs. Merton actually elope with this officer?" Rosamund asked, intrigued.

"No, I don't think so. Before my time, obviously, but according to my mother, the experience made Merton sit up and take a bit more notice of his wife! In any case, I thank you both on his behalf as well as my own. I knew eloping wasn't the thing, but I couldn't think how else to look after her."

Rosamund smiled and offered her hand. "Goodbye, and I wish you luck!"

He bowed over her fingers and shook hands cordially with Giles.

"Actually," Giles allowed, "you managed a difficult situation very well and with your honor intact. Well done, and good luck to you."

The boy blushed with pleasure under the major's praise, although he hastily scowled darkly to cover his emotion. "And to you, Major. Give Boney what for! I don't suppose Wellington would like an extra volunteer?"

"I think you're too necessary at home," Giles said tactfully.

Tom grinned and sauntered out to wave them on their way. "That's a large horse for a lady," he remarked about General.

Rosamund laughed. "At least it means I can talk to Giles as we ride without getting too much of a crick in my neck!"

"Is it always like this for you?" Giles asked, glancing at her as they set off toward the Harwich Road.

"Like what?" she asked, surprised.

"Adopting people, sorting out their problems until they become devoted friends."

"Well, I don't know about devoted friends. I suspect both Izzy and Tom will have forgotten about us within the week when another crisis crops up."

"Oh, I don't know. You're very good at it, you know."

A flush rose into her cheeks. "So are you."

"I'm used to dealing with lads of Tom's age. Still, I would probably have left them to sort things out on their own. I'm glad we didn't."

"So am I." An emotion that was part memory wormed its way to the surface, catching at her throat. "It used to be like that. I liked to make friends, help where I could, or… I used to write to many people I had met on journeys or at social gatherings. And now I don't know them anymore. Even my oldest friends."

"What happened?" he asked.

She tried to smile and managed an unhappy shrug. "Marriage."

There was a pause. "People's lives drift apart. But I think you mean more than that. Rosamund, was your husband unkind?"

"He never struck me, if that's what you mean. But he liked to be in control. I'm sorry, why should we talk about him on such a beautiful day?"

The day *was* beautiful, if muddy after the night's rain.

"Shall we gallop?" Giles suggested. "Give the horses some

fun?"

It wasn't just the horses who enjoyed it. With the wind in her face, General speeding beneath her, and Giles Butler riding beside her, her mood turned back to appreciation and happiness, which she grasped with both hands.

She even lifted up her voice and sang, her voice breathless and bumpy with General's movements. To her delight, Giles joined in with a rich baritone, and by the time they pulled the horses up to rest, they had given up song for laughter.

When she met his gaze, the fierce smile still gleamed in his eyes and around his expressive mouth. Something jolted within her, sweet and heady, spreading tingles through her stomach to her very fingertips, because she loved to see him laugh, she loved his company and his sense of fun and the way he looked. He was the center of this moment of perfect joy in the world.

He dismounted to let Chessy recover from the gallop, and when he reached up for her, she put her hands trustingly on his shoulder and slid to the ground. Still breathless, excitingly aware of his hands at her waist, holding her steady between the horse and his hard, lean body, she wanted suddenly to press closer to him. To feel him everywhere.

Shocked heat swarmed up from his hands into her face. Hopefully, he would think it was still the gallop depriving her of steady breath.

The laughter was dying in his unblinking eyes, replaced by something warmer and much more thrilling. Slowly, deliberately, he dropped his gaze to her mouth. Longing soared, paralyzing her. How would his kiss feel on her lips? She had never wanted to kiss anyone before, or at least not for years since she had stopped being curious about boys. And now she thought she would die if he did not kiss her *immediately*.

She drew in a breath, and abruptly, he stepped back.

Disappointment thudded into her. Only then she realized that he had heard what she had not—the sounds of horses and wheels on the road.

"Someone is in a hurry," he remarked. His voice, though light, was not quite steady. Did that mean he had been as affected as she?

Dear God, I am a married woman! What am I thinking of?

I am a married woman running away from her husband. Is that woman, Rosamund Daryll, not entitled to a lover, even if the Duchess of Cuttyngham is not?

Sophistry. Idiocy. And besides, I do not even want a lover. I just want to know his kiss…

By then, she had somehow taken hold of General's reins, as Giles held Chessy's, and they began to walk sedately along the track toward the crossroads. The newcomers—two outriders and an old carriage pulled by two horses—swept around from the left-hand fork and came to a sudden halt in a welter of mud and equine snorting.

To Rosamund's surprise, two more men spilled out of the carriage, while the outriders waited, pistols drawn.

Giles swore beneath his breath, and his free hand delved into his great coat pocket.

"Don't!" commanded the nearest running man, wheezing to a halt in front of them. "We've got you covered. Major Giles Butler?"

"Who inquires?" Giles said haughtily.

"I do. On behalf of His Majesty's Justice of the Peace, Sir Aubrey Fancott. Are you Major Butler?"

Uncomprehending, Rosamund stared from the pistols by the carriage, to the men confronting them and, finally to Giles.

He stood for an instant, his head thrown back in what looked like simple frustration, and yet she knew it was not. He was taking in the scene, the position of the players, and calculating, surely, his chances of escape.

Why? What had he done? Was this the sin he had mentioned before catching up with him? Whatever it was that had made him declare himself the worst person to be helping her?

He relaxed and met the gaze of the magistrate's representative. "Yes, I'm Butler."

"Then I'm arresting you, and you must come with me to stand before Sir Aubrey."

"What did you do?" Rosamund whispered.

He turned his rather white face toward her. "I killed a man in a duel," he said distinctly. "Rosamund—"

And then everyone whipped around as another set of hooves thundered down the lane at the left. A rider came into view, wheeling to avoid the carriage, then spurring toward Rosamund and Giles.

"Tom?" Giles said, stunned.

"I came as soon as I heard," Tom gasped. "Seems I'm too late."

"No," Giles said with relief in his voice, "you're just in time. Look after my sister. Make sure she completes her journey in safety."

Rosamund all but exploded from her paralysis into speech. "Don't be ridiculous! I'm coming with you to sort out this foolish mistake."

"It's not a mistake, Rosamund." Unexpectedly, he swooped, pressing his lips to her cheek. "Take care and be happy. Tom?"

"Of course," Tom said unhappily as Giles strode forward with a man on either side of him.

"No!" Rosamund started after them, but Tom seized her arm.

"Not now," he breathed. "It's impossible now. But I know where they're taking him, and I know how to break him out."

THE CARRIAGE RIDE was hardly comfortable, although he'd known far worse journeys in Spain. But squashed beside the magistrate's burly, sweaty henchman with another opposite, eyeing him smugly, he at least had time to think.

He was not angry. Not really. This detour had always been a

risk, and he fully deserved his fate. On the other hand, he had not yet given up his ambition to help defeat Boney once and for all. Plus, leaving Rosamund in the care of a stripling of seventeen positively hurt.

God knew why. The stripling was a far better bet than he in almost every conceivable way. Even if the duel was forgiven him somehow, there was no possible future for him with the widow of the man he had killed.

And yet she was everything he had never known he wanted. Sweet and vital and beautiful and funny. Compassionate and kind. And she sang like an angel. He smiled, causing clear alarm to the smug guard opposite him, who scowled instead of smirking. It was an improvement.

He had been within a hair's breadth of kissing Rosamund, too. What had he been thinking? About beauty and desire and how he never wanted to part from her. *No wonder they call me Lune. This is the height of lunacy, where everything has been leading. And it's impossible.*

He drew a sudden breath to pull himself together and found both guards sitting forward as though poised for a fight. Well, he wouldn't give them one, not yet. They were armed and he no longer was. He would bide his time, and who knew? He might yet get to escort Rosamund to her cottage. If he was quick…

The carriage drove up to a pleasant country house and pulled up around the back. The smug guard threw open the door and seized him by the arm.

"There's no need to manhandle me," Giles said impatiently. "I have no intention of either fighting or running before I've spoken to this magistrate of yours."

Warily, the smug one released him, but it rather amused him to be surrounded by his guards as though he were some desperate highwayman or a dangerous French spy. He was led through a side door into the house and down into a basement that he suspected had once been a cellar. Here he was locked in a room behind an iron gate.

There was no comfort save a rough wooden bench, so he sat on that and took off his great coat while his guards stomped away. He looked around him for a way out, but the only window was high up and yards away from his cell. Without candles, it would be unpleasant here in the dark. He doubted there would be opportunity for a quick escape, so he would keep to his original plan of lulling everyone into a false sense of security.

One of his guards returned. "You're to come before the magistrate now. So, no nonsense from you."

"Never," Giles said meekly. To prove it, he even left his great coat in the cell and followed his jailer back up the steps and across a gracious hallway to a comfortable office.

A middle-aged man with graying hair and a distinguished countenance rose from behind a desk. He cast Giles a quick, assessing glance, and dismissed his henchman, who left with apparent disappointment.

"Major Butler, I believe?" the magistrate said, inclining his head with unexpected civility.

"At your service, sir," Giles replied.

"I'm Aubrey Fancott, Justice of the Peace. Please, sit."

Giles blinked but went forward and sat on the other side of the magistrate's desk.

"I'm sorry for the manner of your detainment. It was on my instructions, but I was not aware you would be in the company of a lady. May I do anything for her?"

"I don't believe so, but I thank you for your thoughtful offer. I left her in the care of another gentleman, who I hope will see her to her journey's end."

Sir Aubrey nodded and sat down. "Bit embarrassing, to be honest," he admitted. "I'm not used to having gentlemen up before me. However, there is a warrant issued for your arrest in connection with a duel fought with the late Duke of Cuttyngham. Do you know anything about that?"

"I'm afraid I do. He insulted the memory of my late colonel. I insulted the duke, and His Grace challenged me."

"You fought by all the rules? With seconds and a surgeon present?"

Giles nodded. "We did." He met the magistrate's gaze. "For what it's worth, I didn't mean to kill him. I thought I'd shot well wide of him, but still he died."

"Still, he died," Sir Aubrey repeated. He sighed. "Dueling is a ridiculous and barbaric custom, and I fail to see how it settles anything. If His Grace had not died, I don't suppose we would be having this conversation, but since he did, the matter must be investigated. Not by me, however. I will write to the magistrate concerned and send you on to him tomorrow. In the meantime, I'm afraid I must keep you here."

"I understand."

Sir Aubrey sighed again. "If you give your word you will not try to leave, I can house you more comfortably."

"I'm afraid I can't do that," Giles said regretfully. So much for lulling his captors into a false sense of security. "I am commanded to Brussels to join the Duke of Wellington's forces, and I consider that my first duty. My second would be return to face the law."

The magistrate frowned. "You know that is not good enough."

"I do."

"Then I must send you back to the cell, where your only comfort will be a blanket, and a candle in the evening. I can feed you, but that will be all."

"It's more than I deserve," Giles allowed.

"You are an annoyingly stubborn young man."

"So I've been told. Before I go… Is the duke's death generally known now?"

"It's in the newspapers this morning, though there is no mention of a duel. We knew of it only because some scandal sheet blabbed about it and named you as the other duelist."

Giles nodded and rose to his feet. "I thought it must be something like that," he said vaguely. "Might I ask one favor?"

"Name it."

"Could I have writing materials? There are a couple of letters I should write."

"I'll have them brought down to you."

"Thank you." Giles bowed, and Sir Aubrey called for the guard.

"I am happy to take your parole, if you should change your mind," Fancott said.

Giles smiled with genuine gratitude. "Thank you. I appreciate the courtesy and the kindness."

The magistrate sighed as Giles walked past the guard and into the hall.

Giles cast a quick glance around, wondering if a dash to the front door might be an option. But the smug guard stood in his way. Besides which, he would need a horse. He wondered about the possibilities of simply stealing whatever vehicle they would use to transport him tomorrow. And then his eye was caught by a still figure on the elegant staircase, leaning over the banister to get a look at him.

Izzy Merton.

She cast him a brilliant smile and, amused, he paused to bow elaborately before the guard pushed him forward toward the basement stairs. He didn't glance at the girl again, for he was fairly sure she had winked.

"HE TOLD ME he killed a man in a duel," Rosamund said more to herself than to Tom as they trudged along the road with the horses, including Chessy. Tom seemed to know where he was going, which was enough at the moment for Rosamund, who was still trying to understand what had happened.

"Seems he did," Tom said, "and not just any man, either."

"Duels are illegal," Rosamund stated.

"They are. Though in practice, the law tends to turn a blind eye unless the duelists are caught in the act or kill each other, which Major Butler seems to have done."

"*Seems* to?" Rosamund repeated.

"Well, the *Morning Post* doesn't even mention a duel, but one of the scandal rags does and names a Major Butler. And his opponent is certainly dead. In any case, old Fancott, the magistrate, wouldn't have gone after the major unless there was a warrant out."

"But how did this Fancott even know Giles was in the area?" Rosamund demanded.

"Ah. Well, I'm afraid that was Mr. Merton, Izzy's father. He dislikes army officers as you know, and he dislikes being manipulated."

"It was spite," Rosamund said indignantly. "After we helped his daughter, too!"

Tom looked uncomfortable. "Well, to be fair to the old martinet, Major Butler is a wanted man. I'm sure he imagines he was only doing his duty."

"By depriving me of Giles's protection? By depriving Wellington of an experienced officer in the coming fight?" She paused to draw in a shuddering breath, while Tom regarded her sympathetically. "What will happen to him?"

"He'll be had up before the local beak, wherever it was the duel happened, and then no doubt bound over for trial. Only, we're not going to let that happen."

Rosamund regarded him with resurgent hope. "We're not?"

"No. He'll be locked up in Fancott's house, which is where Izzy is."

"Yes, but does she know what's going on?"

Tom grinned. "Izzy and I have known each other a long time. We can pretty much communicate anywhere. So, let's stop and rest the horses in this village ahead and make plans."

ANTHONY SEVERNE HAD much to do in the wake of his cousin the duke's death, and the last thing he needed was a missing widow. Not that he would object to her death, except that the duke and duchess dying within the space of days would cause the kind of vulgar speculation he wanted to avoid at all costs.

He was in the middle of a letter summoning his daughter Olivia when the butler entered the room and told him in disapproving tones that Gregson from the stables requested a word.

"Send him in," Anthony commanded.

The butler's nostrils flared with disapproval, but he merely backed out, and an instant later Gregson came in and shut the door. He looked about to burst with news.

"Well?" Anthony snapped. "Have you found her?"

"No, but I know what direction she took. She swapped General's saddle for a lady's saddle at the livery stable in Cuttyngham—so she did steal General from under my nose!—and was seen at the inn there in company with a military gentleman. They left the inn together and were seen riding east."

Anthony threw down his pen, splattering ink across his letter. "A military gentleman? *What* military gentleman?" When had she ever had opportunity to even meet one? She was pretty much immured here at Cuttyngs, and even at the house parties and balls she was rarely in evidence as more than a cypher. Even if someone had befriended her, Anthony was sure neither he nor any communications would have made it beyond Gregson or the duke's other henchmen.

No, this must have been a chance-met gentleman doing her a good turn. Or trying his luck. Who would not want to bed a duchess? Or wed one, now that she was a widow, and that was far more alarming. Would the girl even have the grace to wait out her period of mourning?

"What gentleman?" Gregson repeated with some relish. "Well, that is the biggest coincidence of all. His name is Butler. A Major Butler."

Anthony's jaw dropped. "*Butler?* What was he even doing… Actually, it probably doesn't matter." He tapped his fingers on the desk, forming fresh plans. "Butler is the one person in the world she *cannot* marry. Ever."

"Then you don't think they were in on it together?" Gregson sounded disappointed.

"In on what together?" Anthony demanded. He needed to think, not talk.

"The duel. Butler provokes His Grace to a duel, kills him, and marries the rich widow!"

Anthony stared at him. "Have I not just said he is the one man she cannot marry? The man is as likely as not to hang for murder, and only think of the scandal. Even Rosamund cannot marry her husband's murderer. She is naïve, of course, but it is probable she doesn't even know who her escort is. Do we know if she is still with him?"

Gregson shook his head. "I didn't want to go further than Cuttyngham until I'd spoken to you."

Anthony nodded slowly. "And they've gone east, you say? That will take them to Harwich, where I'm sure Butler said he was taking ship for Ostend. He still means to go, probably to seek Wellington's protection, although that duke is more likely to court-martial him by all I ever heard. He detests dueling among his officers and has expressly forbidden it. I wonder if Butler has abducted her to ensure his own safety? Either way, they cannot be allowed to go to Harwich together. She needs to come home and deal with His Grace's burial."

Gregson sighed. "I'll grab a bite to eat and set off again for Harwich."

Anthony thought suddenly of Lord Nimmot, he of the obsessive and gross appetites, and smiled. "Actually…no. There is someone else who will be only too grateful for the task, and I am happy to do him this favor. Go and eat while I write this letter, and then you are bound for London."

Chapter Seven

Giles had just folded his final letter and was scrawling Mrs. Daryll's name upon it, when he heard footsteps on the stairs to his prison, much lighter footsteps than had come with his writing materials, his blanket, and his candle.

He wasn't entirely surprised to behold Miss Isabel Merton, fashionable and pretty in an evening gown of white muslin. He rose to his feet, and she grinned at him conspiratorially before holding up a ring of heavy keys.

A breath of laughter caught in his throat. "Miss Izzy, where on earth did you get those?"

"On the hook at the top of the stairs. Sir Aubrey isn't really used to dealing with prisoners that people actually want to be released."

"You'll get into trouble," he warned.

"Oh, no one will know I'm out of my room," Izzy said blithely. "Except Ellie the maid, and she won't tell. Everyone is changing for dinner, and the servants are all busy, so we should be able to sneak out."

"We?" he repeated as she slid a key into the lock of his iron gate.

"Well, it's only polite to wave you off. I was brought up to observe the courtesies."

"Clearly."

Irritably, she yanked the key out of the lock and tried the next one on the ring. "Tom will have your horse waiting for you outside, as close as he can manage to the side door."

"Why are you helping me?" he asked curiously. "Don't you know what I've done?"

"You fought a duel and your opponent died, which is quite brave and romantic as well as unfortunate since he was a duke. I expect you were fighting over a lady who much prefers you to him, for I hear he was a horrid man. Also…" With a crow of satisfaction, she turned the key in the lock and threw the door wide. Its hinges squealed alarmingly. "I'm afraid it was my father who told Sir Aubrey where you were. Apparently, there is a warrant, and Sir Aubrey was compelled to act. At any rate, it seems horribly ungrateful to me, but parents can be so rigid. So, letting you go is really the least I can do. And Tom agrees."

"How do you know?" He was struggling into his coat and paused to swipe the letters off his rickety desk and shove them in his pocket. On impulse, he picked up the pen and scrawled, *My thanks and apologies, GB.*

"Tom and I always agree about anything that matters." She all but dragged him from the cell and up the stairs. At the top, she rehung the keys on a hook in the wall and peered through the door to the main hall.

Tom could hear the clank of glass and cutlery above, and the muffled chatter of many voices from, presumably, the kitchen and the servants' hall. Izzy crept through, beckoning Giles after her, and ran to the side door.

"You're wonderful, Izzy," Giles murmured, taking hold of the latch. "I hope I get the chance to dance at your wedding." He dropped a quick kiss on her cheek, which reminded him almost unbearably of another kiss on different soft, scented skin. "Thank you."

"My pleasure." Izzy beamed. "I doubt life is ever dull around you."

"Rarely," he said ruefully and opened the door cautiously. In front of him stood Chessy, with Tom holding the reins. The youth grinned and waved, though whether to Izzy or to him, he had no idea and no real interest, for beside Chessy, General shifted impatiently, and Rosamund leaned over his neck to quiet him. Joy surged up so quickly that he almost laughed aloud.

Instead, mindful of the risk Izzy in particular had already taken, he hastened to take the reins from Tom with one hand. "My thanks. I won't forget this."

"Beat Boney for us."

"I'll do my damnedest."

The door to the house closed and not a moment too soon.

"Here!" a male voice exclaimed. "What are you doing there?"

Giles could have bolted with Rosamund. It would have been safest. But he could hardly leave poor Tom there to face the music alone.

"With me!" he barked, holding down one imperious hand.

Tom didn't hesitate but sprang up, heaving himself over Chessy's back behind Giles's saddle, and the two horses took off as if all the fiends of hell were after them.

The smug guard, carrying a tray of food, lunged at Chessy, apparently out of nowhere, and Giles had to haul on the reins. Even so, the horse's shoulder bumped the fool who sat down hard in a puddle with food all over him.

In spite of everything, laughter shook Giles as he spurred forward. A gaggle of chickens flapped, squawking in all directions, and Tom yelled, "Right! Go right!" But to have veered right at that speed risked tangling his horse with Rosamund's—his heart soared just because she was here with him—so he kept going, riding straight at the pen in front, which contained a large sow and several piglets.

Behind him, Tom swore in anguish. They landed inside the pen without difficulty, though the sow, roused to fury by the danger to her offspring, charged them at a run. Chessy, bless him, understood and heaved himself, Giles, and Tom over the pig and pen both, in time to meet with Rosamund on the other side.

Together, they fled along the track leading to the grounds behind the house.

Rosamund's face was brim full of helpless laughter, and though he knew he shouldn't be quite so pleased about involving her in this, he couldn't help the surge of reckless fun which had so often seen him through worse messes than this in wartime.

"You're insane!" Tom yelled in his ear.

"Utterly lunatic," Giles agreed happily.

"No one's following," Tom reported a few minutes later. "Drop me behind the tavern."

They were not on the road the carriage had brought him earlier in the day, but on a track between a couple of lesser cottages and plots of land.

Giles slowed Chessy. "Will you manage?"

"No one saw my face," Tom said optimistically. "Take care, Captain Mad."

"Take care yourself. Jump."

"What?"

"On to the wall."

Tom, who'd clearly planned to dismount and walk through the gate in the wall, gave a breath of laughter and threw himself onto the top of the wall. Giles grinned and nodded and urged Chessy on to catch up with Rosamund, who had slowed, looking around her in apparent bewilderment.

"On to the woods," he called. "And then we can rest." Or poor Chessy could, after her exertions.

At last, they reached the woods and slowed to a walk.

"Will they be able to follow our tracks?" Rosamund asked worriedly.

"If they try. I don't really think they will. Sir Aubrey seemed more embarrassed than pleased to have caught me." He halted Chessy, who was blowing hard, and swung down from the saddle.

Rosamund, her hat dangling disreputably off the back of her head, was already sliding down from General's back, when he caught her and lifted her the rest of the way. For an instant, he resisted, and then he pressed her to him and hugged her.

"You shouldn't have waited for me," he whispered into her hair. She was endlessly soft and sweet and smelled of summer and wonder. "But thank you."

He would have released her then, but with a gasp, she threw her arms around his neck, fiercely hugging him back. She even stood on tiptoe, to press her cheek to his. And suddenly he knew that his breathlessness no longer had anything to do with the hard ride but with the lovely woman in his arms, who felt so right there, who had helped him to escape the law and embraced him like a friend…

No, not quite like a friend. Her breath was too erratic against his sensitive ear, her heartbeat too wild against his ribs. Her fingers had tangled in the hair at the back of his head, and surely it was not ferocity but awareness that fitted her body so deliciously to his? God knew he was aware, in danger of being rampantly so.

He couldn't help sliding his rough cheek against her soft, scented one, turning his face ever so slightly so that their lips almost touched. Her breath caught, trembling. Her fingers grasped his hair harder. She even made a faint, uncertain movement toward him, and he knew.

Slowly, delicately, he touched his lips to hers—the faintest caress which they could both pretend was an accident or a moment of friendship. It gave her time and opportunity to avoid what was otherwise surely inevitable. But she didn't draw back. Her lips moved very slightly, softly kissing his.

He was all too human, and she all too delightful. He brushed his mouth across hers and kissed her gently, lingeringly. Her eyelids fluttered and closed. She sighed into his mouth, and the kiss flowed and deepened.

She tasted divine. He felt all her wonder, all her surprised, awakening passion, and it came to him in disbelief that this beautiful widow had never kissed a man before.

What sort of crass, bumbling, or just plain stupid husband

had she had? And then the query was lost in her mouth, in her taste and scent, and his own deliciously building desire. Her lips, trembling beneath his, were eager while her fingertips traced the bones of his face as though learning him by touch. He could not help sweeping one hand down her back, pressing her even closer. A tiny moan escaped her, and she moved against him, driving his desire to a blaze.

Against all the odds, he was the one with experience, the one who needed to look after them both. With an all-mighty effort, he ended the stunning kiss, murmuring against her lips, "Rosamund Daryll, why do you have to be so beautiful and wonderful and—" He broke off to press his mouth to hers once more, briefly, and then dropped one arm from her so that he could catch Chessy's reins. "We should walk the poor beasts for a little. We might find a stream."

He could almost feel her bewilderment, her effort to adjust from their heady moment of passion to this mundane care for the horses. Kissing her had been insanity. It had been unkind to both of them and complicated even further what was already a ridiculous tangle. And yet, he couldn't leave her bereft. Against his better judgment, as she walked almost blindly beside him, he took her hand.

ROSAMUND, EUPHORIC AT his escape and at the wild ride away from his prison, had rejoiced in his impulsive hug. Hugging him back had been a secret happiness that she knew she would treasure forever. But then, subtly, the embrace had altered, as though he shared that secret. The first touch of his mouth had raised a thousand butterflies in her stomach. The second had devastated her.

Her world had tilted and spun. Had she not yearned to know what his kiss would be like? Dear God, she had never imagined such sweet and yet *earthy* pleasure… And then she was blundering along beside him, with General on her other side, wondering what had just happened. And why, from the delight of moments ago, she felt so lost and alone.

His hand brushed against hers, making her blood tingle, like an echo of the earlier thrill. And then his fingers closed around hers, and she wanted to weep.

Instead, swallowing, she risked a glance at him. He looked serious, even rueful, although the warmth still lingered in his dark eyes and around the lips that had seemed to promise so much.

He said, "I should apologize, but the truth is I'm not sorry for kissing you. It was delightful, as you are. But I'm going to fight Bonaparte and even if I live, I'm wanted for murder. And not just any murder."

His last words distracted her, reminding her of something else she had heard recently, and yet the warm grip of his fingers seemed most important of all.

"Are we still friends?" she blurted.

"I will always be your friend."

"And I yours."

He shook his head and something very like anguish twisted his mouth.

"Will you tell me about the duel?" she blurted.

"If you tell me about your husband."

Guilt at her lie tightened her stomach. "One confession for another."

"But not until we've found some water, fed the horses, and lit a fire."

"A fire?" she repeated.

"It's customary in camp."

She smiled at him in delight. "I have never slept outside before!"

"One thing about campaigning is that you learn to appreciate a good feather bed."

Although still uncertain, she no longer felt bereft. Indeed, there was a new edge of excitement to their camaraderie that both unsettled and delighted her. On top of which, while he amused her with tales of his past camping experiences, he kept hold of her hand. Somehow that anchored her, spreading warmth and comfort as well as deep, insidious pleasure.

Eventually, they found a stream to water the horses. Giles brushed them down while Rosamund collected wood for a fire. He told her where to look for the driest, and in just a little, came to help her carry it back to their "camp," where he had already spread greenery between the thick branches of a chestnut tree to provide a basic shelter.

It was dusk, by then, so Giles built and lit the fire while she assembled the food she and Tom had bought in the village before his escape. To her amazement, Giles emptied his leather flask of water collected at the stream into a can and set it on the fire to boil for tea—which he also carried with him.

"You come prepared," she observed as he sat back down beside her on the covered tree roots.

"I do." He reached for a slice of pie with some appreciation. "Although the tea is courtesy of my mother."

Somehow, she had never imagined him with parents. He always seemed so self-sufficient. "Tell me about your family."

"I am the youngest son of a very minor country gentleman in Lincolnshire. My oldest brother, Ralph, is following in his footsteps. Francis is a vicar. They are both married as is my sister, who now has three children—wonderful, mischievous little brats. My father works hard on the land, alongside his laborers and tenants. My mother is the best-natured woman in the world but somewhat…unworldly. I don't know how, but somehow, she keeps us all together in some important way and makes us laugh."

"Do you miss them?" she asked curiously.

"At first, I did. Dreadfully. Although I was excited to be following my own ambitions. Gradually, I learned to live with it. I love to go home, though, and then hate to leave."

"I envy you that," she said honestly. "Family and home, however far away from them you are. My parents are dead, and my brother and I don't speak.

"Was that your idea or your husband's?"

"Both." She smiled unhappily. "It was the only thing on which we ever agreed."

He frowned. "You said once you had been more or less sold to your husband. Did that not include any provision for your widowhood?"

Now, if ever, was the moment to tell him. *I am not a widow. My husband is the Duke of Cuttyngham.* "Giles," she began helplessly.

"You're right. It's none of my business. You want a home of your own, a life of your own that is not his. Hence the cottage and the herbs."

"Exactly," she said, distracted by his understanding.

Slowly, as though for some reason it took courage, he turned his head to meet her gaze. "Don't you think you might want to marry again one day?"

"No. Marriage and I do not suit."

"In what way?"

"Every way! I hate the helplessness, the lack of freedom, the *duty*—" She broke off, appalled by what she had almost said. But his gaze had not left her face, and it seemed he understood perfectly.

"Marital duty," he murmured. "By which you mean the physical duty of marriage."

She flushed to the roots of her hair, but at least he leaned forward, from where he couldn't see her, in order to retrieve the boiling water in the can from the fire. He poured it over the tea in a smaller can, and she was grateful he could not see her face. There was only the light from the fire now, anyway, casting a warm, flickering glow over his long, capable hands as he delved in his bag and produced a strainer which he placed over a tin mug before he sat back. Shadows beneath his cheekbones emphasized the angles of his lean, handsome face.

He raised his eyes to hers once more. "You hated the physical aspects of your marriage. Was he rough with you?"

"How am I supposed to answer that?" she blurted. "How would I know? The whole business was distasteful, and he enjoyed it no more than I. All that awfulness, and I'm barren anyway."

He leaned forward again and poured the tea through the strainer into the cup. "What makes you think he enjoyed it no more than you? Did he tell you so?"

She nodded, gazing determinedly at her hands until he gently pushed the cup into them. She clutched it as if it were a lifeline. "He told me I was repellent and frigid, even for a wife."

He swore under his breath and unexpectedly, his arm came around her shoulders. "Oh, my sweet, you are neither. He was a mean-spirited boor and a fool and did not deserve you. Any other man would be proud, *awed*, to call you his wife."

She couldn't help smiling at that. "You can't know that."

"I can. I have eyes. And I've kissed you."

"You may kiss me again, if you like," she whispered, turning her face up to his.

He did, without hesitation, and the butterflies in her stomach took flight once more. More than that, it felt somehow healing, as though his kiss was healing the pain of her past, physically and spiritually.

He drew back but kept his arm around her shoulder. "Drink your tea."

Obediently, she drank and passed the cup to him. He took it in one hand, keeping his arm about her shoulder. She had the feeling he wanted to say something, especially when he set down the cup and drew the blankets—his own and Chessy's—over them both. Daringly, she rested her head on his shoulder and gazed up at the night sky with its array of twinkling stars and a half moon. Wispy clouds drifted between.

She sighed with contentment, because of the beauty of the world. And because, against all the odds, she felt safe. And most of all because he held her against him. And she was warm and sleepy.

Somewhere, she was vaguely aware of his voice saying, "Rosamund? I..." And then, she was sure, he smiled. She smiled, too, at least in her mind, as she drifted into sleep.

Halfway through the night, she woke and remembered he still had told her nothing about the duel. But tomorrow was another day, and lying in his arms was too warm and novel and sweet to interrupt. She rejoiced in his every deep, even breath, letting it lull her back to sleep.

SHE WOKE COLD and alone, with a little drizzle beginning to permeate their shelter. It was light, and the fire had gone out.

She sat up quickly, hugging the blankets around her. Giles wandered through the trees from the direction of the stream, leading both horses by the reins.

"Good morning!" he called. "The weather is miserable, so I suggest we breakfast at the inn I'm told is only a mile down the road."

"What road?" she asked.

"That is the question. Shall we look?"

There was no point in regretting his briskness. The weather made such a manner inevitable, and her own shivering cold inspired her to rush into her cloak and bonnet, tidy up their campsite, and saddle General. It was a long time since she had done such things herself, but it seemed one never forgot.

It was rather longer than a mile to the inn, even by the time they found the road, so they were both ravenous by the time they sat down in its unpretentious coffee room and tucked into fresh bread and ham and eggs. And coffee with milk.

"You haven't yet told me about the duel," she mentioned between mouthfuls.

"It's not a pretty story." He drew a deep breath and spoke the rest in a rush as though he had rehearsed it many times or perhaps just spoken the same words to the magistrate yesterday. "A stranger whose company had attached itself to my own, insulted my late colonel and friend. I replied by insulting the stranger, who then challenged me. I accepted and, being in a rush to get to Harwich, insisted we fight the following morning. I didn't mean to kill him or even hit him, but somehow, I did. And he died."

"Don't you think it might be ruled an accident then?" she asked hopefully.

"It's possible," he said gloomily.

"You don't sound very hopeful."

"It doesn't really matter. The man will still be dead, and in any case, there is more to the story. The reason why I should not be with you, why you will hate me. I did not mean to tell you until you were safely at your cottage, but my silence is more dishonest than ever. Several times I have been about to tell you, including last night before you fell asleep. But the truth is, my opponent, my late opponent, was your kinsman."

"My kinsman?" she repeated, uncomprehending, rummaging through her mind for long-forgotten cousins, for her brother would never be involved in anything as nefarious or reckless as a duel. And then she caught his expression, and she knew.

The clues had been there. The other duelist had not been *just anyone*, but a great nobleman. Giles had no possible reason to have been at the Cuttyngs gates that first morning except to confess or to apologize to the family of the dead man.

Her head reeled. "Cuttyngham is dead?" she whispered. "You killed *Cuttyngham*?"

He nodded miserably. "I know you did not care for the man, but it still makes any friendship between us impossible. That is why I should not have kissed you."

She waved that aside while the hugeness of the first point permeated her understanding. "*Cuttyngham is dead!* Oh, damn the man, he's dead… And now I have to go back."

CHAPTER EIGHT

OF ALL THE reactions Giles had imagined and even feared, this one took him completely by surprise. No anger, no sadness, no guilt, only annoyance, like a spurt of fury that she would have to go back to Cuttyngs instead of moving onward with her own life.

"Why?" he asked, baffled. "You have no reason to go back. It is up to his heir and his widow to see to arrangements, and his lawyers to…"

Her gaze had flown to his and he tailed off. *No*, he thought with certainty. *She can't be.*

She rubbed her forehead, and he saw that her hand trembled. There was more here, much deeper feeling behind her irritable first words, almost a return to the hopelessness he had glimpsed on their first meeting.

"Giles, I *am* his widow," she whispered. "I didn't want you to know I was the duchess, but I never dreamed…"

"That I would have killed him?" he said harshly, causing the boy sweeping the floor to look up in alarm. He barely cared. The world was crumbling as it had when Colonel Landon had died and when he'd realized he had killed the Duke of Cuttyngham. Somehow, in this chaotic journey, he had convinced himself that if Rosamund cared for him, there might, in time, be a way for them to be together. A fantasy in which he did his duty against

Bonaparte, was acquitted of murder, and eventually able to marry, to share his life with a distant relative of the duke's.

The duke's widow was another matter entirely.

He knew a surge of cold rage against a fate that would finally show him the possibilities of love when his own actions had already made it *im*possible.

"Oh God, what a mess," Rosamund whispered. She closed her eyes, and he realized that below the table, she was holding his fingers so tightly it hurt.

Abruptly, his anger dissolved. He twisted his hand in order to clasp her fingers in return.

"It is a tangle," he agreed. One day, perhaps, the understatement would be amusing, not today, when he sought only to comfort and soothe. "I have no words to apologize for this."

"Neither do I." She opened her eyes, blinking rapidly. "This was my daring adventure in the company of a charming and heroic stranger."

"Who turns out to be none of those things." Shame washed over him all over again. "I actually came to Cuttyngs with an idea of owning my guilt and apologizing to his widow. Then I realized how intrusive and unwelcome I would be, and instead convinced myself that in helping you, I was somehow atoning." He swallowed. "I have made things worse for you. Now we must make the right plan to send you back without scandal, or the whole world will be looking for the missing duchess. And the last place you need to be found is with me."

"A posting inn," she said. Her fingers no longer clung so tightly as she bent her mind to the immediate problem. "A post-chaise will take me home all the quicker."

"But there will still be speculation as to where you were," he warned. "And who you were with. You need a reason, and a respectable female companion who can pretend to have been with us all the time, even in places where you might have been seen with me."

"I have had enough of lies," she said vehemently. "I will just go home and face the family with the truth. That I ran away because I could no longer stand my life at Cuttyngs and returned when I heard of His Grace's death."

"Word will out that you were seen with me. Someone will have recognized you as the duchess. In fact, Merton said he knew you from somewhere. He has probably remembered by now."

Her eyes widened. "And that will cast even more guilt on you. They will say you deliberately picked a fight with Cuttyngham to make me a widow. Wellington will never defend you then..."

Despite his impatience with her reasoning, he held his tongue. Whatever convinced her to save her own reputation was good.

"Everyone knew I was bored and lonely at Cuttyngs," she said in the voice of one telling a bedtime story to children. In spite of everything, it made him want to smile. "I decided I needed a companion. My sister-in-law's recent correspondence put me in touch with a possible lady, and I went to interview her." Rosamund frowned with dissatisfaction. "Only she never appeared at our arranged meeting place," she ended lamely, "and I heard of His Grace's death and came home at once."

She scowled. "Only that does not explain *you*, should Merton blab. Nor does it explain why the proposed companion did not come to me, which would be more normal in the circumstances."

Giles sat up. "You went to meet her to see if she was suitable because you wanted an excuse to leave Cuttyngs for a few days. And if you liked her, you meant to bring her with you back to Cuttyngs. You might even be able to do that if we can persuade Sophia to stay with you for a little."

"Your childhood friend and one-time betrothed?" she said doubtfully.

"Exactly. Which explains my presence as your escort."

She regarded him with admiration that tugged at his heart. "Only, of course, you could not conduct us all the way back to Cuttyngs because you must take ship at Harwich! So long as neither Sophia nor I mention your name… Oh the devil, Merton knows you as Butler."

"We'll come up with something that sounds alike—Bittner or Battle, maybe. In any case, unless he wants to publicize his daughter's misbehavior, Merton is hardly likely to shout very loudly, if at all. Neither is Sir Aubrey, who hopefully has no idea who you are in any case."

"We might get away with it," Rosamund allowed. "The Severnes won't want any scandal, so I doubt they will dig deeply either. After all, I am only the Dowager Duchess now. Victor will have to marry sooner rather than later. Poor Victor."

Giles's sympathy for poor Victor was strictly limited. By all accounts, the fellow had done nothing to make Rosamund's life more bearable. And her neglect and isolation seemed all the worse for her having been the duchess, the mistress of the great house and grounds at Cuttyngs, and no doubt several other properties, too.

"Then we need to get to Sophia as quickly as possible, convince her to help us, and hire a post-chaise. If you travel through the night, you could both be in Cuttyngs by the morning."

She nodded and tried to smile. But there was a bleakness in her eyes that broke his heart.

ROSAMUND, BATTERED BY emotion, found it easiest to concentrate on practicalities. On reaching Giles's friend Sophia as quickly as possible and hiring a post-chaise. On keeping to the story that should protect Giles as far as was possible.

She had expected him to be angry at her deceit about being the duchess. But then, he had clearly expected her to be angry with him for killing Cuttyngham and keeping it from her. She could not even begin to contemplate the hugeness of that, not yet. Only dealing with the minutiae could keep her sane and keep him safe.

They were both thoughtful on the journey to Sophia's address in the village of Dorwich. Once, during the spell they walked the horses, he said abruptly, "Are you grieving for him?"

Was she? "I don't know. I have barely seen him in three years. We did not like each other. And yet, he was my husband. I am sorry he's dead."

"So am I," he said hollowly.

She couldn't look at him. "I'm sorrier still that you were the one to do it."

"So am I." He took an audible breath. "But we will sort this out as best we can."

She nodded.

They came to Dorwich around midday, and a quick question of a passer-by directed them to the house just beyond it. Guarded by cast-iron gates, it sat at the end of a small, curving drive in the midst of a pleasant garden that stretched away into fields beyond. It seemed his friend Sophia lived in pleasant if not luxurious circumstances, by the standards of Cuttyngs at least.

Nerves tightened her stomach, for she needed Sophia to like her if this was to work. Either way, she could stay away from Cuttyngs no longer. With or without Sophia, she had to go back.

They tied the horses to the gate posts, where they could crop grass from the verges on either side and walked resolutely up the drive to the front door. Giles rapped the knocker, and a few moments later, it was opened by a tired young woman with her hair scraped back under an unbecoming cap. She looked like an overworked housekeeper, with shadows under her eyes and drooping shoulders.

"Good afternoon," Giles said with his pleasant smile. "Is Miss Wallace at home?"

But the housekeeper's face had already changed, her jaw dropping with astonishment, her rather fine blue eyes widening and sparkling at the same time. A huge smile began to dawn on her lips. Suddenly, she didn't look tired at all.

"Giles!" she uttered, and suddenly it was his eyes widening with startlement.

"Good God! Sophia?"

Some of the sparkle died from the young woman's eyes. She glanced from him to Rosamund, and her spontaneous smile froze and grew twisted. With a quick glance over her shoulder, she stepped outside and closed the front door over behind her.

"My knight in shining armor," she said lightly. "I thought you had gone off again to fight Bonaparte."

"I'm on my way," he said, his lips smiling while his eyes scanned her weary face. "Sophia, have you been ill?"

"Thank you," she murmured ironically. "I am merely a little tired. I had quite given you up."

"I was on my way to America when word of Boney's escape changed the orders, and now I'm en route to Harwich and Ostend. May we not come in?"

"God, no, I'd be packing my bags within the hour. Go away. Turn right at the gate and follow the road to the fork. Take the lesser road to the left and wait for me at the bridge." With that, she whisked herself back inside and closed the door, leaving Giles blinking at Rosamund.

"What just happened?" he asked, not quite amused.

Without thinking, Rosamund took his arm and urged him back down the path. "I don't know, but your old friend's situation is clearly not as happy as you assumed. Let's go and find this bridge."

"I had hoped we'd find the horses some oats," he muttered. "To say nothing of luncheon. I'm starving."

"How do you manage on campaign?" she wondered.

"With difficulty and a good deal of complaining. Sophia's in trouble as well, isn't she? I should have gone to see her before this."

"Why didn't you?"

He gave her a crooked half-smile. "I suppose I was afraid she might have changed her mind and want to marry me again.

Though I did indeed mean to come en route to Harwich. My mother thought her happily settled with her cousins, but she doesn't look very happy to me."

She did when she first saw you.

They did not encounter a soul on either the main road out of the village or the track that led over the hill to the bridge Sophia had mentioned.

"I'm sorry your plans are upset," he said as they let the horses crop at the greenery nearby.

She nodded, feeling his gaze on her face.

"Do you know what your circumstances will be in widowhood?" he asked.

She shook her head. "Neither my father nor Cuttyngham saw fit to tell me, and I never thought to ask."

"Perhaps you can be a wise duchess instead of a mere wise woman," he suggested. "Dispensing herbs and advice from slightly greater comfort than a servantless cottage."

She tried to smile. "Perhaps."

He produced the last piece of his toast he had purloined from the inn at breakfast and broke it in two. She took one and chewed it half-heartedly, until a female figure came into view, hurrying toward them in a thin, gray cloak and battered bonnet.

Giles eased his shoulder off the side of the bridge, frowning, as if sure now that something was wrong.

"I have ten minutes before they'll notice I'm gone," Sophia said. "What is it you want?"

"Does he have to want anything?" Rosamund asked, annoyed by the woman's attitude.

"Oh, I think so," Sophia flung over her shoulder, her gaze still on Giles.

She loves him, Rosamund thought bleakly. *He has neglected her and doesn't know she has loved him all this time.*

"I'll start by introducing you to Her Grace the Duchess of Cuttyngham," Giles said. "Your Grace, my old friend, Miss Sophia Wallace. Sophia, are you some kind of *servant* in that house?"

"No, for servants are generally paid in coin. My payment is a roof over my head and the privilege of eating—although an undisturbed meal occasionally would be pleasant—with the family if they do not have guests. I believe I said my time is short, and you still haven't told me why you are here."

Giles was frowning. "You never told my mother that. Or me."

"I wouldn't have told you now if you hadn't taken me by surprise."

Rosamund believed her. Pride would have prevented her, as pride had prevented Rosamund from telling anyone the circumstances of her marriage. Until Giles. And Giles, she saw, had been Sophia's strength through this ordeal. Just at first, she had thought he had come to rescue her, as though it had been her dream. And pride would never allow her to admit that either.

One day, I might be that strong.

"Well?" Sophia prompted impatiently.

Giles raised his gaze from her face and glanced at Rosamund, who nodded once. He said, "We came to ask for your help, but in the circumstances, I think perhaps we might help each other. Am I right in thinking you would not be with your cousins had you any other choice?"

"Your intelligence is wasted on the army."

"As your sharp tongue is wasted in servitude. How would you like to practice it on Her Grace instead? She will give as good or better in return."

Sophia's eyebrows flew up, and her gaze shifted reluctantly to Rosamund. "Your Grace wishes some verbal abuse?"

"My Grace wishes for a lady's companion. It may be temporary for a few weeks or more permanent, depending on many things, including my circumstances and how well you and I thole each other. If it proves to be temporary, I will provide a glowing reference and use what influence I have to secure you another position in a decent household. And my payment will be in coin. Don't ask me how much, for I have no idea what remuneration companions receive."

Sophia's mouth showed a tendency to drop open, but she recovered quickly. "You've never done this before, have you?"

"No. We are both novices in the art of companionship. I am, as you have undoubtedly guessed, in trouble. Not that kind of trouble," she added hastily as Sophia threw an indignant glare in Giles's direction. She blushed furiously, though Giles let out a crack of laughter. "On the contrary, Major Butler has been most kind and helpful, not least in bringing me here to you."

A hint of intrigue crept into Sophia's expression. "You had better tell me all."

"On my way to Harwich, I killed the Duke of Cuttyngham in a duel," Giles said bluntly. "In a moment of entirely *unempathetic* guilt, I decided to apologize to his widow and children. Fortunately, sense stopped me at the gates of Cuttyngs."

"Where he ran into me. I was making a bid for freedom," Rosamund said.

"To Little Fiddleton," Giles put in, and suddenly she wanted to laugh. Since she thought the mirth might emerge as tears instead, she choked it back.

"I stole my husband's groom's horse," she went on, "and Giles helped me escape his pursuit. He has kindly escorted me all the way since, unaware that I was the duchess."

"And she allowed it, unaware that I had killed the duke," Giles added.

"And now, having discovered my husband is dead, I need to return to Cuttyngs as quickly as may be, before there is some massive hunt to find me. Under no circumstances can it become known that the duke's widow has been in the company of the duke's killer. Sorry," she flung at Giles as he winced.

Sophia, who had been looking from one to the other in growing astonishment, now said faintly, "No, of course not. I quite see that."

"Besides, Major Butler needs to get to Harwich and board his ship before any other over-enthusiastic justice of the peace tries to arrest him," Rosamund finished. "So that he can fight Bonaparte."

Sophia's lips tightened. "I hope you don't mean to get yourself heroically killed in battle just to avoid the public shame of a trial for murder."

Rosamund felt the blood drain from her face so quickly that dizziness compelled her to reach for the side of the bridge. As if it a distance, she heard Giles say sharply, "Of course I do not. If I die, who will look after my men?" And a terrible, tragic longing vanquished her dizziness.

"Will you help me, Miss Wallace?" she managed.

Sophia met her gaze, her own thoughtful and just a little secretive. "I believe we would be helping each other. And Giles. So yes, I will be your companion."

Rosamund let herself sag with relief. "Thank you. Our aim is to hire a post-chaise at the next town. Could you possibly be ready to leave in two hours?"

"I am ready now," Sophia said flatly. "Lead the way.

CHAPTER NINE

WITHOUT ANY OBVIOUS regret, Sophia strode on over the bridge, her stated intention being to borrow a gig from the nearby farmer, as she often did when she had errands in the town. Rosamund exchanged glances with Giles. Then, with an expressive twitch of one eyebrow, he merely fetched General and bent with his hands joined to boost her into the saddle.

Two hours later, they reached the Coach and Horses, where Giles hired a chaise with postilions and outriders for the journey to Cuttyngs. It cost Rosamund the last of her savings, but she would let Giles pay for none of it. Quarrelling over the matter kept her mind off the inevitable parting, which had begun to weigh her down, almost like panic. By mutual if silent consent, they did not speak of that, only of what needed to be done. But she was aware of trying to store up every moment of his company, every word, every look, every accidental touch, as though they could give her the strength to deal with the next ordeal and the inevitable loneliness that would follow.

While she dealt with funeral arrangements and her late husband's aloof son and daughter, Giles would sail to Ostend and join the gathering army. She would write to Wellington himself on Major Butler's behalf. It might help, although it would not keep him alive in the coming confrontation with Bonaparte.

When Sophia entered the private parlor where they waited,

Rosamund was conscious of both relief that she had come and disappointment that her time alone with Giles had ended.

"Your household will find it odd that I arrive with no baggage at all," Sophia said as though this had just struck her as she ate from the cold collation still spread on the table.

"Oh, we'll make up some tale of it falling off the back of the carriage," Rosamund said vaguely. "It will be an excuse to buy more. Part of your salary," she added as Sophia frowned. "We leave in about an hour. Perhaps I will take a turn about the yard first."

She hoped desperately and reprehensibly that Giles would join her. At any rate, she was not paying attention as she opened the parlor door and walked into the coffee room. A gentleman stood deliberately in front of her.

Forced to halt by such rudeness, she blinked up at a familiar face and person that jolted her out of her reverie. A broad, overfed body that somehow conveyed both softness and strength; a cold, aristocratic face that had begun to sag with the lines and puffiness of dissipation; the eyes that spoke of voracious appetites, corruption, and greed.

Of all the people she had encountered as the duke's consort, Lord Nimmot was the one she had seen most and liked least. The man made her skin crawl at the best of times. Right now, his presence raised all sorts of alarms.

"Your Grace, how fortunate." His voice always grated, too, its pitch too soft and high for so large a body, which bent toward her in as much of a bow as he could manage.

"And how surprising," she managed, inclining her head in return. "How do you do, my lord? You must excuse me, I'm afraid. I am in a hurry to go home, and my carriage awaits."

"I came to offer mine, but no matter, I shall dismiss it if you prefer. Allow me to offer my deepest condolences."

Forcing herself, she nodded again. "Thank you. Then you have heard the sad news of His Grace?"

"Indeed I have. And I am selfishly relieved, at least, that I do not have to be the one to break the news to Your Grace. I have been asked by your family to escort you home to Cuttyngs."

She blinked, wrestling down the spurt of fear. "By my *family*?"

"Lord Dean, whom I must remember to call His Grace."

"Victor?" she said in disbelief. She doubted either she or her absence had entered her stepson's head.

Lord Nimmot appeared to understand her doubt, for he smiled faintly. "At the suggestion of his cousin, Mr. Severne."

"Mr. Severne is very good," Rosamund said. "But he has no right and less reason to put you out in such a way. As I said, my post-chaise awaits."

He blinked at her, almost sleepily, although behind his heavy eyelids, his eyes were hot. "You must know it is not fitting for a duchess to travel alone. Especially when so recently widowed."

Panic surged, for she could not, *would* not, be shut up alone in a closed carriage with Lord Nimmot, for she knew instinctively her recent widowhood would not protect her from him. And then, like a child's comfort blanket, she inhaled the presence of Major Butler at her side and immediately calmed.

"But, of course, I am not alone," she said pleasantly.

Nimmot raised a disdainful eyebrow as his gaze whipped over Giles. His full, slightly slack lips curled into a sneer. "And this is…?"

"Captain Battle," she murmured, instinctively changing his rank as well as his name. "Lord Nimmot."

Nimmot did not bow this time. A frown flickered across his brow, though, as if the name had taken him by surprise. Because he was expecting it to be Butler?

"My dear lady," he drawled. "You cannot go galivanting across the country alone with a young man who is not even known to your family."

"Of course I cannot," Rosamund agreed. "And you quite mistake the matter. Captain Battle has given us his escort thus far but leaves us now for Harwich."

This time Nimmot's frown was more definite. "Us?" he repeated blankly.

Rosamund turned to her other side, where Sophia had materialized. "Indeed. This is my companion, Miss Wallace. Sophia, Lord Nimmot."

"Companion?" Nimmot said sharply. "I'm aware of no—"

"Indeed, why should you be?" Rosamund interrupted pleasantly. "Miss Wallace is betrothed to Captain Battle which is, of course, the reason he has escorted us thus far. But you must excuse us. I do not care to linger in the public rooms, though I can recommend the food. Goodbye, my lord, and I thank you for your condolences."

She stepped around him. Nimmot moved, as though he would block her way once more. But unexpectedly, Giles's arm, bent at the elbow to receive her hand, was between her and Nimmot. She took his arm as though she hadn't even noticed Nimmot's movement. It was Giles who caught and held Nimmot's gaze.

Nimmot could cause a scene, or he could stand aside. Perhaps he read something in the officer's reckless eyes, for suddenly he was no longer there, and she was strolling toward the door on Major Butler's arm, with Sophia on her other side.

"Who the devil is that bag of wind?" Giles demanded once they were in the fresh air of the busy inn yard.

"An acquaintance of my late husband's," Rosamund said with a shiver. "Though God knows why Anthony sent *him* of all people, and how did either of them know where to look for me?"

"Your people must have been searching," Giles said. "Probably from the day you left Cuttyngs."

"Oh dear... At any rate, our plan seems to be working, for though I'm almost sure he knew who you were, he seemed to accept your name as Battle."

"He is at least doubtful," Giles agreed.

"I apologize for demoting you," she added with a forced smile.

He shrugged. "You didn't really. I was given the rank of major in the regiment, but I haven't yet bought the new commission. Sophia, I apologize for betrothing myself to you once more."

"Once more?" Sophia repeated. "One is either betrothed or one is not. Let us go around to the other part of the yard, where the hired carriages depart."

Rosamund, whose stomach seemed to plummet at Sophia's words on betrothal, walked blindly with the others.

"It might be ready now," Giles said. "I put it off for half an hour because I wasn't sure how long you would be."

He is anxious to be gone from us, and I can't blame him... I'm not fond of drawn-out partings either.

The horses were already being harnessed, and Rosamund's carpetbag and saddlebags stowed beneath the backward facing seat of the bright yellow carriage. The parting was upon her, and she was not ready. She would never be ready.

Something more than panic seized her. So many words were left unsaid, leaving them heavy and aching within her. Without warning, Sophia walked away, and Rosamund seized her moment. Grasping his hand, she yanked, all but hauling him through the open side door to the empty carriage house.

"I need you to know—" she began desperately, before his mouth swallowed the rest, coming down on hers, hard and wild, and all too brief.

"I could have loved you so much," he whispered against her lips as though he could not bring himself to leave them. "You'll be with me always."

A sob rose up her throat, and she fastened her mouth to his once more, another quick, hard, kiss, because there was no time for more, and if she kissed him for longer, she would ruin everything and never let him go.

"I do love you," she said fiercely and broke free, bolting out of the door before her resolve broke in two with her heart.

In front of her, Sophia was trying to snatch her arm from the grip of a respectable looking young man at whom she was glaring.

"Unhand me this instant!" Sophia commanded.

"Don't dare speak to me that way when you should not even be out of the house," the stranger said furiously. "Get into the carriage right now and—"

With a bolt of something very like relief, Rosamund threw herself into the breach. "My good sir," she uttered in what she thought of as her duchess voice, "by what right do you assault my companion?"

The young man, caught in ungentlemanly conduct by an unknown lady of quality and considerable haughtiness, flushed and dropped Sophia's arm.

"You are mistaken, ma'am," he muttered. "The lady is my cousin and should be at home with my mother."

"On the contrary, the misapprehension is yours, sir. The lady is engaged as my companion, and I shall not allow her to be manhandled."

The cousin bristled. "My dear lady—"

"I am not your dear lady. You may address me as Your Grace."

"And I," Giles said, opening the carriage door and handing Sophia inside, "take exception to your treatment of my betrothed. Another word, and I might be forced to call you out." He bowed to Rosamund. "Your Grace?"

The young man's jaw had dropped during this speech. His mouth now began to open and close silently like that of a landed fish. Rosamund swept regally past him and gave Giles her hand. Her fingers clung tightly to his, but this was it. There would be no more.

Whatever he read in the major's gaze, Sophia's cousin fell back before it. Through the carriage window, Rosamund saw him try to bluster, but Giles simply turned his back and spoke to the postilions now mounting the horses. The outriders lined up on either side.

Rosamund's head pounded. Her ears sang, and she clutched

her fingers together hard in her lap. All she saw was Giles as he stood back out of the way of the horses. How had he come to mean so much to her so quickly? For she had spoken the truth. She did love him. An explosion of feeling that must be silent now and forever. She could not even raise her hand to him, nor he, it seemed to her. He turned away, throwing some last remark to Sophia's cousin and walked out of her sight.

A huge sob surged up within her. She swallowed it back and closed her eyes, only to open them again a few moments later on the hostile face of her new companion.

ANTHONY SEVERNE WAS both restless and annoyed. None of the letters he had sent out since his arrival at Cuttyngs had been answered. For most, he did not mind, since the news of the duke's death would likely have led to condolence letters to the duchess and to Victor. But there was no sign of communication from his daughter Olivia, let alone of her arrival, and even Nimmot was silent, although according to Gregson, his lordship had promised to oblige Mr. Severne.

Lady Hera, the duke's daughter, had arrived with her aunt and uncle, Lord and Lady Hadleigh. Anthony, frowning out of the window and drumming his fingers impatiently on the morning room desk, contemplated joining them for tea. Friday-faced Victor was unlikely to be there, and the pleasure of Letitia Hadleigh's company was drawing him.

Through the window, he saw a rider approach and dismount in front of the house. One of the well-trained stable boys appeared immediately to take the horse around to the stables. The visitor did not much interest Anthony. His horse was decent and his garb darkly respectable, although there was something vaguely familiar about him. Anthony assumed him to be some lawyer or man of business and waited to see him before joining the Hadleighs and Hera for tea.

When no one showed the newcomer into the room, he began to scowl. Perhaps it was merely a neighbor who had been shown to the drawing room instead. Anthony stopped drumming his fingers and rose to straighten his cravat before the ornate glass on the wall. With a final, satisfied pat of his fashionably styled hair, he left the room and sauntered along to the drawing room.

Here, he found only Hera and Lady Hadleigh, Lord Hadleigh having apparently taken to his bed following the atrocious journey from London.

Taken to the brandy, more like.

Anthony accepted his cup of tea from Lady Hadleigh, allowing their fingers to touch casually. "Victor is not joining us?" he murmured.

"Leave Victor to his books," Hera said with a touch of impatience. "It's all he has now."

Anthony blinked. "All he has? He has just inherited a dukedom!"

"And how much do you imagine he wants that?"

"Hera, grief does not excuse rudeness," Lady Hadleigh reminded her.

"No, but it makes it understandable," Anthony said peaceably.

Hera said nothing, possibly because her dainty little mouth was full of scone.

Anthony drank his tea, discussing arrangements for the burial, then left the ladies to go in search of the mysterious visitor, whom he discovered, surprisingly, in the library with Victor.

The boy looked much as he always did, darkly frowning and distracted. He barely looked up at Anthony's entrance, although his visitor rose courteously from the chair on the other side of the desk.

"Am I interrupting?" Anthony asked lightly.

"No," Victor said, unusually decisive. "In fact, you might be able to help since you knew His Grace better than I did. This is

Dr. Rivers, who attended my father in his final moments. Dr. Rivers, my cousin Mr. Anthony Severne."

Anthony bowed but did not offer his hand. "Of course. That is where I've seen you before. You attended the duel."

"I did."

"Of course," Victor said. "I had forgotten you were his second in that foolishness, Anthony."

"Have you ever tried to talk your father out of anything, foolish or otherwise?" Anthony retorted. "As it was, at least I could be there to see the matter conducted honorably."

"And was it?" Victor asked with insolent irony, which he then waved away with impatience. "The doctor's concerns are with the physical rather than the honorable. Was His Grace well, Anthony?"

Whatever Anthony had expected, it was not that.

"Well?" he repeated. "Yes, of course. Right up until the pistol ball entered his body."

"You are sure?" the doctor insisted, his eyes curiously piercing.

"I believe I said so," Anthony replied haughtily. "Although I was not in his every confidence. There is a family physician in London, I believe, who could be more help, were it any of your business."

"But it is my business," Dr. Rivers said, "both on account of the reason for my presence at the duel, and my failure to save the patient's life."

"I understand your soul-searching," Anthony said. "Believe me, I feel it, too. The unnecessary waste of a valuable life, decades before his time, the helplessness of the watcher. But what on earth leads you to question His Grace's health?"

"Did it not seem to you, sir, that at the moment of firing, or a fraction before it, His Grace staggered?"

Anthony's chest contracted painfully, but he allowed himself time to consider. "No. It seemed to me that he staggered when he was shot."

"And yet the wound was not so very serious."

Anthony raised one eyebrow. "Are you an expert on wounds of this nature?"

"Yes," said Dr. Rivers. "I served as an army surgeon on the Peninsula for several years. It is…unusual for a wound like that to be so instantly fatal."

"Unusual?" Victor picked up the word at once, saving Anthony the trouble. "Not impossible?"

Rivers shrugged. "Any wound might corrupt and kill the patient. In this case, there was no time. My concern is that there may have been some underlying health issue. If the shock of the ball caused his heart to fail, or there was some other condition to have caused him to stagger, it would be helpful to know."

Victor grimaced. "Would it bring my father back?"

"No," Rivers allowed. "But it might provide some relief for an honorable young man accused of murder."

"And there we have it," Anthony said contemptuously. "You are a friend of Major Butler who killed him."

"I am," Rivers said, "and have never pretended otherwise. Nor did I ever pretend to approve of the duel, not to Butler or His Grace or anyone else."

"It is to your credit," Victor said abruptly before Anthony could open his mouth. "Grown men playing like children with lethal toys."

"Exactly," Rivers said grimly. "Do I have your permission to speak to the duchess? If she will receive me?"

"You have my permission," Victor said. "But we're damned if we know where she is. Stay the night, and if she turns up by morning, you can speak to her then. But I give you warning, she's unlikely to know more of his health than I do. I suppose Aunt Hadleigh might, or even my sister," he added thoughtfully. "At least they were, mostly, in the same city."

IN THE SWAYING coach that thundered through the gathering dusk, Rosamund met the glare of her new "companion." She wondered bleakly if she had either the strength or the will to fight. There was certainly no reason.

"How have I offended you?" she asked wearily.

"You are in love with Giles Butler." The words sounded dragged from her, as though the other woman was loathe to admit she cared enough to notice.

"So are you," Rosamund retorted.

Sophia blinked, and a flush began to stain her cheeks, making her appear less severe and more beautiful. "All my life. It is a habit, but one I cannot break."

"Well, don't try on my account," Rosamund said ruefully. "You must see that anything between him and me is impossible."

"I see that it might be difficult. And that he didn't come near me, although he has been home for months, until *you* needed my help. How long has this been going on?"

Rosamund laughed. "*Going on?* Sophia, I have known him three days, and if he hadn't killed my husband, he would not have felt obliged to help me. Whatever or whoever kept him from you, it was not I."

"Meaning it was me?" Sophia said harshly. She dragged her gaze free of Rosamund, who already felt her pain as though it was her own.

Rosamund swallowed. "Giles told me that the betrothal was informal, made by your mothers when you were infants. That neither of you had taken it seriously since childhood."

"I might have said I did not," she admitted with clear reluctance.

"It seems to me," Rosamund said, feeling her way, "that he had a life apart from you, a career and a purpose. While you were left in an impossible situation, waiting, perhaps to be rescued. I have been in a similar situation and finally worked out that no one was going to rescue me. I was going to have to do it myself. As you just did, by agreeing to come with me at once when you neither know nor like me. I'm guessing that however awful I am, I can't be worse than your cousins."

The flicker of an unhappy smile twitched the corner of Sophia's mouth. "At least you agreed to pay me for my drudgery."

"I will even promise not to treat you as a drudge." She drew in a breath. "Whatever might happen in the future between you and Major Butler, you must see that I am no threat to you."

Sophia did not look noticeably happier. But her heart could not have been more desolate than Rosamund's.

CHAPTER TEN

IT WAS STILL dark when the post-chaise deposited them at Cuttyngs. Once reaching their state of armed neutrality, they had spent the journey partly in discussing their supposed connection.

Rosamund had told her new companion, "I heard about you through my brother's wife, who sends me the occasional duty letter, but never visits or has anything to do with the Severnes. I thought you could be her goddaughter, to explain why I chose to travel to meet you. Your betrothed, one Captain Battle, escorted you to meet me, and then accompanied us both on a brief tour of the countryside before we heard of my husband's death via the newspapers and hired the chaise to return. At no point, did either of us spend a night without the other."

"If you say so," Sophia had said doubtfully. "But it would be easy enough for your family to find out the truth."

"They won't bother. They will only have noticed I'm gone because they need my presence at Cuttyngs after the burial."

"Yet they sent that man after you."

"Yes, that was odd," Rosamund had agreed, frowning. "Although Nimmot might well have taken it upon himself. He has pursued me on each occasion we have met."

Sophia had stared. "I thought he was a friend of the duke's."

"He was. His Grace found it amusing—when he noticed. Of

course, Nimmot never overstepped in public, and I don't believe he would have done anything much even in private while Cuttyngham lived, but still, the man repels me."

"I'm not surprised. If he appears for the funeral, you should lock your bedchamber door. Also, carry a large hatpin or a letter opener in your reticule. If you can't get to them, a knee brought up sharply between his legs should incapacitate him and give his thoughts a different turn."

Rosamund had probably goggled at her, wondering how and why she had learned such measures, though they were certainly sensible enough. But Sophia had closed her eyes as though trying to snatch some rest on the bouncing coach.

Bleary-eyed stable boys had dealt with the postilions and a semi-dressed footman had let the travelers into the house. Both ladies were so tired that Rosamund swept them straight up to her bedchamber.

"I've no idea what guest chambers are occupied right now," Rosamund uttered, "but there's a comfortable couch in my dressing room if you can bear that for a few hours."

"I could happily sleep on the floor providing it does not jostle me."

"Good girl," Rosamund said, pointing her through the door before collapsing on her bed and sleeping like the dead.

Three hours later, she was woken by Perry, her superior dresser, with a cup of coffee and a disdainful, "Good morning, Your Grace. Welcome home."

"Thank you," Rosamund said blearily.

"I took the liberty of ordering Your Grace a bath, though there is a female residing in the dressing room."

"Bring the bath in here and send for another for the lady. Miss Wallace is my new companion."

"Very good, Your Grace. May I help you out of those clothes?"

"Not until I've drunk this coffee and the bath is ready. You had better tell me who is in the house."

"His Grace, of course."

"Of course."

"Lady Hera with Lord and Lady Hadleigh. Mr. Severne. And a Dr. Rivers stayed last night, though I believe he departs today."

The doctor's name sounded vaguely familiar, though she couldn't remember why.

"I have taken the liberty of dyeing two of your morning gowns and an evening gown. Black, of course."

"Oh, well done!" Rosamund said gratefully. "I was just wondering if I had anything dark enough not to set tongues wagging."

To her surprise, the maid flushed with pleasure at her casual praise. For the first time, Rosamund wondered if the woman was not quite as disdainful as she always appeared.

"Also, we have managed to lose Miss Wallace's baggage on the road," Rosamund added. "Perhaps you could find her something of mine until we can sort out more permanent apparel?"

"Of course, Your Grace."

After a soothing bath, when she was dressed in a plain black morning gown, with a black shawl and her hair dressed in Perry's idea of plainness, a maid brought a message from Dr. Rivers, who wondered if she could possibly receive him before he departed for London.

Intrigued, Rosamund had the man summoned to her private sitting room. He was younger than she had expected, perhaps not yet even thirty years old, straight-backed like a soldier, his face harsh featured, though with saving laughter lines around his eyes. Or perhaps they were squinting-into-the-sun lines, for his complexion seemed to be darkened by stronger sun than was usual in England.

He bowed with perfect courtesy. "Your Grace. Thank you for seeing me. Please accept my condolences and my apologies for disturbing you at such a time."

"Thank you. What might I do for you, Doctor?" She waved one hand to offer him the chair opposite her own.

He came forward and sat with what looked like reluctance. "I should tell you at the outset that I was the medical man who attended the duel where your late husband died."

Her gaze flew to his, and she had to squash a sudden upsurge of questions that might have betrayed an unseemly interest in the wrong things. "I see."

"And since that hasn't appalled you, I will further confess that I count myself a friend of His Grace's opponent at that sad affair."

Her heart lurched, causing her hand to reach up to her chest as though to calm it. "Go on," she managed steadily.

"May I be so intrusive as to inquire about His Grace's general state of health?"

Rosamund blinked. "He seemed to be hale and hearty. I never heard him complain, but then he and I did not see a great deal of each other. Why do you ask?"

"To be frank, Your Grace, the duel casts up a couple of medical mysteries for me. From the wound your husband received, I should have been able to save him, bullet wounds being something of a specialty of mine from my years on the Peninsular campaign. And yet, he was dead before I could do anything for him at all. And then there is the matter of him staggering."

"Does one *not* stagger when hit by a pistol ball at twenty paces?" Rosamund asked bewildered.

The doctor sighed. "There's the rub. To me, he staggered the instant *before* the shot was fired. Though His Grace's second saw it happen the instant after."

"Hence your interest in His Grace's health before the duel," Rosamund murmured.

"Exactly."

She shook her head. "I don't know what to tell you, because in truth, I do not know. Any gossip will inform you that His Grace and I were not close. In the last three years, we have spent perhaps two weeks or less under the same roof. I don't believe he was a confiding sort of man, but he might have spoken to Victor or Anthony Severne. Or his physician in London."

"I am on my way to London now."

She was nodding before, belatedly, the significance of his investigation struck her and seemed to empty her lungs.

"You want to know if he died of natural causes instead of the duel itself," she blurted. "You want to prove the innocence of M—" She narrowly avoided saying his name. "Of your friend."

"I do," the doctor said frankly. "Major Butler aimed wide by his own account and had the impression His Grace stumbled into the ball. In conjunction with the fact that the ball should not have killed him… You see my problem?"

"I do…"

"Would you have described His Grace as a melancholic man?"

"No," she said flatly. "And if you are suggesting deliberate suicide, I would very much doubt it."

"I certainly saw no signs of it."

"Then you knew my husband?"

"Hardly, but we spent an evening in the same company when his party and my own found ourselves sharing a private parlor at the inn."

She fixed his rather fierce eyes with her own. "Then you witnessed the challenge?"

"I did. If I am honest, it sprung out of the duke's belief that he knew a certain colonel better than his comrades did. This colonel was beloved by his men and particularly close to Major Butler."

Rosamund nodded. This was more or less what Giles had already told her.

Dr. Rivers said, "It was inevitable that Butler should rise to the colonel's defense even if the rest of us could bite our tongues. But I have to admit he didn't need to be so insulting. He has a somewhat reckless temper."

She licked her rather dry lips and tried to talk herself out of it. "Tell me," she said, inevitably, "about this Major Butler. I heard his men call him Lunatic."

An involuntary smile flickered across the doctor's lips. "Major

Lune, usually. It was the fault of Captain MacDonald who yelled at him that he was a da—er…dashed lunatic, after Butler saved his life in a highly unorthodox and dangerous manner. Occasionally, he sees those red mists and charges where he should fear to tread at all. Yet he always comes out of it, and so, usually, do his men. Bravest man I ever saw, though also the most fool hardy. And good-natured."

"Did those…red mists come down the night my husband challenged him?" she asked carefully.

"A little," the doctor admitted. "He would not otherwise have called His Grace what he did. But his temper was well in check by the morning. He told his seconds he would not kill the duke, though neither would he apologize. I cannot condone the duel, Your Grace. I would have stopped it if I could."

"It was a waste of a life," she said sadly. "Two, if you count the major's. What will happen to him?"

"It probably depends on Wellington," Rivers said. "I'm sure he'll let Butler fight Boney. But after that… Let's just say it would help him if your husband's health was in doubt. Not," he added hastily, "that I would suggest anyone lie on that score, but I would like to know exactly what killed His Grace. Forgive my bluntness."

"There is nothing to forgive. I'm glad you were with him, even if you could do nothing."

"Thank you," Dr. Rivers said ruefully. "I suspect none of us present had all the information. With your permission, I'll make inquiries of his physician in London."

"Of course. Although Victor, the new duke—"

"I already have his permission."

"And Hera's?" Rosamund asked doubtfully.

"I believe her ladyship sniffed."

In spite of everything, Rosamund's lip twitched.

WHEN THE DOCTOR had gone, she collected Sophia and went down to breakfast, where she was rather surprised to discover both her stepchildren, the Hadleighs, and Anthony Severne.

They all stopped talking when she entered the room and turned to gaze at her. Which was more attention than they had ever given her before, including on her wedding day. Inevitably, Anthony was the first to speak, rising from the table and coming toward her with both hands held out.

"Your Grace. I am so sorry."

"As are we all," Rosamund said, allowing him to take her hands and kiss her cheek before stepping out of his reach. "Allow me to present to you all my companion, Miss Wallace. Sophia, His Grace of Cuttyngham, Lady Hera Severne, His Late Grace's daughter, Lord and Lady Hadleigh, and Mr. Severne, his cousin."

"Companion!" Lady Hadleigh uttered in the same tones as she might have said, *Spider!* "We heard some such nonsense and couldn't believe it. You are a young woman. What in the world do you want with a companion?"

"I believe the answer is in the description," Rosamund said tartly. "Sophia, our custom is to help ourselves from the sideboard. There is tea and coffee on the table."

She didn't need to look at them to know they were all exchanging bewildered expressions. But her few days away from Cuttyngs had made her realize they could not intimidate her and never really had. She had been so desperate to please them, to make them like her, that she had accepted every neglect, every minor rudeness, and let them hurt her.

"Of course, you must do as you please," Anthony said placatingly. "It is just an odd time to add to the expenses of the duchy."

"The decision was made before His Grace took it into his head to fight a duel. And in any case, the expense will be from my existing funds." She and the still silent Sophia sat down beside Victor. "I understand His Grace will be laid to rest tomorrow."

"He will," Victor said shortly, "and the solicitors will be here to read the will afterward. Mrs. Irwin is arranging tea, whatever that means in the circumstances. I should think brandy of more use after such a day."

"Victor," Lady Hadleigh scowled.

"Aunt," he replied with his usual mockery.

"Do you know what is in the will?" Hera asked Victor curiously.

He shrugged. "No. Never expected to need to quite so soon. Why, wondering if there's any more to your dowery?"

"Wondering if there's any provision for me if I don't marry."

The answer surprised Rosamund. But then it seemed to surprise everyone. The eyes of the brother and sister met.

Victor shrugged. "There will be, one way or another. You can do what you want."

"What she wants," Lady Hadleigh scolded, "is what every young lady wants. An advantageous marriage to a good man. I have several in mind."

"I draw the line at several," Victor said. "I'm an easy-going fellow, but more than one husband is too many."

"Depending on the husband, *one* can be too many," Hera observed.

Rosamund glanced from her to her brother and found Victor's gaze on her, not with sarcasm or malice, but something much less readable.

"Is that the conversation to be having right now?" Anthony wondered. "When your stepmother has just lost a husband?"

"Oh, for goodness' sake, she didn't mislay him in the undergrowth," Victor snapped. "He brought it on himself when he was old enough to know better."

"Unless Dr. Rivers is right," Rosamund said before she meant to.

Victor's dark eyebrows flew up. "You spoke to him? Do you think there's something in his theory?"

"That His Grace died of something other than a bullet wound? I don't know. He never seemed unhealthy, but it's worth looking into, for the sake of the young man who fought with him if for no other."

"A Major Butler, I believe," Anthony said, "for whom we should have no sympathy whatsoever."

"Oh, I don't know," Victor said provokingly. "Can't go around calling a fellow's heroic commanding officer a bumbling coward and hope not to be challenged. In any case, it was His Grace who issued the challenge."

"Because Butler called him a crassly ignorant, pampered imbecile!" Anthony retorted.

Inappropriate laughter tugged at Rosamund's breath and had to be expelled with a cough.

"The man had a point," Victor allowed unexpectedly.

"Victor!" Both Hadleighs and Anthony uttered his name at the same shocked tones.

Hera said, "We can't all be academic geniuses, Vic." And raised her teacup to him.

Victor sighed. "No. And the academically inclined don't necessarily make good dukes. I'd pass it to you if I could, Anthony."

"Never speak of such a thing," Anthony said severely. "We have enough grief in the family for the present!"

Only, grief seemed to be remarkably absent from the room. Even Lady Hadleigh, who dabbed her eyes with her handkerchief, had no actual tears that Rosamund could see. Which was sad. To die with no one to miss you…

For the first time since she had begun to hate her husband, she pitied him. And that *almost* made her weep.

SOPHIA WAS OF a similar height to Rosamund, so it wasn't difficult to find her gowns and undergarments to wear. Some of the gowns were gray, left over from mourning her parents. Others were sent to be died black, along with a few shawls and hats. Spare sets of hairbrushes and other personal items were also removed to Sophia's new room across the hall from Rosamund's apartments.

"You don't need to do all this for me," Sophia said, sounding harsh, when Rosamund stuck her head around the door to see if she was comfortable. "My role here is not real. Even if it were—"

"It's as real as mine," Rosamund interrupted. "I was never truly the duchess here, and after the will is read tomorrow, I may well be banished elsewhere. Circumstances may have thrown us together, but I see no reason why we should not be allies, at least until we each decide what to do with our lives."

Sophia, arranging the hairbrushes and combs on her dressing table, swung on Rosamund in consternation. "But you should not have to *keep* me."

"Why not? I dragged you away from your family."

Sophia smiled reluctantly. "You did not drag me. I leapt, clinging to your skirts. My life was one of unappreciated and often malicious drudgery. Whatever happens, I will never go back."

"Then live in the present. Whatever else, we keep a good table here. Take time to get well and strong. Join me for a luncheon, which I have asked to be served in my sitting room in an hour. Afterward, we could take a walk if you like. The gardens are pretty."

"Lady Hera said you made them so."

Surprised her stepdaughter had even noticed, Rosamund said, "Only the one nearest the house." She had never been allowed to touch the others, which her predecessors had ordered to their own liking.

At the door, she was stayed once more by Sophia's voice. "You are, you know."

"I am what?" Rosamund asked over her shoulder as she opened the door.

"The duchess."

Returning to her own sitting room to deal with the mountain of black-edged correspondence awaiting her attention, it struck her that in fact she felt more like the duchess than she ever had when the duke was alive.

She sat down at her desk, looking at the list of people who needed to be formally informed of her husband's death. The list had been compiled by Anthony—certainly it was in his hand—and he had further taken it upon himself to begin with those at the top who might well attend the funeral tomorrow.

Beginning with the first name that had not been scored out, she began her first letter. *It is my sad duty to inform you of the death of His Grace, the Duke of Cuttyngham...*

Even after a mere few minutes, the knock on her door was a relief. "Enter," she called over her shoulder, and was surprised to hear the halting step of the new duke.

She rose, turning to face him as he limped in and waved impatiently for her to sit once more. "Would you like some tea?" she offered civilly, hovering by the bell pull.

"Lord, no, I can never understand why people are so eager to addle their insides with that stuff. It tastes nasty and has no healthful properties so far as I can gather."

"Another example of human stupidity, I daresay," she said gravely, sitting on the chair beside the fire.

He dropped onto the sofa opposite and laid his stick beside him. To her surprise, a crooked smile curled one corner of his mouth. "And another proof of my superior genius, naturally."

She had never known him to poke fun at his own cleverness before and regarded him closely to make sure he was not serious.

The sardonic humor died on his face. "We don't know each other very well, do we? Considering you were married to my father for a hellish five years."

"Were they as bad as that for him?" she asked ruefully.

He stared. "For you, Rosamund,"

She blinked. She couldn't ever remember him using her name before, hadn't been aware he paid any attention to her whatsoever.

Victor's lips twisted. "He was in clover. Everything ordered as he liked it and a beautiful, biddable young wife to trot out whenever he needed her. While you wasted away here, forbidden to change anything, do anything, go anywhere. Hera and I didn't help, did we?"

"It was understandable," she managed. "A young woman of your own age brought in to replace your mother…"

Victor emitted a crack of laughter, shocking her into silence. "We did not *resent* you, Rosamund. We kept out of your way because that was what our own mother preferred. And to be frank, we had no real idea how else to go on. Ours was hardly a warm house. Hera and I couldn't wait to escape. And I had my books."

He skewered her with his dark gaze once more. "You fought my corner for Oxford. I should have thanked you, but I never forgot it."

"I didn't succeed."

"No. You wouldn't have. He was determined not to let the cripple out where he could be seen by other people's sons."

"Victor!"

"It's true," Victor said with no obvious pain. It was something he had come to terms with long ago, in his own way. "Hera, who told me about the subsequent battle, incidentally. She was very impressed by your bravery. Oh, and don't feel badly about Hera either. It was my father who insisted she go to my aunt for her come out. He didn't want the trouble of squiring the pair of you to tedious balls or holding parties in his own house."

"I didn't know that either," Rosamund murmured.

"No, well, we never told you," Victor said with a trace of ruefulness. "Communication in this house has never been great. Hera and I were used to relying on ourselves or each other, but that hardly helped you. Anyway, I'm sorry for it, which is what I came to say. Also, whatever is in His Grace's will, this house is your home for as long as you wish it to be. If you'd rather live somewhere else—and who could blame you?—I'll make sure that is possible for all or part of the year. In any case, do what you will with this place, house and grounds."

Rosamund took a moment to find her breath. "That is generous and kind, Victor, and I thank you from the bottom of my heart. But when you marry—"

"Don't be silly," he said impatiently. "We all know I shall never marry."

"Your duty to the succession—"

He stared at her. "Who would marry a cripple? Who would give their daughter to me?"

"Victor, have you ever *looked* in a mirror?"

He blinked in rare confusion. "What?"

"You are an extraordinarily handsome young man." Besides which, what parent would not want their daughter a duchess and be prepared to overlook far greater flaws than Victor's in the pursuit of it, though she doubted that was what he needed to hear.

Color seeped along the beautiful blades of his cheek bones. "I don't require flattery," he muttered. "I'm well aware where I stand. I just want you to know." Snatching up his stick, he levered himself to his feet.

"Victor?" she said quickly.

"What?" he asked, apparently suspicious now of what she would say next.

"Don't let Anthony take over. It will be harder to shake him off later."

Victor's lips twisted into the widest smile she had seen on him. "It won't be hard at all. I'll enjoy throwing the whole pack of them out after the funeral."

Chapter Eleven

ROSAMUND WAS SURPRISED to see that for the second day running, all the family present at Cuttyngs gathered in the drawing room before dinner. Even Victor had abandoned his books again, almost as though he planned to take his position of duke and head of the family seriously.

As Rosamund entered with Sophia behind her, she heard Lady Hadleigh saying waspishly, "She has countermanded several of my orders concerning tea after the burial and my allotment of bedchambers for—"

She broke off as she caught sight of Rosamund and sniffed. Rosamund didn't break her stride. "For Lord Frostbrook and Lord Nimmot," she said smoothly. "You had assigned Nimmot to the room that is now Miss Wallace's. Nor do I wish any stranger so close to my apartments. I wasn't even aware these gentlemen were staying until Mrs. Irwin informed me."

Rosamund and Sophia accepted the glasses of sherry offered by the footman, who then departed.

"I invited them," Anthony said apologetically. "I'm sorry if it displeases you, but old Dorrick told me they were mentioned in His Grace's will."

Lady Hadleigh smiled, as though that was Rosamund's guns spiked. "And the catering matter—"

"Will remain as I ordered," Rosamund said pleasantly.

Lady Hadleigh's eyes spat venom, though she swung hastily on her nephew. "Victor—"

"Oh, for God's sake, Aunt, let it be!" Victor snapped. "Her Grace is undoubted mistress of Cuttyngs and will order things as she sees fit."

"Though it was kind of you to try to help," Hera soothed, causing Rosamund to glance at her shrewdly. *Try* to help. It seemed to Rosamund that there was more malice than comfort in Hera's words, and the tiniest flicker of the girl's gleaming gaze in Rosamund's direction confirmed it.

Once, such support from her stepchildren would have meant the world to Rosamund. Now, it still warmed the edges of her heart, for her brief conversation with Victor had given her an understanding of their cold, lonely lives that she had never truly grasped before. Beneath it, they were struggling to be good people, as though their father's death had finally granted them permission.

It began to seem that she could actually be comfortable here. Now that mere comfort was no longer enough. The image of Giles Butler, never far away, swam in front of her eyes and she had to banish it.

But there was one more matter to make clear, so she accepted Anthony's arm to lead her into the dining room. Forcing him to walk a little faster than those behind, she said, "You invited Lord Nimmot to stay. Did you also invite him to escort me back to Cuttyngs?"

"He was happy to help. In fact, I believe he was hurt by your brusque rejection of his escort."

"Is that what you believe?" Rosamund said, making no effort to hide her sarcasm. "Then please note my instruction. You will never invite him anywhere near my presence again. I will tolerate his staying tomorrow night, but unless Victor bids it, he will never stay under this roof again."

Surprise widened his eyes. "Your Grace, I don't think you quite understand—"

"I understand perfectly." She released his arm and allowed the footman to seat her. "And I shall not put up with attempts to intimidate me or maul me in my own home or anyone else's. I trust we are clear?"

Anthony sat down at her side with something of a snap. "I am. I trust you are also clear that upon Victor's marriage, your opinions will not matter a jot."

It was honest. Which surprised her, though not as much as his obvious assumption that Victor would marry. Somehow, she had imagined he would oppose the new duke's marriage since it was likely to remove him from his position as heir to the dukedom. Perhaps she had maligned Anthony. After all, her resentments had festered for several years.

"I do feel strongly on this issue, though I apologize if I offended you," she said more gently. "And be assured, I would not dream of opposing Victor's wife."

Anthony looked mollified and chose to be gracious.

DESPITE HER LONG-TERM exhaustion and the comfort of her new bed, Sophia still woke before dawn. Unable to go back to sleep, she rose, washed, and dressed in her borrowed dark garb, which, although a trifle loose on her, fitted well enough for a mere companion. Since the room across the passage was still quiet, she set off alone to explore the house, discovering the fabulous library, which was the young duke's domain, a series of ornate salons, and a large, glass-fronted ballroom at the back of the house.

She had just returned to the main front hall when a yawning footman laid down a pile of letters on the table there and went off in answer to the butler's sharp command. Sophia, curious to know if the cousins she had just left had chosen to write to her already, went and rifled through the letters.

None were addressed to her. She hadn't really expected there to be. But she paused over one epistle. It was addressed to the duchess, and in a hand she recognized only too well.

Jealousy stirred. She had seen them at the inn. She knew Giles would never see her now, as long as the duchess stood before him. The duchess who was unattainable and as such, someone with whom Sophia could never compete.

In a moment of impulse, she snatched up the letter and hid it in her skirts before she ran lightly back upstairs to her bedchamber.

WHILE THE MEN attended the duke's funeral, the women took up their places in the drawing room to receive the mourners on their return. Rosamund chose a sofa facing the door, and Sophia obligingly sat beside her. A little later, Hera and Lady Hadleigh came in together, although Hera sat apart from her aunt.

"What will you do, Hera?" Rosamund asked. "Stay here or return to London?"

"I would rather stay here for a little. In mourning, there's little enough to do in London. I would rather walk and ride here, read some of Victor's naughtier texts—"

"Hera!" exclaimed her aunt. "As you very well know, Victor's interests are in the *classics*."

"Aunt, have you never read Catullus?" Hera asked, and Rosamund had to stifle a laugh.

"No," Lady Hadleigh said crossly, "and I'll make sure you don't, either!"

"I believe he isn't the worst of them, either," Sophia remarked unexpectedly, and this time Hera and Rosamund both laughed aloud.

Which was probably not the best time for the gentlemen mourners to walk into the room.

They were not led by the new duke, but by Anthony. However, Rosamund didn't believe that was necessarily the "taking over" she had warned Victor about. She had noticed before that if obliged to enter a room with others, Victor fell back to the rear, presumably so as not to impede by his more halting step. Or to hide from pitying or deriding eyes.

Behind Anthony came Lord Nimmot, Lord Hadleigh, Lord Frostbrook, a couple of neighboring landowners, and Mr. Dorrick, the solicitor.

Each of them approached Rosamund in turn to greet her and offer condolences, which she felt a fraud for receiving. It was a ritual they all had to go through, but she found it a strain on her nerves and her sense of guilt, because she had not loved or respected her husband. Even in the early days when she had been so eager to win his approval and acceptance, she had known in her heart he was not worthy of her love, or even the honor one owed one's husband.

While she had tried not to notice, part of her had already acknowledged he was unkind, selfish, opinionated, and not really clever enough to wield the control he enjoyed over his family. He had largely ignored his children, except to deny their requests or jibe at Victor for his physical failings. The servants tiptoed around him for fear of his sharp tongue or even dismissal. Rosamund had not been allowed to engage or dismiss staff, even her own personal maid. According to the duke, it was beneath her, as was the ordering of the house, its decoration, making or receiving calls with lowlier neighbors, or arranging hospitality of any kind.

All this she had forgiven in the early months of her marriage and endured for the rest, without ever clearly acknowledging more than her own unutterable boredom and her growing need to escape.

She recognized fully now, for the first time, that this need was not due to her own failings but to the duke's. To his unrelenting, unnecessary cruelty, exerted merely because he could. Her pity now was for his children and for the servants and tenants who were the subjects of his whims.

An inconvenient revelation, she thought, for a supposedly grieving widow accepting the sympathy of her husband's friends. How did such a man even *have* friends? Had he treated Nimmot and Frostbrook as equals?

At least Nimmot did no more than pat her black-gloved hand, since they were in public. Frostbrook, who had been Cuttyngham's second in the duel, bowed over her fingers with perfect civility. He had always seemed a cool, even cold man, to Rosamund, but unlike her husband, he had at least shown her every respect. He had even danced with her at one of the awful autumn balls she had hosted.

"It was good of you to come," she murmured now. "Might I speak with you later on?"

"Of course," he replied with no sign of dismay or surprise and moved on to make way for the local squire.

Her opportunity came when tea had been served—and brandy for the gentlemen—and slightly awkward conversation had started up. Lord Frostbrook stood alone by the table where an elegant repast had already been quietly ravaged. Thoughtfully, he consumed a small pastry.

He straightened as Rosamund approached him. "Your Grace. May I help you to a little nourishment?"

"Thank you, no." She laid down her teacup. "I really wished to consult you on the matter of the duel."

His expression betrayed nothing, although he did sigh. "I was afraid you would. I can only apologize for my part in what turned out to be so deadly an event."

"*Turned out to be*?" she repeated. "Is the deadliness not inherent in the challenge?"

"It is, of course. But few who indulge in the pastime truly wish to make it a killing matter. Even His Grace did not. The officer had given him what he felt to be an insurmountable insult before witnesses, and so he felt obliged to do something about it. I only wish the young man had the sense to apologize. Then we would not be standing here."

Rosamund's hackles stood up, though she retained sense enough to hide the fact. "I heard that the officer had reacted to Cuttyngham's insult of his commanding officer. Could His Grace not have apologized?"

Frostbrook met her gaze. "He could. And probably should have. But it was not in His Grace's nature, was it? His Grace had no intention of killing, and for what it's worth, I don't believe the officer had either. And yet, we have tragedy, including that of the young officer who has, I believe, been mentioned in dispatches several times during the Peninsular campaign, and now faces a charge of murder."

"That is what I wanted to speak to you about," she said, moving aside as Lady Hadleigh and the solicitor came a little too close. "Dr. Rivers called on me. I understand he attended the duel in his medical capacity. He is of the opinion that the duke's wound should not have killed him."

"Certainly not so instantaneously," Frostbrook agreed. "Though it could have been shock that stopped his heart. The human body is still largely a mystery, even to the medical profession, not least because every one of us appears to react differently to similar events."

She nodded slowly. Simple bad luck, not Giles, had probably killed her husband, and yet it was Giles who must pay the price.

She said, "Dr. Rivers appeared concerned about His Grace's health before the duel. In fact, he thought Cuttyngham staggered *before* the ball hit him. Was that your impression, my lord?"

Frostbrook hesitated. Rosamund counted it in his favor that he had not refused to discuss the duel with her and didn't want him to clam up now. But it seemed he was only edging away from eavesdroppers. He reached for his glass of brandy as an excuse, and she followed him.

"It happened too quickly to be sure," he murmured. "I would not rule out Rivers's theory, but nor can I state categorically that it was the case. Butler claims he shot well to the left to be sure of missing Cuttyngham. So, it's possible that the duke merely stumbled into the path of the bullet that would otherwise have missed him—a case that would help Major Butler but sadly makes His Grace no less dead."

"You were his friend," she said bluntly. "*Was* he ill?"

"If he was, he never mentioned it to me. But then, our acquaintance was not of a confiding nature. Shall we sit?"

Rosamund walked with him and sat on the nearest sofa. He sat beside her, presenting her with a small slice of cake on a plate.

Frostbrook said in a rush, "He seemed...stiff that morning. He would not eat or even drink the coffee I brought him before we left. I put it down to nerves over the upcoming duel. It is never an easy thing to anticipate meeting one's maker. But it's possible he was hiding illness."

"Did you tell this to Dr. Rivers?"

"Of course. But it is not proof, is it? I would not condemn an honorable soldier if I could save him, and I suspect neither would you. Rivers, of course, is biased. Butler is his friend."

"He admitted as much." She stopped her fingers from crumbling the cake on her plate. "Is the doubt enough to save Major Butler?"

"I'm no lawyer, Your Grace. My suspicion is, he would normally face the lesser charge of manslaughter. But in the circumstances, I would say everything depends on whether or not Wellington chooses to exert himself on Buter's behalf. But I have taken up enough of your time. Please accept my sympathy and my best wishes for Your Grace's future."

He rose as Mr. Dorrick, the solicitor, approached, but Dorrick said hastily, "No, no, my lord, there is no need to rise on my account. In fact, I came over to ask that you remain for the reading of the will. You are included."

"I am?" Frostbrook said, clearly and unusually startled.

"In a small way."

The neighboring landowners were now approaching, too, so Rosamund stood to allow them to take their leave of her and to thank them for the kindness of their presence.

When they had gone, Victor said, "Let's get the will over with. Mr. Dorrick?"

Sophia materialized by Rosamund's side. "Should I go?" she murmured. "This is family business, and I feel awkward."

Rosamund nodded. "By all means. I wish I could join you…"

But there were no final humiliations for Rosamund in the will. If His Grace had not been over-generous, neither had he been mean. Her allowance remained for her lifetime, or until she remarried. And she was likewise given the use of the dower house for life or until she remarried. And, of course, she also had the settlements she had brought to the marriage. There were no conditions, which she had more than half expected. But it seemed his desire to control her did not extend beyond his life.

Victor, of course, was the main beneficiary, inheriting all the unentailed estate as well as the entailed. Hera received nothing more than her already generous dowry, except her father's fob watch, an odd gift that caused a sardonic smile to curve the girl's silent lips.

The Hadleighs received nothing since, the duke intoned from beyond the grave, they had already milked him enough for his daughter's Seasons. Nor, rather to Rosamund's surprise, was Anthony remembered in the will, beyond a signet ring he had apparently admired. Anthony's face remained expressionless, although he nodded as though that was all he had ever desired of his ducal cousin.

Frostbrook received a horse, Nimmot a collection of books already set aside in the library.

There were no bequests to servants, not even Gregson.

When Dorrick stopped talking and took off his spectacles, there was silence in the room.

"Well," Victor said. "There we have it. You will, of course, all stay to dinner, and I know Her Grace has prepared rooms for you to spend the night at Cuttyngs. I'll have your carriages brought up to the door after breakfast tomorrow, unless you prefer to leave earlier, in which case we shall accommodate you with pleasure. Nimmot, I'll have your books sent to your London address, shall I? Frostbrook, you will let me know where to send the horse."

With that, Victor picked up his stick and left the room.

"He doesn't mean *us*," Lady Hadleigh murmured uncertainly.

"He does," Hera responded. "And I wouldn't underestimate his determination, either."

DINNER WAS A slightly awkward affair, but since no one expected a widow to entertain, Rosamund made the most of her position to excuse herself immediately afterward, Sophia solicitously at her elbow.

Sophia followed her into her sitting room. "Shall I ring for tea?" she asked.

Rosamund shuddered. "Only if you want some. I drank so much this afternoon that I still feel I'm drowning in the stuff."

"Me, too," Sophia admitted. She hesitated, then sat down opposite Rosamund. "Lord Frostbrook told me you were asking him about the duel. About Giles's part in the duke's death."

"I told you what Dr. Rivers suspected. It seems all the more harsh that Giles's career, or even his life, must end because His Grace put him in an impossible situation."

"It does," Sophia agreed. A look of desolation had entered her eyes. "But I… I never even thought of inquiring, and he is my oldest friend, the man I once believed I would marry."

"The man you still might," Rosamund forced herself to say. "And I have known about the duel for longer."

Sophia shook her head. "Not much longer, but that isn't really the issue, is it? You would move heaven and earth for him."

Rosamund thought of her letter already on its way to the Duke of Wellington in Brussels. And of Giles, who should have sailed by now, and the constant ache in her heart seemed to spread through all her veins. "If I need to. If I can."

Sophia's smile was difficult. "I may have loved him longer than you have, but I don't love him *more*, do I?"

"I don't think you can," Rosamund whispered, and dashed her hand angrily across her eyes.

Sophia's breath caught. "Your Grace—"

"It makes no sense," Rosamund interrupted, almost angrily. "I'm aware of that. I knew him only a few days in bizarre circumstances. And yet I feel I am *alive* now, that I am stronger just for knowing him. He has given me a purpose, even if nothing more can ever be between us. And it can't."

Sophia was silent. Then she said bleakly, "Never is a very long time. Who knows what will be possible once Bonaparte is defeated?"

Neither of them said what was surely at the front of both their minds. That even if Giles were never prosecuted for the duel, his survival in the coming fight with Bonaparte was by no means secure.

ANTHONY SEVERNE WAS in a filthy mood that was hardly improved when, after a brief knock on his bedchamber door, which he ignored, Lord Nimmot walked in anyway. The baron took one look at the brandy glass in Anthony's hand and said, "I'll have one of those."

"What do you want with brandy?" Anthony demanded. "He wasn't your damned cousin, and at least you got a collection of valuable books out of him."

"They're not valuable, they're just filthy," Nimmot said bluntly. "I imagine he hoped to embarrass me, or at least insult me."

"Why would he do that?"

"Because he knew I coveted his wife."

Anthony considered that, then, without standing up, reached for the decanter and a spare glass from the shelf behind him, and poured some brandy for Nimmot.

"Isn't your ring valuable either?" Nimmot asked, raising his glass perfunctorily to his host.

Anthony shrugged. "Not particularly. It was his grandfather's and was meant to be passed from heir to heir."

"Then perhaps he knows you will be duke one day after all. No one believes the boy will live long, do they?"

"No, he gave me it so that the world would see I wanted it," Anthony said bitterly. "For years I danced attendance on the moron, ran his errands, and kept his damned family secrets, and this is all I get for it? Even Frostbrook got a damned horse out of him—a decent horse, too—and they weren't even close."

Nimmot drank in sympathy. "Perhaps the boy will do something more handsome by you."

"Not he," Anthony said with contempt. "You heard him. He's throwing us all out tomorrow morning."

Nimmot's brows rose. "Even you?"

"Even me." Anthony curled his lip with malice. "So, you're running out of time. Better have at the grieving widow while you can, for she won't have you under her roof again."

Nimmot blinked sleepily, his eyes gleaming. It was odd, but even with such signs of life and emotion, his eyes always looked curiously dead. As though there were no one behind them.

"*Have at her*?" Nimmot repeated. "I thought I wasn't meant to touch her until the world could be sure no son of hers was the duke's?"

"I lift my embargo," Anthony said recklessly. "There are plenty of witnesses to the fact that the duke never touched her in at least two years. And if she whelps, I'm more than happy to embroil the family in lawsuits."

Nimmot downed the rest of his brandy and left without a word.

CHAPTER TWELVE

ROSAMUND WOKE THE following morning after a profound sleep. She had every intention of using her widow's prerogative to hide in her rooms for breakfast, until Sophia, fully dressed and neat as a new pin, came into her room.

"I caught Lord Nimmot rattling your door last night," Sophia said without preamble.

Rosamund, her eyes widening, met Sophia's gaze in the glass.

"How dare he?" Perry the maid gasped. "And you so recently widowed! Was *that* why the door was locked this morning?"

"Well, yes, and I'm very glad it was locked last night, too, on Miss Wallace's sound advice." Now Rosamund thought of it, she had been vaguely aware of a faint disturbance from the passage—closing doors and muffled voices… "I hope he gave *you* no insolence, Sophia."

"Not precisely. He seemed more irritated that I had caught him skulking at your door. He had no choice but to retreat without creating a bigger disturbance that would not have looked well for him."

Rosamund scowled. "Then I *shall* go down for breakfast, if only to show I'll not be intimidated by his ridiculous, vulgar games."

Accordingly, she marched for the door with Sophia trotting after her.

She again found Victor in the breakfast parlor with his guests. Not that he said much. Anthony and Lord Frostbrook made the odd, civil remark to the ladies, but otherwise, everyone appeared to eat in a somewhat strained silence.

Only as he finished eating and rose to his feet with the aid of his stick, did Victor speak.

"My stepmother and I would both like to thank you for taking this trouble to pay your last respects to His Grace. And for everything you did for him in his life. We will not forget. But I know you will not begrudge my family this coming solitude." He nodded curtly and limped from the room.

"Well," Lady Hadleigh said tight-lipped. "Am *I* not family? Did I not know Cuttyngham longer than anyone?"

"He would not immure your ladyship in this house of mourning," Rosamund said smoothly. "Knowing you have family of your own to care for in London."

Lady Hadleigh sniffed and seemed to become aware she had said too much in front of strangers, for she bit her lip and lapsed into silence with the rest of the room.

Having made her point to Nimmot by her mere presence, without so much as addressing a word to him, Rosamund also left her guests to finish their breakfast. Dutifully, Sophia trailed after her.

"Do you ride, Sophia?" Rosamund asked abruptly.

"I haven't for years."

"Then when this lot have gone, shall we go for a hack? Let me find you a riding habit."

Victor was as good as his word. By the time Rosamund had changed into her habit, the various horses and carriages were lined up in the courtyard, ready to receive their owners and their baggage.

"He appears to have a ruthless streak," Rosamund observed. "Surprisingly like his father's." Although tempered, it would appear, by a generosity quite alien to Rosamund's late husband. "Come, if we go the back way to the stables, no one will see us. I feel I will explode without fresh air."

Sophia, her riding habit slightly too loose on her thinner frame, seemed equally eager as they walked quietly through the house to a side door and followed the path to the stables. Low voices drifted to them from inside. Rosamund was about to call to the grooms, when she recognized one of the voices as Gregson's, and on impulse, closed her mouth again, walking closer.

"Nah, they were warned to wait for him in Harwich. If he isn't already banged-up, he soon will be," Gregson said impatiently.

The answering grunt seemed familiar, too. And the reference to someone being "banged up" in Harwich rang uncomfortable warning bells in Rosamund's head.

"I don't get the hurry, sir," Gregson added. "Left to his own devices, he'll just go and get himself killed abroad. It'll cause more talk if he's arrested."

"Look," came the clear, determined voice of Cousin Anthony, "whatever she says and whatever her reasons, Her Grace was with Butler, not this mysterious Battle no one has ever heard of, supposedly the betrothed of the equally mysterious companion. I won't have that spread across the British army in Brussels or anywhere else. Now go and find out if he's taken yet."

Rosamund dragged Sophia around the side of the building just in time. Anthony emerged, leading his horse by the reins, then mounted up and trotted off toward the front of the house and the main drive.

"He should have sailed by now, should he not?" Sophia murmured uneasily. "Would we not have heard if he had been arrested in Harwich or anywhere else?"

"I suppose Victor might have been informed as a courtesy," Rosamund said, tugging at her lip. "He certainly hasn't mentioned it."

"Then we should go for a ride as planned," Sophia said firmly, "and then you can speak to Victor when he has had a chance to read his post."

It was sensible advice, but a knot of unease had formed in Rosamund's stomach that would not be dispelled by exercise or common sense.

"HAVE YOU HEARD any more about the other duelists?" she asked Victor, bearding him in the library for the purpose.

"No," he replied. He appeared to be buried in ledgers rather than the more usual classical volumes, and he didn't look up. "And unless you feel differently, I've no intention of pursuing him."

"No," Rosamund said tightly. "I don't feel differently."

She left him to his estate books, her brain churning, not least with whether what she was considering came from common sense or simple desire.

Alone in her sitting room, she paced several times to the window and back, until Sophia entered, and she halted, frowning at her companion.

"Should we warn him?" Rosamund demanded.

Sophia's brows flew up. "That the law might be waiting for him in Harwich? Don't you think he already knows? In any case, he could already be in Ostend."

Rosamund threw herself onto the sofa. "I know," she muttered. "I know. I'm looking for a reason, an excuse to go and look for him, and there is no point. My warnings are unnecessary, and I cannot protect him."

Sophia did not answer that, although she closed her eyes as though stricken. Eventually, without looking at Rosamund, she took a folded paper from the pocket of her gown and dropped it in Rosamund's lap.

"That came for you yesterday. I hid it on impulse and then convinced myself I was doing you a kindness. But you had better at least read what he has to say."

"He?" Rosamund stared from the letter in her lap up to Sophia's rigid face. "This is from Giles?"

Sophia nodded. "I recognized his hand."

Her fingers shaking unaccountably, Rosamund took hold of the letter and broke the seal. *My dear Rosamund…* Silly tears started to her eyes.

It seemed he had written it while imprisoned in Sir Aubrey Fancott's cellar. A surprisingly humble apology for everything he had done from the duel to his reticence over his part in it and his foolish effort to redeem himself by helping a member of the duke's family.

At least, that is how I justified it in the beginning, he wrote. *Since then, I have reveled in your friendship and found myself increasingly reluctant to let it—or you—go. But I want you to know that at all times, I acted out of respect for you, and that my only regret in our shared adventure is that I may have made things harder for you. I will do everything in my power to make that right, and though we will never meet again, I will never forget you.*

The writing ended abruptly, as though he had been interrupted, and then, written with a different pen, he had added under the fresh date of the day before yesterday, *Let me be honest since none but you will read the words. I told you when we parted that I could have loved you. You were both more generous and more courageous in your reply, so let me at least write the words I should have said to you in person, in the hope that they ease your heart and encourage you to fresh hope. I love you to distraction, to despair, to utter, all-consuming joy. I seem to have waited my whole life and yet never even hoped to find what I feel for you, my one and only love. GB.*

Tears streamed down her face.

"For five years," she sobbed, "I was married to an unworthy man who crushed my spirit and every hope of happiness I'd ever had. Even in death, he thwarts me…" She flapped her hand in apology, still holding the letter. "I'm sorry. Ignore me."

Sophia drew in a shuddering breath. "Even now, you don't scold me. For God's sake, what apology do you owe me? Rosamund, you have been too much ignored." She flung herself across the room and crouched at Rosamund's feet. "Your Grace, Rosamund, he thwarts you only if you let him. You deprive *yourself* of happiness."

Rosamund blinked at her in surprise. "Even if Rivers is right, and Giles is not responsible for Cuttyngham's death, think of the scandal if I marry the man who is known to have dueled with him. They will say I was the reason."

"Who will say?" Sophia demanded.

"Everyone!"

Sophia sat back on her heels. "Do you care?"

Rosamund stared at her, considering. "No…but scandal would damage his career…"

"My dear, look at Wellington's own scandals," Sophia said dryly. "Giles is not a politician, he is a soldier of a line regiment and marriage to a former duchess is unlikely to harm his career. Moreover, I gather from your tears that he loves you. If you are not willing to fight for him, if you will not even try, then forget him."

"There is no point in whining," Rosamund said slowly, "if I will not fight." Her eyes refocused on Sophia's. "I meant to stand aside for you."

Sophia's smile was crooked. "No, you didn't."

A choke of laughter took her by surprise. "No, perhaps I didn't. Will you come with me?"

"I don't know that I am quite that selfless."

Rosamund frowned. "Besides, it would leave Hera without a chaperone. Perhaps you should stay, and I will send you word."

"You'll follow him to Ostend? Alone?"

"If I have to. I just hope I'm in time to warn him about Harwich."

IN FACT, GILES had already discovered that he was watched for in

Harwich, when Mac and Elton hustled him away from the docks and told him to find another port.

"We'll see to the men, and you can meet us in Ostend," Mac said.

Giles hesitated, but only for a moment. "It's either that," Mac said brutally, "or miss the last battles, and I know for a fact you're needed. You're their lucky lunatic."

And so, Giles found himself on the road to Dover, his head and his heart full of Rosamund instead of the coming fight.

He was ambling along the road, leading Chessy in order to give the beast a rest, when a very sporting curricle and pair came thundering up beside him.

"Good God, it *is* you!" exclaimed a familiar voice. "There's only one man in the whole British army who manages to *slouch* in a soldierly manner. Where you off to, Lune?"

"Dover." Grinning, Giles veered toward his old friend Captain Cornelius Cornhill, and reached up his free hand. "You?"

"My mother's." Cornhill wrinkled his nose. "Truth is, I'd rather not. Wretched ball tomorrow evening. Worse than that, a masked ball."

"My dear fellow," Giles said in sympathy. "Aren't you under orders to Ostend, too?"

"Yes, but my mother found out my ship doesn't sail until the end of the week. I didn't know you fellows were with us."

"We're not. Only me. Mine sailed yesterday from Harwich."

"Missed them, did you? Bad luck." Cornhill grinned suddenly. "Tell you what, old fellow, you could do a comrade a favor and come to my mother's ball. She'll love to have an extra man—she's short apparently, which is why she's so damned insistent about my presence."

"Can't, Corny."

"Don't give me that. You can sail with me, no trouble at all."

"Not sure that's true," Giles said ruefully. "Thing is, I'm in a bit of trouble."

Cornhill grinned. "No!"

"Haven't you heard? I found myself in a duel, and the fellow died, and now they want to haul me off for trial. Which is fair enough. I'll go."

"Just not until we've beaten Boney," Cornhill said, nodding as though that were perfectly proper.

"Exactly. But you see why I can't sully your mother's house and hospitality. Or even yours."

"Nonsense." Cornhill's eyes began to gleam. "My mother need never know. It's a masked ball, isn't it?"

"Corny—"

"Excellent plan," Cornhill pronounced. "Stay tonight at the Horse and Hound. Tomorrow, I smuggle you into the house, tell Mama you're there for the ball, and you turn up all masked and costumed. Not only will no one know you, no one will ever accuse my *mother* of knowing you. Being masked."

A breath of laughter shook Giles. "That's what I always liked about you, Corny. You make the unthinkable seem quite commonplace."

"Funnily enough that's what I always feel about you!"

In truth, with his men already sailing, there was no real rush, and Giles's bruised, still-reckless spirit was sorely tempted, if only to distract himself from the worry and pain over Rosamund.

Of course, over several pints of ale and some suspiciously good brandy in the Horse and Hound, Giles found himself telling Corny about the wonderful, stunningly beautiful girl he was leaving behind.

Cornhill listened with interest, nodding in all the right places, after which he frowned with the effort of considering Giles's plight.

"Don't see why you have to leave her behind forever," he said at last. "For the campaign, maybe it's best, but chances are you'll come home. You always do. Besides which, you may not be rich, but your family's good. You're a handsome fellow and will probably make colonel after this campaign. You're a good catch, if you ask me."

"Not for her," Giles said morosely. "Not for her."

"Married already, is she?" Cornhill asked.

"Widowed."

"Well, that's fine, then," Cornhill encouraged.

"By me," Giles said, reaching for the brandy.

Cornhill paused with his own glass halfway to his lips. "What?"

"Widowed by me."

Cornhill's jaw dropped, and he set the glass back down on the table. "You shot *her husband* in this duel?" At that, something else seemed to permeate his jug-bitten brain. "Good God, Lune, it was never you who killed the Duke of Cuttyngham?"

"I'll understand if you want me to go," Giles said stiffly.

"Don't be an ass, old bean." He rubbed his hands together. "Now it will be even more fun flaunting you under the noses of Mama's very correct cronies!"

In spite of himself, Giles let out a shout of laughter. "It might at that," he uttered. "It might at that."

"THERE ARE SOME things I need to set right," Rosamund told Victor. "I'll leave as soon as the carriage is ready, if you don't mind my using the private coach and your horses."

"Use what you need," Victor said. A certain sparkle had lit his eyes, as though he envied her the adventure. "Including changes en route. My father has horses stabled along all the major turnpikes."

"Thank you. I will. I'll take Perry with me and leave Sophia to play chaperone to Hera if it proves necessary."

"It might," Victor said doubtfully. "Though I doubt she'll be here long enough."

"She's going back to Lady Hadleigh in London?" Rosamund asked, not quite pleased.

"Lord, no. I just think she's up to something. Like you." His teeth flashed in a rare, dazzling smile. "I wish you joy, Rosamund."

"I will be back," she assured him. "I'm just not sure when."

"Well, I doubt *I'll* be going anywhere."

He spoke without bitterness, though with enough subtle feeling for her to vow to help him somehow, after she had saved Giles.

How had she ever thought to fit in herbalism?

By means of changing horses frequently, she reached Harwich before nightfall. She thought they might have to spend the night in the town in order to track down news of Major Butler. But when she alighted from the carriage for a quick supper, the first person she saw was Gregson.

"Good Lord," she exclaimed, although she shouldn't have been surprised. "What are you doing here?"

He looked as if he wanted to ask her the same question, though in the end, sense won out and he only said, "Errand for His Grace."

"For Mr. Severne, I think," Rosamund said tartly.

Gregson's chin tilted. "I don't know what you mean."

"In pursuit of Major Butler," she said, making it easy for him. "Have you found him?"

Gregson sighed. "No, Your Grace. Seems he was warned off and decamped, though the rest of his regiment sailed already. He went south… Look, I have to dash on to… er… His Grace, but I could see you settled here before I go."

"That's quite all right, Gregson, we'll bespeak our own accommodation. You get back to His Grace." She didn't even wait until he was out of sight before she told the ostlers to harness a new team. Perry, her once-superior dresser, groaned.

By morning, Rosamund was sure they were on Major Butler's trail. Perry turned out to be remarkably useful in asking questions about the officer, making her interest sound like a case of unrequited love that she wished to keep from her mistress.

However, by the time they reached the Horse and Hound in Kent, Rosamund was no clearer as to which port Giles was aiming for. But out of consideration for Perry, if not herself, she decided they should spend the night here and recover from growing exhaustion.

Perry, returning from a foray downstairs to obtain some warm milk for them both, entered the bedchamber, her eyes gleaming with fresh news.

"He has been here, Your Grace," she said with satisfaction, depositing the milk on the table. "Spent the night, along with another officer the staff seem to know well, a Captain Cornhill. The pair of them got drunk together and left together the following morning. Captain Cornhill was apparently going home and taking his friend with him."

Rosamund, reaching for her hot milk, threw an admiring glance at her maid. "And of course, you have discovered where home is?"

"Braxley Manor," Perry said with some relish. "About fifteen miles from here. Apparently, Mrs. Cornhill, is holding a masked ball—like the ones they're always having at that Congress in Vienna—and Captain Cornhill wanted his friend to go, too, by way of moral support."

"And did your informant have the impression that the friend would oblige?"

"He did. At least when they were foxed, they thought it would be a great lark, though the tap boy doesn't understand why."

"Let's hope he never does," Rosamund murmured. She hugged her milk to her, then sipped thoughtfully. "Then we may spend the night quite comfortably here and reach him at Braxley Manor tomorrow. Providing he stays."

"Well and good," Perry said, frowning. "But where are we going to stay? You can't turn up at some stranger's party and expect to be welcomed just because you're a duchess."

Rosamund lowered her cup. "Actually, I probably could, but since I don't really wish to advertise my name or rank, I have no intention of doing so." She took another sip. "We'll have to reconnoiter. Well done, Perry. I can't think how it is I haven't made use of your talents before!"

"Neither can I," Perry said smugly.

CHAPTER THIRTEEN

THERE WAS A village inn at Braxley, which was fortunate. There was even a room available since Mrs. Cornhill's guests appeared to be all staying either at the manor house or with neighbors—a fact that clearly miffed the innkeeper's wife, although she perked when she heard that Rosamund—now Mrs. Daryll, once more—would stay.

"It's a surprise," Rosamund said inventively. "A secret surprise. I'll just take a stroll up there to make final arrangements."

Perry was outraged not to be accompanying her on this expedition.

"Actually, I need you to do something else for me while I'm gone," Rosamund said. "If I can't speak to him now, I shall have to try again later, and for that, I'll need a mask and domino cloak at the very least. Could you manage to beg, borrow, or steal one?"

"You know," Perry confided, "I once thought it was rather dull working for the Duchess of Cuttyngham."

"It was," Rosamund said apologetically. "Hopefully, I should only be an hour or two."

Her hopes, however, were frustrated.

She found the manor house easily enough. It proved to be a gracious stone building, bigger than she had expected, with pleasant gardens surrounding it. There was a great deal of coming and going, but the front door was constantly guarded by footmen on the lookout for arriving guests. The back doors receiving luggage and kitchen goods, were also in constant use.

Rosamund hid herself amongst the undergrowth just beyond the formal garden, watching the guests who strolled there, and then took tea. There were a few military uniforms amongst them—one of them seemed to be the son of the house, Captain Cornhill—but there was no sign of Giles.

What if he had not stayed here after all? What if he was already boarding a ship at Dover or one of the other ports along the south coast?

Then he will be safely out of the country, and all will be well. I can write to him.

This scenario would, probably be best and safest, she acknowledged, and yet her longing to see him, to speak to him, just to touch his hand, was like a pain. She wanted him to know he was everything to her. Her arms ached to hold him.

Annoyingly, everyone went inside after tea, as the blink of sunshine passed. It seemed likely that time now would be spent preparing for the ball, and her chances of spying Giles, let alone of speaking to him, were diminishing. She began to wish she had brought Perry, who would be able to move more easily among the servants and even get a message to the captain. But since she hadn't, she decided to return to the inn and wait until the evening made mingling with the guests easier.

THE EVENING WAS too cold and her domino cloak too thin for Rosamund to want to spend much more time out of doors. From the darkness of the sheltering trees, she could slip into the lantern-lit part of the garden and from there meander through the helpfully open French doors into the ballroom.

Her decision made, she stepped out from under the oak tree and moved toward the gate in the low hedge.

"My, what have we here?" drawled an amused voice. "A solitary nymph, perhaps, longing for company?"

She whipped around to see a youngish man in ordinary evening dress. A black domino hung carelessly off one shoulder, and a matching mask dangled from his fingers.

"Something like that," she said cautiously. Surreptitiously, she checked her mask and hood were in place, for the man looked and sounded vaguely familiar, and the last thing she wanted was to be recognized.

"Are you escaping your chaperone?" he asked lightly. "Or perhaps you find the ballroom a little too much?"

"Just a very little, but now I am cold and would definitely like to go back inside."

Gallantly, he offered his arm. "Allow me to escort you."

She took his arm somewhat warily, but he did indeed open the gate and walk toward the light. His name came back to her. Sir Lyndsay Haverton, the Member of Parliament for…somewhere or other. At any rate, he had been at Cuttyngs for one of the autumn balls. Naturally, she had barely spoken to him, so his chances of recognizing her were slim, but even so, she thought she should probably further his assumption that she was a debutante with a chaperone somewhere in the vicinity.

"Perhaps," Haverton said, "you would even do me the huge favor of dancing with me? If all your dances are not already promised."

"I avoided promising any," she replied, glad for once to be able to speak the truth, more or less. "And I would be glad to dance with you." If only to warm up, though there was an endearing humility to the man that made her like him.

Many of Mrs. Cornhill's guests were in costume, spectacular and otherwise. Sir Walter Raleigh danced by with a Roman matron in his arms. In an antechamber, Henry VIII played cards with a highwayman and two cavaliers, while a gaggle of bejeweled milkmaids held court with a bizarre collection of historical figures and army officers.

Rosamund looked carefully at everyone in uniform but none of them resembled Giles. Even masked, she knew she would recognize him just by his posture, the way he walked…

"Since the waltz is so informal, we could just join in," Haverton suggested at her elbow. "Or we could take a stroll and see if there is any champagne left."

Did debutantes drink champagne? She couldn't remember, having been thrust into marriage before her first Season. "I believe I would like to dance," she said hastily.

Haverton obliged once more, turning her around the dance floor and enabling her to glimpse, surely, all the waltzing gentlemen, none of whom appeared to be Giles. Although from Haverton's conversation, she did discover which of the military gentlemen was Captain Cornhill, a large, amiable personage resplendent in a scarlet domino and black mask worn across his forehead.

Haverton was a comfortable partner, a decent dancer, who neither trod on her toes nor tried to hold her too close while he made unthreatening and occasionally witty small talk. And then he said, "I can't help thinking I know you."

"Oh, no," she said at once.

"You sound very certain, and yet something in your voice and manner is familiar. Are you one of Mrs. Cornhill's neighbors? Or are you staying here in the house?"

"You are trying to identify me," she said with mock severity. "I consider that ungentlemanly."

He tried another tack. "Perhaps you have identified me."

She regarded him, sensing a trap. Since he was unmasked, she could easily be expected to know him. If she didn't, she might give away more than she meant to. "You are trying to trick me. I shall not be tricked."

He laughed, and fortunately, the dance came to a close a few moments later.

"Allow me to escort you in search of that champagne I mentioned earlier," he suggested, offering his arm. "Unless I should be returning you to your chaperone?"

"Well, that might give me away."

"Then she isn't masked?"

"You are incorrigible, sir. I will have that champagne since you offer, but I make no promises to keep you company thereafter."

"Cruel," he mourned, making her laugh.

As they made their way to the other side of the room, she noticed that Captain Cornhill was with a group of other men, both military and costumed. Surreptitiously, she peered at them, but found no one resembling Giles. It began to seem that she was wrong, and he was not here. In which case, she was wasting her time and abusing a stranger's hospitality for nothing.

Haverton took two glasses of champagne and presented her with one. By then, the sets had begun to form for a country dance, and Captain Cornhill was leading a Queen Cleopatra on to the floor. Which was annoying, for she'd thought if she kept an eye on him, Giles would surely materialize by his side at some point.

Some younger men came to join her and Haverton. Since it was too late to join the dance under way, they began to compete for the following dance, which they were sure was a waltz. Rosamund kept a smile on her face, committing to nothing, while Haverton watched her, looking, no doubt, for clues. Eventually, since her growing court was blocking her view of everyone else in the room, she murmured her excuses and simply walked away.

She looked into the card room, where a table of exotically dressed ladies were concentrating ferociously on their cards, and another of gentlemen seemed equally interested in the wine. She moved on around the ballroom to the open doors. A few people were drifting in and out of cloakrooms. A couple of men were deep in conversation by a pillar. None of them remotely resembled Giles.

Increasingly frustrated, she returned to the ballroom. She began to feel she was running out of time. She needed to find him before the unmasking, or she was undone. More to the point, he would probably vanish by then for his own self-preservation.

In desperation, she decided to attach herself to Captain Cornhill and at least find out what she could. Accordingly, as the dance came to an end, she walked in parallel with him as he returned his Cleopatra to her masked chaperone. So that when he had exchanged civil words and bowed, he turned directly toward her, and she smiled as dazzlingly as she knew how.

His response was instantaneous, slightly surprised but definitely pleased. "Mysterious madame, might I beg your company for the waltz?"

"That rather depends," she replied.

"On what?"

"On your entertaining conversation, of course," she teased.

His eyes gleamed. "You intrigue me, madame, but sadly I am more a man of action."

"I can tell that by your uniform." She flicked a glance along the ballroom and saw Haverton approaching from one side, and two of her other admirers from the other. How long before the music started up again? "There are several officers present, I think. Are you all going to join His Grace of Wellington in Brussels?"

"Most of us. The dancing there will be superb, you know. Half the *ton* has migrated there already, and His Grace does love to waltz. In between the fighting, of course."

"You sound as if the dancing is of more importance."

"Isn't it?"

"I suppose it depends on who one is dancing…" A masked soldier with a dark blue domino trailing from one shoulder sauntered through the French doors into the room. His uniform was blue and gold. Rosamund's heart dived and seemed to land with a mighty thump. "…with," she finished breathlessly.

The newcomer, surely Giles Butler at last, paused for a moment, just inside the room, perhaps looking for her companion, for his gaze seemed to halt when it reached them. The orchestra struck up the introduction to the next waltz, but for Rosamund, the music, and the chatter around her faded. Cornhill, the couples tripping onto the dance floor, Haverton, and the other young men might not have been there at all. There was only the man walking steadily toward her, loose-limbed and predatory enough to keep her heart drumming, and yet dearer than life itself. Gladness swamped her, just to see him, just to breathe the same air.

Their eyes locked. A couple moved back out of his way, and though she didn't think her limbs would move, she took a step nearer him. She had meant to be so discreet, and yet now the moment was at hand, the whole world seemed to be watching them. At the same time, they were part of another world, as though she and Giles were completely separate.

She could not read his full expression beneath the mask, only his steady, devouring eyes as he advanced upon her and commandingly held out his hand. Mechanically, she placed her fingers on his palm, and the shock of his touch almost made her gasp. He bowed over her hand, and a gentle tug caused her to walk by his side onto the dance floor.

She thought a couple of her earlier admirers might have complained about military high-handedness, but they were like the distant buzzling of flies.

Giles did not speak, and for the first time it hit her with a jolt that he might not be pleased to see her. Somehow, she had caused a scene, a situation where both of them were noticed where neither of them should have been.

He turned, taking her hand, his other arm slipping around her waist, and the dance began.

"What in God's name are you doing here?" he all but groaned.

"How did you know me?" she blurted. She could not think for his closeness, his scent, the feel of his hand at her back, guiding her to turn and step in perfect time with him.

"I will always know you." He sounded almost impatient.

"Were you looking for me? What is wrong?"

"I came to warn you that they were watching for you in Harwich. I think Anthony informed on you. He can't prove it, but he suspects you are the same man as Battle."

"I was warned at Harwich and was on my way to Dover when I met Cornhill. My plan is to sail with him the day after tomorrow. Who knows you are here?"

"My maid."

The mask twitched as though he frowned beneath it. "You knew I wasn't taken at Harwich, yet you followed me?"

A lump seemed to have sprung into her throat. She tried to swallow it down. "I had to. I read your letter."

His fingers tightened on hers. "I meant it to comfort you, not endanger you," he whispered.

"I'm sorry. I'll go once everyone has stopped staring…"

"No," he said quickly, then his breath seemed to catch. "Oh, the devil, Rosamund, I can't be other than glad and yet… How did you even obtain an invitation when you're in mourning?"

"I didn't. I skulked and let someone else escort me inside."

"You're not short of initiative, are you?" His voice was unsteady again, as though he were laughing, and through the mask, his eyes danced, banishing the anguish she had seen before.

"It seems not. I feel I have been in some miserable sleep for five years and now I'm finally awake and remember who I am. And because those five years were wasted, I find I am impatient."

He spun her around, a little too fast. "Impatient for what?"

Heat flooded her face, but she held his gaze. "For you."

His lips moved, though no sound came out. Something like desperation shone in his eyes, though they never left hers for a moment as they danced and spun in silence. It didn't seem to matter. It was as if the music and their every movement proclaimed their feelings to each other.

"At the village inn."

"I'll take you back there when the dance is finished."

"My plan was never to drag you away," she said in sudden

distress. "Just to tell you—"

"We can tell each other everything," he interrupted, his quiet voice thrilling through her. "In privacy."

"And Dover?"

"Dover is for tomorrow." Intense feeling blazed out of his eyes, at once exciting and calming. How was that even possible?

Because her spirit was soothed by his presence. Every other part of her was wildly aroused by his nearness, the way he moved, almost touching her at hip and thigh, the low vibrations of his voice. For the first time, she began to understand melodramatic declarations of being unable to live without one's beloved. One might live, but one was not truly *alive.*

Now, she was alive. And because of that, she smiled into his eyes.

GILES WAS IN danger of drowning in that smile. In the beauty he held in his arms. His heart clamored with joy because she had come to him, however foolishly. It seemed she loved him beyond reason, which was both heady and humbling, for he could think of nothing to account for such feelings. But then he could think of very little except the sweet curve of her lips and their nearness to his.

Nothing had changed, of course. He still could see no way out for them, but somehow, her being here drowned all that out. His body had very definite ideas of its own about how close they should be and how soon.

For the first time, he was grateful for the enveloping domino cloak which Corny had given him, and which he could subtly let swing around him as the music ended and he bowed to Rosamund and offered her his arm.

"A little air on the terrace?" he suggested for the benefit of any listeners.

"That would be pleasant," she replied primly and allowed him to guide her across the room. He thought her hand trembled, but it might have been him.

At the last moment, he swept Cornhill up with them. "Come and join us," he said, yanking his friend by the arm.

"Dashed right I will," Cornhill said indignantly. "You deprived me of my mysterious madame!"

They stepped together on to the terrace, where a couple of officers smoked cigarillos, and a youthful couple in disguise talked in whispers in one corner.

"I'm about to do so again," Giles murmured. "If I'm not here by morning, will you bring my horse and my things and meet me at the inn?"

Cornhill frowned and opened his mouth.

"Say everything that is proper to your mother, give her my regards and my sincere thanks."

Cornhill closed his mouth. His frown smoothed as he gazed at Rosamund. "It's *her*, isn't it?"

"Don't make me lie to you, Corny."

"I don't know whether to be shocked or delighted." Cornhill sighed. "I suppose I'd better show you the rose garden."

Giles grinned, and they wandered together off the terrace to the formal gardens beyond.

"There's a gate here," Corny said. "Follow the road around the wood, and you'll come to the village."

Rosamund held out her hand. "My thanks, Captain. And my apologies. I do need to speak privately with Major Butler."

"I know. And we all stand his friend. And Your Grace's," he added with a rueful smile as he dropped her hand and shoved Giles's shoulder. "Be gone, you Lune. I'll see you tomorrow, if not before."

Giles cast him a quick grin and opened the gate to let Rosamund walk through.

CHAPTER FOURTEEN

ROSAMUND RETRIEVED HER lantern from beneath the oak tree and took the flint from her reticule to light it. Her hands had stopped shaking, though her heart still drummed, and every inch of her was aware of Giles standing beside her, then reaching down to take the lantern from her and draw her upright.

The glow swept across his still-masked face, and a moment of panic flared with it. Because in harsh reality, she knew him so little, and she had already been wrong about Victor and Hera and even Perry, when her acquaintance with them had been far longer. She would not even think of Cuttyngham here, but she was clearly a poor judge of character. And she had just placed her person and her reputation in the hands of a light-hearted and, by his own account and everyone else's, *reckless* officer.

"I wish I knew what it meant," he said huskily, "that you came here…" And what she saw in his eyes by the lantern's light was not recklessness but worry, helplessness and something much softer. Then he took her hand, leading her toward the path, and her sudden anxiety dissolved.

"It means I will waste no more time on unhappiness," she said. "That if you wish it, I will stay with you up until the instant you step aboard your ship."

His fingers tightened briefly on hers, though he didn't, as she more than half hoped, put his arm around her. "I wish it. But you are not some comely, happy-go-lucky tavern wench, glad to snatch an hour of fun with a passing soldier."

Her body flushed. "I wouldn't mind," she confessed. "Providing you came back."

"If I could guarantee that, I would not be much of a soldier. But if I live, Rosamund, I will always come back to you." He groaned. "How can I ask you, a duchess—*this* duchess!—to wait for *me*? We have only known each other a week! How long would we need to wait? Even supposing I am not hanged for the murder of your husband, no one will quickly forget that I shot him." He kicked a stone in his path. "In five years, or ten, maybe no one will care."

"It is no one else's business but yours and mine," she said firmly. "Why should I care for society's opinion? I would rather follow the drum with you."

His head whipped round to her. "You would?"

"Of course, I would. My herbal knowledge might even be useful."

A faint smile lurked around his lips, making her want to kiss them. "The officers' wives have opinions, too," he warned. "And they are not always kind."

"I am a duchess. I can out-disdain them."

A breath of laughter brushed her cheek, reminding her how closely they walked. "I believe you. But I'm not sure you fully understand the rigors, the discomforts, and sheer unpleasantness of campaign life. And then there are the dangers. Once Boney is beaten, I could be sent anywhere in the world—the Americas, India, the Caribbean. Quite aside from fighting, there are dangers from the climate, disease…"

"I won't come if you don't want me to."

She thought he swore under his breath, but she didn't care, for quite abruptly, he halted and wrapped his arms around her.

"My dear, my sweet, of course I *want* you to! But what kind of a man would I be if I did not consider your safety, your comfort?"

"My only comfort is being with you," she said brokenly. "I don't know why or how, but it has bec—" The rest was lost in his mouth, which devoured hers; in his lean, hard body to which she was pressed so tightly that she gasped in wonder and new, flaring delight.

With a muffled sob, she freed her arms and flung them around his neck, kissing him back with blind, instinctive passion.

This kiss was different to his earlier embraces—hotter, wilder, at once more desperate and on his part, it seemed, more purposeful. He knew so much more than she did. Most astounding of all, he knew *her*, how to please and excite and coax her, just with his lips, his tongue, his fingers playing on her back, her cheek, the corner of her mouth.

The lantern, which he had dropped to the ground with a dull *thunk*, somehow remained lit, so when Giles finally, unsteadily, lifted his head, she immediately saw the interested head of the cow watching them over the hedge.

With a snort of laughter, she buried her face in Giles's neck, trying to fight through the gladness and dizzying desire back to reason. That seemed to be a lost cause, for his fingers caressed her nape in sweet, arousing circles that parted her lips. She pressed them to his skin, inhaling his scent, his taste, and wanted, wanted… She wasn't sure what, but it overwhelmed her.

His whole body moved against hers. Her fingers tangled desperately in his hair, and she flung up her head once more, seeking and finding his devastating mouth.

She could have stayed there all night, lost in feeling, wherever it led. It was he who, reluctantly, took his mouth and his arms away. In one swift movement, he swiped the domino cloak from his shoulders and draped it around hers.

"You will be cold," he said unsteadily. "Come." He swiped up the lantern, and yet, since he kept one arm around her shoulders, she did not feel bereft, just stunned, bewildered, and ridiculously happy.

Until he said, "I cannot ask you to wait five years, or ten."

Her heart twisted. "Would you? Wait that long?"

He groaned. "I'd wait forever, but it wouldn't make me happy. Or you."

"Then what are we to do?"

His arm tightened around her. "I don't know."

She listened to the strong, rapid beats of her heart. "I do."

He dropped a kiss on her hair. "Tell."

"We could *not* wait. We could marry now."

He inhaled, his breath ragged. "There is no time. I sail the day after tomorrow."

"If you are worried," she pursued determinedly, "about having to bring up another man's child as your own, I assure you Cuttyngham has not touched me in more than two years."

His mouth fell open. "Rosamund," he said helplessly. "I would be thrilled, honored, *delighted* to bring up *any* child of yours. But if you marry me, especially so soon, no one will believe you are not complicit in my killing Cuttyngham."

"That is one way of looking at things," she allowed. "Another is that by marrying you, I tell the world of your innocence."

"Days after burying your previous husband, whom I shot?"

"Whom you shot by accident but very probably did not kill. Your friend Dr. Rivers believes he died of something else entirely, that caused him to stagger into your shot. That bullet would otherwise have gone wide as you intended. Also, I've discovered that no one believes my husband to have been a good or pleasant man. People might be scandalized by my marrying again so quickly, they might shun me in public, but they will not blame me. And I, following the drum with you, would not care if they did."

He gazed down at her as though fascinated. "What did I ever do in my life to deserve such devotion?"

"You are you."

He swallowed audibly and looked away at the road ahead. "Honesty compels me to point out that I am not the only man who will ever be kind to you. Corny, for one, is clearly at your feet, and from my glimpse of the ballroom when I first saw you, you had several other admirers, too."

"You are not, in effect," she said slowly, "the only fish in the sea?"

"Exactly."

At least he didn't sound happy about it. "Am I?"

He blinked. "Are you what?"

"The only fish in your sea? I know about Sophia, who was never your choice in any case, but you have been about the world. You have lived. Is there someone else competing for your affections or even your duty?"

He closed his eyes. "I should tell you yes, for your own sake, so that you will give me up. But I can't lie, and I can't hurt you. As you say, I have been about the world. And I have not been a saint, but I pine for no one, and no one pines for me."

"No one?" she said wistfully, and he tugged her hard against his side.

"Only you, God help us both. Only you." He drew another ragged breath. "But the point is, Rosamund, you have been married and more or less immured for five years and widowed one week. You need time to find your feet, to discover what and who you really want. Whether that is your reclusive cottage in Little Fiddlesticks or a grand marriage or the life of a merry widow. Or all three in turn. I cannot tie you to *me*. Even if I didn't have to leave the country to fight and return to face trial for the murder of your husband."

She swallowed, taking what comfort she could from his arm around her shoulders and his warmth at her side. "You make it sound hopeless."

"It *is*," he said hoarsely. "I wish it was not, God knows how much. But it is."

"Then we are saying goodbye?" she said desolately. "For five years or ten?"

An owl hooted in the distance. Something small scurried across the road in front of them and vanished into the darkness.

"Yes," he said low, and in that one word she heard all his grief and loss, his love and his determination to do right, as he saw it, by her.

She leaned her head against his shoulder as they walked on, and the village came into view. She had to recognize that he was right in so many ways. She *was* growing and finding her wings in the short time of her widowhood. Yet so much of that was due to him. He was so much more than the first man to have been kind to her since her marriage. It was as if she *recognized* him on some deep, unfathomable level. He was her soul mate, and she loved him.

More than that, he loved her and believed she was his.

She knew this from his kiss, his touch, the anguish of his voice, the tenderness in his care for her.

"Will you grant me one favor?" she asked.

"Anything,"

She turned her head against his shoulder, looking up at him while the swinging lantern waved light back and forth across his face. "Stay with me tonight."

GILES'S HEART BROKE in two. The reaction of his nether regions was much more straightforward, like a clap of thunder.

"Rosamund," he groaned.

"It would be a gift," she interrupted, "to hug to myself through the years you say we must be apart. Will you not help me? Would it not help you?"

"It's more likely to make me behave badly and never let you go."

"Would that be so bad?"

"Yes. For all the reasons we've just talked about. And *you* might well find parting harder. On top of which, what if there are consequences? What if we conceive a child?"

"Then I will worry about that if it happens. I suspect it won't, since my marriage is barren. I will love any child of yours until you can be with us."

"The Cuttynghams would have the say in that, since the child would technically be your late husband's."

"Not if I go abroad. And in any case, I believe I trust Victor to do the right thing. We…misunderstood each other, I think."

He regarded her with fresh fascination. "You have thought all this through."

"I have. I have had plenty time to think about it. I would give you the same time, only we don't seem to have much of that particular commodity."

Struck by the desolation in her voice, he hugged her to his side, burying his lips in his hair.

"I am a good soldier," he said, low but intense. "An instinctive one. I think on my feet, and I *always* know what to do when battle situations change, even in the worst of circumstances. Now, for the first time in my life, I am floundering. I don't know what to do. I don't know what is right." And it was tearing him apart, killing him in any way that mattered.

Her fingertips brushed his cheek, his lips. "Do you trust me, Giles?"

He stared at her in surprise. "You know I do."

"Then you do know what is right. For both of us."

Relief washed off him in waves. God, he was glad.

THEY ENTERED THE inn through the deserted coffee room, where the chatter and noise of the taproom was a mere, muffled echo. Leaving him there, she went up to her chamber and sent the curious Perry to bed in her own attic room. Then she threw her domino cloak and reticule onto a chair and stared at herself in the black-spotted glass.

Her eyes seemed huge in her pale face. It did not look like the face of beauty or seduction. What did she know of such things? She, who had endured her husband's attentions with ever-growing revulsion for three whole years, was voluntarily contemplating seducing the man she loved into such an act. Which was unlikely to satisfy him more than it had satisfied Cuttyngham. And yet…

And yet excitement stirred in her blood, in her bones. She wanted this. She needed to be close to him.

"It's more likely to make me behave badly and never let you go," he had said with intense desperation. She was not just gambling on that. She was counting on it.

She patted her hair with hands that shook and swung away from the glass before she lost the courage to fight for her love, her happiness, her future.

And his, please, God.

He stood in the coffee room, almost where she had left him, under the pale light of a single lamp. When he turned quickly toward her, she paused on the stairs and beckoned.

He didn't smile. She had never seen him so serious. He walked toward her and climbed the stairs, his every movement slow and deliberate. Her heart thundered as he took her trembling hand. His gaze never left her face as they crossed the landing and entered her bedchamber.

It was he who turned the key in the lock and then turned to face her.

Her breath came in ragged pants as he raised her hand to his lips. "Sweetheart, we need do nothing. If you prefer, I will lie by your side until morning and kiss you farewell before we part."

"Really?" she said.

His crooked smile dawned. "Really. It might kill me, but just being with you for a few hours is more sweetness than I ever imagined in my life."

She twisted her fingers among his. "I want to be with you, as though I am truly your wife."

"My lover," he said low, and heat swirled through her.

She dragged his hand to her cheek, hoping it would hide her shame. "I want this, Giles. I want you. I just…I just don't know what to do."

"Whatever you like," he whispered, "and only what you like. You must tell me." He took her face between her hands, "Promise you will tell me."

She barely understood him, though she nodded because it was obviously important to him. Then he kissed her, softly, tenderly, yet as though he would never stop. When his mouth left hers, she took it back with a gasp, and the kiss grew in heat and urgency, like those on the roadside. Only this time they were alone, and his hands swept up and down her back as she arched into him and then settled on her rear.

The excitement of novel arousal galloped under the caresses of his mouth, and his hands, on her nape, her breasts, her waist, and hips. She found the hot, smooth skin of his back and stroked it in wonder, loving his instant reaction to her touch. He threw off his uniform coat and cravat to make it easier for her, and she found the hollow of his throat with her lips.

"You smell divine," he whispered. "Like summer flowers and sunshine."

She smiled, wordlessly inhaling the male scent of his own skin. This time, when she kissed him, his fingers efficiently unhooked the fastening of her gown and unlaced her stays. He lifted her out of them and twirled her around, making her laugh before letting her slip back to her feet against his hard, warm body before he fastened his lips to hers once more.

This was all beguilingly new and heady. She had never dreamed of such kisses, such luscious, intimate caresses. They made her body both weak and eager, tingling with a pleasure she had never known and a strange, desperate heaviness that wanted…more.

Only when he lifted her in his arms again and brought her to the bed did reality pierce. But she had learned from him already and would learn to please him in this, too, even through gritted teeth which she would never show him. Because she loved him so much.

Her chemise was untied and gone. She had never been naked in front of a man before, and now she had no time for embarrassment, for he was naked, too. The sight of him, almost golden in the candlelight, from his broad, scarred shoulders to his muscular thighs and the male parts between, was oddly, breathtakingly beautiful. Before she could help herself, she had reached for him, stroking his shoulders and chest, and as he came down over her, his long, undulating back, his slim hips and rear.

"Dear God, you are lovely," he whispered. "I dreamed, but I never guessed *this*." His mouth glided over her nipples, making her moan with pleasure, even while her heart sang because he thought she was lovely, because he still liked her, because his weight on her, his *everything* felt so good, and still she wanted more.

His hand caressed her thigh, moving inward as his body shifted, and he kissed her mouth as his fingers found the heat between her thighs. She gasped, arching instinctively into his hand, and her astonished moans of bliss were lost in his smiling mouth.

That had never happened before. She was so taken with the intensity of feeling that she hugged him with her arms and legs as he slowly, gently entered her body.

At some point it occurred to her that it was barely even the same act as her husband had perpetrated upon her. Giles did not force himself to duty. He made love with clear, obvious joy, and received it. As Rosamund did.

FROM HIS PLACE by the taproom window, Gregson had seen the duchess arrive wearing a bright, theatrical cloak with its hood up. Beside her was a man in a similar but darker cloak. They looked like Quality, but only a careful observer who knew her well could have recognized the recently widowed Duchess of Cuttyngham.

Her escort wore no hood, though his identity was more problematic. If he wore military uniform, his cloak covered it, and his face was turned away from Gregson toward the duchess. It could easily have been Captain Butler or Battle, whatever his name was, the duke's killer. Gregson elected to wait until the man left to get a better look.

But by the time the innkeeper had emptied everyone out of the taproom, the duchess's escort had made neither an appearance nor an exit from the inn. Gregson was thoughtful as he mounted his horse to begin the long ride through the night to London.

On a personal level, he did not begrudge the duchess whatever fling she was indulging in. On a professional one, he was sure Mr. Severne would want to know. As he would know the major was sailing from Dover.

Chapter Fifteen

Giles woke wrapped around a luscious female form. The scent of Rosamund's hair, her skin, filled his nostrils and made him smile, even before he opened his eyes. It wasn't quite light, but still, he'd slept longer than he meant to.

Somehow, their first gentle, tender loving had been followed very shortly after by something shorter and wilder and even more satisfying. Although Rosamund was clearly new to more than the mechanics of coupling, she gave and received passion with an eager, addictive joy that thrilled him beyond anything he had ever known.

Softly, he kissed the silky skin of her shoulder, and she moved immediately, turning her sleepy head toward him and smiling.

"Giles."

"Rosamund," he said, and kissed her.

Instant passion flared, but he curbed it, for their time had run out, and they needed to talk about the future, so before things got out of hand, he rearranged the pillows and hauled them both into a semi-sitting position, keeping his arm around her and trying very hard not to push the sheet down another inch.

"Have we complicated matters furthers, Rosamund?" he asked ruefully.

She nodded. "I could never understand why women took lovers from choice." She cast him a shy, mischievous smile. "I would take you from choice. Now, if you like."

"Then we'll solve nothing," he said hastily, catching her roving hand, although he loved this new boldness in her, felt a strange new pride that he was the one who had taught her pleasure.

"I love you, and I want to marry you," she said candidly. "Last night only confirmed that."

"There are other men who could give you pleasure, Rosamund."

An expression of hurt entered her beautiful eyes. "They are not you."

He groaned. "And God knows you are not 'other women.' What are we to do? Will you wait a year for me? Providing I do not hang."

"It is better than five or ten," she allowed. She twisted around to touch his cheek, and he felt her weighing her words with care. "There is another alternative."

His heart beat with hope. "Go on."

"That I immediately instruct my solicitor to obtain us a special license and send it to Brussels. And that I travel there with you. As soon as the license reaches us, we may be married. There must be many Church of England clergymen there, since I believe half the ton has congregated in the city."

How was it that the impossible had become merely a little difficult? "You know what accusations we would face?"

"Perhaps the fact that this is wartime actually helps us," she said ruefully. "Our little scandal doesn't matter much beside the huge threat of Bonaparte, death, and battle."

"It will matter before and after," he said frankly. "I think… I think our best hope is to get Wellington on our side. Then, at least if I avoid trial, I will still have a career. There will still be talk and probably unpleasantness. Are you really prepared for that?"

To his surprise, she actually considered it. He could almost see her mulling over backs turned on her, cuts direct, whispers… And weighing them against nights in his arms and a life spent together in companionship and fun. After all, they would always have the support of friends.

Was it more than possible?

"We could wait a year or five or ten, but Giles, why waste what we have been given? I am so tired of wasting time." She smiled a little uncertainly. "It is different for you, I know..."

He hauled her into his lap, burying his face in her tangled hair, as though inhaling her like air. "No. God knows I am reckless and impulsive by nature, but I would do anything, sacrifice anything, to keep you safe and happy."

"Then marry me," she whispered and kissed him as though she would never stop.

By the time she did, he had made up his mind.

"We will go to Ostend on Corny's ship, taking your maid with us," he said sternly. "We will travel with perfect propriety until we can be married. By which time, I hope to have at least won Wellington's acceptance if not his blessing. For what follows, we will just have to brazen it out."

"Yes, Giles," she said meekly, although she was grinning like a hungry child presented with cake.

CORNY, WHEN HE turned up at the inn with Giles's horse and saddlebags, accepted the new arrangements with his usual good nature. Fortunately, Rosamund's carriage was not emblazoned with coats of arms, but even so, Giles stuck to his rules. Rosamund climbed into the carriage with her maid and baggage, and Giles and Corny rode beside the coach like outriders.

"Well?" Corny murmured to him once.

And Giles, who was almost bursting with fresh happiness and hope and the possibilities of the new life before him, only grinned.

"I see," Corny said dubiously.

"I don't suppose you do. She wants to marry me, Corny, though I'm damned if I can see a way to manage it without miring her in scandal."

"That's the odd thing about the supposedly Polite World," Corny observed. "They'd probably rather a discreet affair between you than an honest marriage. Makes no sense to me."

"It wouldn't be a discreet affair if she followed the drum."

Corny blinked. "She means to do so? Good God, she's a duchess! Has she any idea…?"

"More than you'd think. And she'll do it with grace, too, and be useful. She'd be a huge asset, Corny, and not just to me."

"Apart from being mired in scandal."

"Apart from that."

"Oh well," Corny said philosophically, "perhaps no one will care after we beat Boney once and for all."

It was, of course, crazily optimistic, but on this sunny day, with the scent of her lingering in his nostrils and the memory of her passionate embraces vivid in his mind, he was far too happy to do more than agree.

They reached Dover in the early afternoon and went immediately to the Ship Inn on Custom House Quay, dramatically placed at the foot of the cliffs. Since the whole town was heaving with people, including huge numbers of soldiers, Giles didn't hold out much hope for rooms at such a convenient and respectable a house. But as it turned out, a ship had sailed only that morning, and he was able to obtain two rooms and even a private parlor.

Leaving Rosamund to settle in, Giles went off with Cornhill onto the Quay to search out their ship and see if he could negotiate a cabin for Rosamund and her maid. Not that he particularly wanted her on a ship full of soldiers, certainly not without the protection of his name, but if she could be located near the captain's quarters…

"Major! Major Butler!"

"Another one," Corny said admiringly, "How do you do it, Lune?"

Dragging himself out of his reverie, Giles turned in the direction of the female voice hailing him and discovered an unexpected figure all but hauling another across the cobbles in his direction.

"Major Butler, it *is* you!" Miss Merton exclaimed, apparently delighted. "I knew it was. Oh, Fanny, this is Major Butler who was so kind to us last week. Captain, my aunt, Mrs. Edwards."

Mrs. Edwards was a rather fashionable-looking lady, only just on the wrong side of thirty, both elegant and pretty. Despite being dragged across the quay to speak to strange soldiers, her face expressed only mild disapproval at her niece, which quickly dissolved into a civil smile at Giles.

She seemed an odd choice of chaperone for such a willful handful as Miss Merton, until Miss Merton confided artlessly, "Fanny is going to Brussels, so they sent me with her hoping all those gallant officers will distract me from my engagement to Tom."

"Izzy!" complained her startled aunt.

"Oh, Major Butler knows all about Tom," Izzy said cheerfully.

"How do you do, ma'am?" Giles cut in with a bow. "Allow me to present my friend, Captain Cornhill. Cornhill, Miss Merton."

While everyone bowed and curtseyed and murmured polite nonentities, Izzy said eagerly, "How is Mrs. Daryll? I hope she managed to get home comfortably?"

"Ah, yes, she did," Giles said. "Thank you for asking."

"Mrs. Daryll is the major's sister, the kind lady I told you about," Miss Merton told her aunt.

Cornhill, who knew perfectly well that Giles's sister was not called Daryll, cast him a startled glance. But Giles's mind had sprung two moves ahead.

"You are going to Brussels?" he said. "When do you sail?"

"With tomorrow's morning tide, apparently," Mrs. Edwards replied. "My husband is a keen yachtsman. That is his vessel just at the end of the quay. I suppose you gentlemen will sail on the Royal Navy vessel behind you."

"That is the plan," Giles agreed, already formulating others. "But you spoke of Mrs. Daryll. It so happens she is staying at the Ship Inn there. I know she would be glad to see you if you have a moment to call on her."

"Oh, how lovely!" Miss Merton cried. "Is she going to Brussels, too? Oh, come Fanny, let us go now."

"Allow me to escort you," Giles said at once, and in a low aside to Corny. "Get me passage if you can. I'll join you as soon as I'm able."

THERE WAS LITTLE settling in to do for one night at the inn, and since Perry attended to Rosamund's belongings, she flopped on the window seat and gazed over the quay with its vast variety of ships—cargo vessels, a magnificent Royal Navy warship, passenger packets and even private yachts further along. Sailing ships dotted the sea into the distance.

It was tempting just to gaze dreamily out of the window, remembering in vivid detail the night spent in Giles's arms. But after five minutes of such delightful indulgence, she sighed and went to the table, where Perry had already set out her writing implements.

Sitting, she drew a sheet of paper toward her and tapped the quill feather against her lips. She needed to write to Victor and Hera, but how much to tell them?

She dipped the quill in ink and began *The Ship Hotel, Dover, 18th May 1815. My dear Victor…* That was the easy part. Fortunately, a knock on the door disturbed her. She twisted around in time to see Perry open it to Captain Butler. Instantly, Rosamund jumped to her feet and hurried toward them.

She loved the way his eyes lit up at sight of her. It set butterflies soaring in her stomach. "Giles? Is all well?" she said breathlessly. She wished he would touch her, but he didn't, though he did take a step nearer and lean toward her.

"Better than well," he said low. "I've brought Izzy Merton and her aunt to meet you. They're traveling to Ostend by private yacht. I'm sure you could go with them."

"But I don't want—" she protested.

"A day or so apart, Rosamund, and I'd meet you at Ostend. It could give you a reason to be in Brussels and protect you as I cannot yet do. Think about it. They're in the private parlor. I have to go back to Corny…" He glanced quickly up and down the passage, and then dropped a swift, all-too-brief kiss on her lips. Then, ignoring Perry's outrage, he grinned and strode off toward the stairs.

For a moment, Rosamund stared after him, then pulled herself together and walked in the other direction toward the private parlor.

Izzy immediately launched herself at Rosamund with cries of delight. "Mrs. Daryll! How absolutely wonderful to find you here!"

Rosamund submitted, laughing to the enthusiastic embrace. "What a surprise indeed! Are you here with the rest of your family?"

"Only my aunt and uncle. This is my aunt, Mrs. Edwards," she said with a shade of pride. "The only one of my family who is not appallingly stuffy."

"*Stuffy*!" Mrs. Edwards repeated, clearly scandalized. "Izzy, *please* will you mind your—"

"Oh, please don't worry on my account," Rosamund interrupted. "I'm afraid we are rather too far in each other's confidences to worry about such trifles. How do you do, Mrs. Edwards?"

"Mrs. Daryll," the aunt said, clearly taking in her old but well-made black gown. "You are recently widowed?"

"Sadly, yes," Rosamund replied. "Let me send for tea and

then I must make a confession..."

If she really meant to make use of these people, she would do so only with full honesty. Her faith in Izzy's discretion was not great, but there was no spite in the girl or, she suspected, in the aunt, who was clearly out of her depth playing chaperone to her lively niece.

While they waited for tea and watched Rosamund pour it out, Izzy chattered blithely about her life since parting from Rosamund.

"Papa shouted at me all the way home from Sir Aubrey's, though he never suspected Tom and I had anything to do with the major's escape."

"What major?" Mrs. Edward said suspiciously. "What escape?"

"Dear Fanny," Izzy said affectionately, giving her aunt's arm a quick hug. "Then Papa stopped speaking to me altogether. Until he heard that Tom was back. Thanks to you, ma'am, both sets of parents agreed to our engagement, although both clearly think we'll grow out of it. Hence my being sent to Aunt and Uncle Edwards as soon as we knew they were leaving the country."

"When does Tom sail?" Rosamund inquired.

Izzy grinned at her. "Not for a bit. He has responsibilities at home. He probably won't come at all, unless for a mere few days, but it makes no real difference, you know. We won't give each other up."

"Isabel, my dear, I wish you would not talk in company with quite such passion?" Mrs. Edwards tried.

"Oh, I shan't to anyone else. But Mrs. Daryll knows everything." Izzy rose and accepted the teacups from Rosamund, then ferried one to her aunt. "Now, I am on tenterhooks. Confess all, Mrs. Daryll."

"Well," Rosamund said, sipping her tea with some discomfort. "I'm afraid my name is no longer Daryll. And it was never *Mrs.* Daryll."

"Oh." Izzy set down her cup. "Are...are you not a cousin of

the Duke of Cuttyngham either?"

"No, I'm not. I'm the Duchess of Cuttyngham."

Izzy frowned, distracted. "I didn't know he was married. We thought he was the country's most eligible bachelor."

"You are thinking of my stepson, the new, current duke."

Izzy brightened with understanding. "Of course! You wear black now because you are widowed!"

Mrs. Edwards frowned at her. "You needn't sound so delighted about it."

But Izzy had moved on, staring at Rosamund as the full implications of this confession hit her. "But that means Major—"

"Precisely," Rosamund said. "The major is not my brother. He felt obliged to help me get home. And now things have changed, and I wish to go to Brussels. The world will not understand."

Izzy, for once, appeared to be speechless.

Her aunt said carefully, "There is someone in Brussels Your Grace wishes to be near?"

"Yes," Rosamund said frankly. "My aim is not to attend all the reviews and parties I understand are so prevalent there, but to live as quietly as I may, for a few weeks at least. Another officer friend is trying to arrange passage for me on the ship that is carrying him—"

Mrs. Edwards's jaw dropped. She looked appalled. "Your Grace cannot sail on a ship full of soldiers!"

"I hope I can."

"Fanny," Izzy said impulsively. "Mrs. Daryll—Her Grace—must come with us. Uncle Edwards will not mind, will he?"

"Well, no, of course not, but…" Mrs. Edward's glanced from her niece to Rosamund in some consternation.

"Of course," Rosamund said with some relief. She did not want to be on a different ship to Giles, after all. "I quite understand you cannot risk your niece with possible scandal."

Mrs. Edwards's breath caught. "With a widowed duchess? On the contrary, it rather raises us above the middling society to which we belong. I believe Izzy's parents would be pleased."

Rosamund met her gaze. "You understand my aim is not to go out in society? And that once it's known I am there, all sorts of talk and scandal may abound? I am not behaving like a conventional widow and that is even before—"

"I think it's the most wonderful, romantic thing ever," Izzy interrupted. "And most assuredly we will help you. It's the least we can do."

Mrs. Edwards, perhaps with not all the facts but certainly with a heavy dose of worldly ambition, nodded emphatically. "It will be our pleasure if Your Grace will accept passage on our yacht. If you have a large retinue…?"

"There is only my maid."

Mrs. Edwards smiled. "Then we have no problems at all."

VICTOR, THE NEW Duke of Cuttyngham, looked surprisingly well upon a horse. At any other time, Anthony would have been glad of it, if only to prove the old duke wrong. But he had timed his visit badly. Victor had quite annoyingly chosen to return from his ride while the Cuttyngs grooms were up at the kitchen, leaving only Gregson in privacy to receive Anthony's commands.

When Victor trotted into the yard, there was nowhere for Anthony to hide. Forced to brazen it out, he stepped away from Gregson to wave and smile at his cousin as though pleased to see him.

Victor didn't bother to wave back. Perhaps he needed both hands to control the huge horse he was mounted on, even though the beast was clearly tired after a presumably long morning out.

"Well met, Cousin!" Anthony said cheerfully.

"Back so soon?" Victor replied without heat. "Perhaps it's just as well. You can take Arabia with you when you go."

Anthony's brows flew up. Used to the old duke's tricks, he said carefully, "You're giving me Arabia?"

"The old man was pretty mean, considering how much you put up with him," Victor observed. Although Gregson went forward to take his horse, the young duke dismounted unaided and regarded the groom. "You might as well go with him, too, since you're barely here as it is. I gather it's my cousin's business you are about."

Gregson flushed and rolled his eyes wildly at Anthony for help.

"You are turning him off?" Anthony said, unwilling to lose his spy in the ducal household.

"I'll give him a character if you want one," Victor said, a light of amusement in his eyes. "You should be able to afford him with the increase in your allowance."

Anthony smiled. "I dropped by to thank you for that. You are generous."

"Only compared to His Grace." Victor petted the neck and nose of his horse and fed him a carrot from his coat pocket. "Will you take a glass of sherry before you go?"

A glass of sherry. Not even a meal, let alone an invitation to stay. It struck Anthony that Victor might become even more formidable than the old duke, not least because there was intelligence behind his malice.

"I don't believe I'll trouble you, Cousin," Anthony said pleasantly. "I have said my thanks and will add further gratitude for the gift of the horse and Gregson, here, and be on my way. You'll allow Gregson to take care of your horse? His last duty before he leaves your employ for mine."

With a final pat to the horse's neck, Victor tossed the reins to Gregson and limped off toward the house, once more his familiar, ungainly self.

Anthony swore under his breath.

"Never thought he'd notice," Gregson said, aggrieved.

"Don't worry, you won't lose by it," Anthony snapped. "So,

Her Grace is in Dover? With *Butler*? In what capacity?"

Gregson gave him a look.

"Good God," Anthony said faintly. "This is terrible. The last thing we want is Butler's bastard masquerading as Victor's heir! We must inform the magistrates at once."

"Already done, sir," Gregson said smugly. "I went to Bow Street, got the Runners involved."

Anthony blinked at him, impressed in spite of himself. "That, Gregson, was a clever move, though I'm surprised they paid any attention to you."

"I used your name," Gregson confessed. "And His Grace's."

"Even better! Then let us to Dover and gather back up this bolting duchess. I wonder if Victor could be persuaded to find her so irritating that he has her declared insane…?"

"If her antics interrupt his books often enough, he just might," Gregson said cynically and went to prepare the horses.

CHAPTER SIXTEEN

GILES'S NOTIONS WERE not quite what Rosamund had planned, but she did see that it would be more comfortable on the Edwardses' yacht and would, besides, provide a glimmering of respectability. In gratitude, she invited them to dine at the Ship Inn, where they were also joined by Giles and Captain Cornhill. Perry, at her most severe and supercilious, supervised the serving of the meal.

Mr. Edwards, Izzy's uncle, turned out to be a bluff, good-natured man with shrewd eyes. Though not, as Rosamund's brother might have put it, out of the top drawer, he was clearly a wealthy man, having expanded the fortune his father made in manufacturing by moving into banking and other ventures. He touched on those only lightly, knowing enough not to talk money with the aristocracy, mentioning them only, it appeared, to prove he was proud of his origins and had no intention of hiding them to try and impress a duchess.

On the other hand, he did, in fact, seem very impressed with Rosamund. If he and his wife were surprised she should be jaunting about the world so soon after the death of her husband—and in such a way—he said nothing of it.

Rosamund soon discovered why.

"Has your godbrother found you lodgings in the town, Duchess?" he asked, over the beef course.

Bewildered, she glanced up at him. "Godbrother?"

Izzy laughed. "Sorry, Your Grace. I invented the word! I was explaining to my aunt and uncle how close you were to your godmother's own children growing up, and how the youngest of those is with Wellington."

"Your Grace's anxiety is most understandable," Mr. Edwards declared. "The gentleman being so young and untried. A terrible extra burden for you to bear at such a time."

Rosamund met Izzy's limpid blue eyes, torn between annoyance—so much for honesty—and amusement because she could hardly expose the girl for trying to help her.

"Terrible," Cornhill agreed with apparent sincerity.

"I doubt he will have had time to arrange accommodation," Giles said smoothly. "He will be training hard for the coming action. Her Grace means to stay at a hotel until she can find somewhere suitable."

"We have taken a little house close to the center of Brussels," Mr. Edwards said.

"And would be delighted if Your Grace would join us there," his wife finished eagerly. A duchess, after all, even an eccentric and possibly scandalous one, was a boost to one's social standing.

"Oh, no, I could not possibly put you out in such a way," Rosamund said at once. She could feel herself being tugged back into the prison of conformity, away from Giles and the life they had chosen only last night.

"There is plenty of room," Mrs. Edwards assured her. "And of course, we would not intrude upon your privacy."

"It might be more comfortable," Izzy put in. "Just until you find something else to suit you. And then you may devote your time to your godbrother rather than rooms and houses."

In panic, Rosamund found Giles's gaze. His nod was infinitesimal, and the rueful understanding in his eyes calmed her enough to consider. They would not intrude upon her privacy, but would she able to spend time with him? His approval of the scheme seemed to say yes. And after all, it need only be for a night or two.

"You are very kind," she managed to Mrs. Edwards. "I accept with gratitude and promise to get out from under your feet as soon as I can."

Everyone beamed at her, and she realized in a rush that Giles wanted her to be somewhere safe if he had to leave suddenly before they could me married. And even if they were, if Boney attacked without warning, it was possible women and children would be left behind with the baggage. She would have to get used to the idea of spending days and nights, even weeks, away from him.

Since everyone was sailing the following morning, no one stayed long after coffee. Giles and Captain Cornhill were the first to depart, no doubt to maintain the duchess's respectability.

Rosamund, feeling slightly bereft, forced herself to keep smiling—after all, she had had a good deal of practice at that over the years—while making final arrangements with the Edwardses to collect her luggage and conduct her to the yacht. She was very glad she had decided to pack properly this time. The Edwardses would have found it extremely odd to discover a duchess traveling abroad with a mere carpetbag.

The thought amused her, raising her spirits and her trust in Giles. They were beginning an adventure, one that was a little uncertain as yet, but one she relished. Moreover, she recognized that if she was to be the good officer's wife she wished to be, she must not cling and whine and add to his burdens. She wanted to *enhance* his life as he somehow completed her.

So, she accompanied Perry back to their bedchamber and allowed the maid to loosen her gown and take down her hair.

"You go to bed," she told Perry. "Leave the candle. I'll just sit by the window for a little." And think how to keep her lies straight, now that Izzy had invented a "godbrother" for her, too. At least the Edwardses had not seemed to connect Major Butler with the duel that had killed Cuttyngham, and for Giles's sake, she had to keep it that way, at least until his ship departed.

The quay had quietened, though she could still hear distant male voices raised in song over the pleasant, rushing sound of the sea and the occasional creaking of the docked ships. She hugged her shawl around her and thought about how her intolerable life had changed so suddenly. Of course, she had decided to change it herself when she took the cottage in Little Fiddleton and set about escaping there. Without that, she would never have met Giles. Although nature, it seemed, would have freed her anyway, through the cruel trick of fate that was Cuttyngham's death.

Reluctantly, she dwelled on that death. On the duel that should never have killed him. The tragic accident that would forever be associated with Giles now, whether the duke had died of natural causes or of his wound. She did not underestimate the difficulties of a life with Giles, especially if the authorities insisted on trying him. But together, surely, they would overcome.

She could no longer hear the sea for the hefty snores emerging from Perry's truckle bed on the other side of the room. Deciding to go to bed herself, she rose from the window seat. Brisk footsteps in the passage were coming this way. In spite of herself, her heartbeat quickened. Giles would not come to her here—*could* not with Perry in her room, and Cornhill in his.

And, of course, they paused before they reached her door. Another opened gently and did not close. The door next to her own. The private parlor.

Her breath caught. She moved impulsively toward her bedchamber door and unlocked it before she reached for the candle and left the room. Glancing into the parlor to see who was there would do no harm. It could be the manager making sure the room had been cleared, as indeed it had been by his efficient staff.

The parlor door stood ajar, a faint light glowing inside the room. After making sure the passage was empty, she hurried along and glanced inside.

By the glow of a single candle on the table beside him, Giles rose from the settle. His coat was unbuttoned, his hair was tousled, and he had never looked so handsome. She retained enough sense to softly close the door and turn the key. And then she was in his arms, his rough, stubbly cheek pressed to hers.

"I wanted to say a proper goodnight," he said with relief. "I didn't want to leave you so casually. There will be so little time tomorrow, and we will always be in public…"

She stopped his mouth with a kiss. After a moment's tenderness, he took rather wild, exciting control of the embrace, thrilling her to her toes. Slowly, gradually, he gentled things once more, and then drew her on the settle beside him, his arm around her.

"You are content with these arrangements?" he asked with a hint of anxiety.

"I meant to be more honest," she said ruefully. "But now Izzy has given me a 'godbrother.' That girl is incorrigible!"

"Yes, but it's actually quite a good idea, so long as you can avoid details."

"No doubt I can apply to Izzy for them." She glanced up at him. "She knows about us, doesn't she? This is why she's trying to help us. She sees us like herself and Tom Yates."

"I suspect so. And if you come down to basics, our situations are not so dissimilar. She is kind-hearted. Though I don't see the Edwardses being able to keep her much under control. I suspect your presence will be valued there."

She couldn't help smiling. "You are trying to get around me, aren't you?"

"Reminding you that you and the Edwardses are helping each other."

"You know me too well." She laid her head on his shoulder, and he stroked her hair.

"In some ways. In others, I barely know you at all." She felt his breath, his lips on the top of her head. "You gave yourself to me so beautifully last night."

Warmth suffused her. "I wanted to so much. I've never wanted to before."

"Because of your husband?"

She nodded. And then, haltingly, she began to tell him something of her marriage, things she had thought she would never tell anyone because they made her feel ashamed and ugly, inside and out. Part of her listened to her own words, appalled and frightened in case he would draw back from her in disgust. But instead, his arm tightened around her, and the anger that stiffened his body was not aimed at her.

"My poor darling," he whispered into her hair. "My brave, wonderful love. You have such strength, such spirit."

"I do?" She raised her head to look at him in surprise.

He didn't smile. "He wanted to crush you. It's how such men feed their own sense of worth. He had to belittle a brave man like Colonel Landon to show his own superiority. And subjugate his wife to make her feel she was nothing compared to him. I'm almost glad I killed him. But you had already defeated him."

It was a novel way of looking at the corrosive relationship, but a few layers of cold and shame seemed to have slid away. Because she had done her best. Because Giles, wonderful, kind, brave, honorable Giles, loved her.

"I'm not at all convinced you *did* kill him," she said stoutly, and they talked a little more about Dr. Rivers's suspicions and what difference they could make. Despite the unpleasantness of these subjects, a warm, comforting bubble seemed to have enclosed them. Last night, there had been little time for words. Their bodies and passions had spoken in their own ways and brought them a closeness Rosamund had never imagined. Tonight, with confessions and plans for the future, they drew closer yet.

And when they parted with no more than a long, tender kiss, she felt a deeper, quieter happiness than she had ever known.

DESPITE THE IMMINENT parting, Rosamund woke with the excitement of her new life beckoning. She had never sailed on anything wider than the lake at home. She had never left England. And she had never known the comfort, the joy, of a man's love. Despite all the dangers still to be faced, life felt wonderful.

She took a hasty, early breakfast in the private parlor with Giles and Cornhill, and then the Edwardses' footman arrived to carry her luggage. While Cornhill went off to pay their shot—she would sort her share out later, she assured him anxiously—Giles loaded the footman with her smaller bags and Perry's. He picked up her trunk and led the way downstairs.

Although still early, the foyer was bustling with travelers of all kinds, including soldiers. Apparently, a ship had just docked. Somehow Giles, with the trunk somewhat jauntily on his shoulder, cut a path through the milling throng, Rosamund and Perry at his heels, with the footman following.

At the door, he stood aside to let someone enter, and Rosamund came face to face with Anthony Severne.

There was no time to avoid him, let alone to hide. He halted, and so did she. Their eyes seemed to clash together, and for no obvious reason, her blood ran cold in her veins. He was part of her old, discarded life. She did not want him here at the start of the new.

He bowed. "Your Grace."

"Anthony." She recovered enough to smile. "What brings you to Dover?"

"Business," he replied, smiling back. "And Your Grace?"

"I'm traveling," she said with a slight tilt of her chin.

He inclined his head. "Then I won't keep you. Don't forget to write to His Grace."

"I already have." She inclined her head and swept by him, her heart hammering. Anthony's eyes had never once flickered to Giles or Perry. He had shown no surprise on finding her here.

He knew exactly where I was.

The wind whipped off the sea, making her gasp. She grasped Giles's arm. "That was the duke's cousin. I don't trust him, Giles. Leave the trunk to the footman and board your ship. *At once,*

Giles."

He turned to her, frowning, though he kept walking, even increased his pace to suit hers. "Our ship is on the way to yours."

"But he knew I was here. He must know you are with me. Why else would he be so distant? He still wants revenge for Cuttyngham, despite the will…"

The Royal Navy ship loomed over all the others on the quay. Soldiers lined the decks, shouting and waving to those gathered on the shore to see them off. A small group of four red-coated marines stood on the quay at the gangway, talking to two very serious men in civilian dress. Rosamund had no reason to suppose they were a danger and yet, somehow, she knew they were. The civilians both wore red waistcoats, a flash of bright color in their otherwise sober dress that bothered her.

Red breasts. Where had she heard that? Talk among the servants down from London, one autumn, on the subject of some theft or other… *Bow Street Runners!*

"Giles," she said in growing panic. "I think these men are from Bow Street! They'll be looking for an officer with a woman—Anthony will have told them—so I'm going to leave you now…"

Before Giles could speak or she could veer away from him, Cornhill caught up with them at a run. "What's the matter?" he asked cheerfully, glancing from one to the other.

"Take him on board, disguise him somehow," Rosamund said wildly. "Pretend he's your batman or something!"

Cornhill frowned in consternation.

"I'm sure *they* are waiting for him, to arrest him!" she said impatiently, jerking her head toward the marines and their companions. "Please, Captain. Ostend, Giles."

It was hardly the way she had meant to part from him, but there was more at stake here than her dignity, or her trunk, which she abandoned without a thought. She walked away from him without a word or a glance.

But it was too late.

Even over the yards between them, she heard the accusation,

"Major Giles Butler?" She halted, and saw the Bow Street Runners approaching Giles, two of the waiting marines at their heels.

Cornhill said, "Captain Cornhill, actually. In a bit of a rush, so you'll have to excuse us."

"Can't. I have a warrant for the arrest of Major Butler. Sir, you must come with us."

One of the runners stood in front of Cornhill, who showed every sign of interfering. The other glared at Giles. On board the ship, the soldiers had clearly noticed the excitement, for they had grown silent and were watching the scene below.

Giles said clearly, "Sorry, I have a war to fight. I'll answer any warrants when I come home."

It won him an unexpected cheer from the ship's decks, which seemed to make the arresting officers nervous. "Now," one snarled, and made the mistake of reaching for Giles's arm.

Giles threw the trunk at him, and the runner caught it instinctively, staggering under the unexpected weight. While a choke of shocked laughter shook Rosamund, and the soldiers on deck howled with glee, Giles leapt around them all and bounded toward the gangway.

The soldiers guarding it snapped to attention.

"Stand aside!" Giles yelled.

"Can't sir!" cried one in clear distress as he raised his rifle.

At the last minute, Giles veered again, leaping to his left to avoid the magistrate's men and then running in a wide circle, dodging between passengers, leaping over someone's scowling pet pug on a leash, and shoving empty crates into the path of his pursuers. The soldiers on board cheered him on, chanting "Major! Major!"

Giles ran them in circles, like some wild, childish game of tag. Rosamund didn't know whether to laugh or shout at him in anger, for in these moments at least he was actually enjoying himself. She could hear his sudden breaths of laughter as he dodged one of his would-be captors and saw the other "accidentally" tripped by Captain Cornhill.

But there was method in his madness. The farcical difficulty of catching him had drawn the other pair of marines away from the gangway. Cornhill was edging nearer it, and so, in his erratic way, was Giles. Both of them seemed to think he would be safe aboard the ship, and perhaps he would, for no one told the soldiers off for cheering on one of their own.

Rosamund, feeling utterly helpless, still could not move away, even at Perry's urging. And then, as she cast a quick, desperate glance around the quay, she saw Anthony again.

He stood directly opposite her, at the front of the watching crowd, though his gaze was not on the action but on Rosamund.

What the devil is he about?

Before she could even think of an answer, someone seized her arm from behind and tugged hard, almost yanking her off her feet. From instinct, or perhaps sheer panic, she flung up her free arm, swinging her reticule into her attacker's face. Recovering her balance, she stamped hard on his foot.

But apart from a muffled grunt, her attacker made no acknowledgment. Certainly, his grip didn't loosen. At least she managed to twist around—and gazed into the affronted face of Gregson the groom.

She blinked. "Gregson? Unhand me this instant! What on earth do you think you are doing?"

Her sharp scold finally distracted a few of the gathered crowd, who were still more interested in Giles's antics. She could not even see the Edwardses' footman, lost somewhere in the crowds.

"Sorry, Your—ma'am. You've got to come home," Gregson muttered. "Come along with me now."

"I most certainly will not!" She tried again to shake him off, causing the man nearest her to frown with angry disapproval at Gregson.

"Your family needs you home," Gregson said with more than a shade of desperation, just before a large hand clamped over his wrist, hard enough to force a grimace and the loosening of his fingers.

"Run," Giles said to Rosamund and drew back his fist.

"She can't do that," Anthony said pleasantly. "It would hardly be dignified. And you, Butler or Battle or whatever your name is, are under arrest. Come, Rosamund."

Rosamund evaded him easily, glaring at him with her haughtiest expression. "My dear cous—"

And then disaster struck. Two of the marines took hold of Giles's arms.

Anthony laughed.

"Got you," said the burlier of the Bow Street Runners with a satisfied grin.

"A moment, if you please!" The authoritative voice cut through the clamor of the soldiers on the ship and the buzz of avid interest among the crowd of watchers on the quay. Everyone looked toward him.

A man in red and gold uniform, a black cloak hanging from his shoulders, strode off the gangway onto the quay. Miraculously, a passage formed for him as he marched toward Rosamund and Giles.

"Release him," this personage commanded, almost casually—the orders of a man who knows he will be obeyed instantly and without question.

And he was, although the men looked slightly baffled as to why they had done so.

"Colonel Davidson?" Giles said in some astonishment.

With a swish of his cloak, the newcomer swung to face him. "Major. You are an elusive man. The duke wants you."

So does the duchess. She must be growing hysterical…

The colonel raised his hand, and all four marines materialized at his shoulder. "Escort Major Butler on board and inform the captain he may sail whenever convenient."

"No, sir!" exclaimed one of the runners in outrage. "There is a warrant for this man's arrest. He is accused of nothing less than murder."

"So I believe." Colonel Davidson did not appear to be interested. While he spoke, he delved into the dispatch case he had been carrying under his arm. "The Duke of Wellington believes there is some doubt in the case and that his need of Major Butler is greater than the law's. The duke himself will vouch for Major Butler until the country is safe, and we might all cooperate in any unresolved investigations." Extracting a sealed document, he presented it to the furious officer of the law. "This is my authority. Now, gentlemen, if you will excuse me, I have other dispatches to deliver. Good—"

"Sir," Giles interrupted. Clapping Rosamund's hand to his arm, he took a step nearer the colonel and spoke in a low, urgent voice. "This lady is the Duchess of Cuttyngham, and she is, in the purest sense, under my protection. I need to see her safely aboard her friends' yacht."

The colonel's cool eyes landed on her at last, with the first hint of curiosity she had seen in them. "Ah." He bowed to her. "Your Grace's servant. My orders concern you, too. One moment." He swung back to the soldiers. "*You* two will escort the lady to her yacht, making sure she is safe. When you have all completed your tasks, come and find me."

Now that the danger to Giles appeared to be over—thanks to the Duke of Wellington himself—Rosamund's knees began to buckle with relief. All four marines, as well as Cornhill and some indignant looking gentlemen, now stood between her and Anthony and Gregson.

The men on the ship were cheering and calling insults to the Bow Street Runners who looked more frustrated than angry. Rosamund almost felt sorry for them.

"You'll be safe now," Giles murmured, bowing formally over her hand. A hint of the mischievous smile touched his lips. "At least until Izzy's next trick."

"Will *you*?" she asked bluntly.

"Be safe? Oh yes. Wellington's word is law in the army."

"And out of it," she said, thinking of the rejected warrant. "His influence is huge."

"And this before he's beaten Boney."

Their eyes met, and she longed to be alone with him, just to give him one more sweet, life-affirming kiss. But they appeared to be the center of attention, and she could not even let her eyes express what they wanted to. All she could do was smile brightly, straighten her shoulders, and walk away, escorted by two soldiers, one of whom was obliging enough to carry her trunk.

When an even louder cheer went up from the ship, she couldn't resist glancing back just once. Walking up the gangway behind Cornhill, Giles waved his hat at the soldiers in a self-deprecating salute. She swallowed the lump in her throat, unsure if it brought tears or laughter.

Of Anthony and Gregson, there was no sign at all.

"WHAT NOW?" GREGSON demanded over his ale in a quiet tavern some distance from the sea front. "Do we follow her?"

Anthony drank angrily and set down the mug. "We'll have to. Which is what I really don't need. I never imagined her behaving like this… Still, they're separated for now, so I have time to speak to my daughter, who is dragging her heels. Not that I blame her, but everyone has to make sacrifices for the family, and she will hardly lose by it. Perhaps I could just write to her, while you make inquiries about passage to Ostend, or any other port within easy distance of Brussels. Wait, though, what of the companion woman? Where is she? There was no sign of her with the duchess."

"She's still at Cuttyngs, preparing the Dower House for Her Grace and keeping Lady Hera company. Officially at least."

"Well, she's probably better there than in Brussels for now. As am I! Damn it, how did this nobody get to be Wellington's protégé?"

Gregson shrugged. "Probably a clever fellow," he said, not without malice. "Clever enough to beat us at every turn."

"And as I'm sure His Grace of Wellington will tell you, it's not winning the battle but winning the war that counts!"

CHAPTER SEVENTEEN

As it happened, Rosamund did find she was useful to her hosts on the voyage to Ostend, for both Izzy and her aunt succumbed to seasickness. So, it was up to Rosamund to nurse them and coax them onto the deck to find what Mr. Edwards called their sea legs. Like Rosamund, he seemed immune to the rolling of the yacht and the fierceness of the waves.

Before nightfall, the weather calmed, and Izzy began to bounce back to her usual ebullient self, which meant Rosamund had to balance caring for Mrs. Edwards with entertaining Izzy enough to keep her out of trouble.

"Are you *flirting* with the sailors?" Rosamund asked her once.

Izzy giggled. "Don't be silly. I'm only practicing. And telling them all about Tom."

Rosamund wasn't quite sure how that worked, but at least two of the sailors seemed to be dazedly in love with Izzy by the time they reached Ostend.

By then, even Mrs. Edwards had recovered enough to declare her mortification at being nursed by a duchess. At which Rosamund laughed. "My dear ma'am, it's quite my specialty."

As the yacht approached Ostend, excitement grew. Rosamund, watching on deck with Izzy, tried not to *rely* on a reunion with Giles here. After all, he would have to obey orders to go wherever he was sent. But she could not help hoping…

"Have you and Major Butler been in love for a long time?" Izzy asked.

Rosamund blinked and blushed.

"Well, you know all about Tom and me," Izzy said. "It's only fair that I know about you and the major."

"No, it isn't!"

"Why? Because you were married?"

"Actually, I wasn't," Rosamund said ruefully. "His Grace was already dead by the time we met, though I didn't know at once. I didn't know he had fought a duel with my husband, and he didn't know I was the duchess."

Izzy's eyes were shining. "Then how did you meet him?"

Rosamund hesitated. Her behavior was hardly a good example for a very young lady. "He felt compelled to apologize to the family for what had happened in the duel. I encountered him hovering outside Cuttyngs, wondering if his presence was not more insulting than respectful. I…wished to move to another residence without all the trappings of my position. But he was right. No one should travel quite alone, whatever their station. And he thought I was a member of the duke's family."

"So, he accompanied you? To make amends for the duel?" Izzy said, wide-eyed.

"I think so."

"How romantic. It must have been love at first sight."

Rosamund scoffed. "Don't be…" But, actually, Izzy was probably close to the truth. She might not have fallen starry-eyed at his feet outside the gates of Cuttyngs, but she had instinctively liked and trusted him, far beyond what was acceptable naivety. She couldn't pin down the actual moment her liking had become love, but it had been swift. So swift that were she giving advice to anyone else, whether Izzy or Hera or Sophia or any stranger, she would advise caution and waiting. Hence the advice she had given Izzy's father about a long engagement. "You must think me quite the hypocrite."

Izzy linked her arm through Rosamund's. "No. I am only

sixteen. Even Tom thinks we should wait. While you and the major are quite old."

Rosamund scowled. "Pass me my walking stick, child."

Izzy laughed, and then was immediately distracted. "Look! Isn't the town pretty?"

THE TOWN WAS busy. And if Dover had been full of soldiers, Ostend was packed with them. The task of finding one officer, who was probably apart from his own regiment, daunted even Rosamund, staring eagerly at every passing uniform of the correct color.

Mr. Edwards, installing her with his family in the inn booked for them, promised to set inquiries in motion. Although kind and helpful, it was no longer enough for Rosamund simply to rely on other people.

Accordingly, as soon as they had eaten and Mrs. Edwards had retired for a nap, Rosamund took Izzy off for a walk. Perry and a footman came with them for respectability. Between them, they soon discovered that the soldiers in the town were waiting for transport to Ghent, from where they could march to their stations around Brussels. Some were going by road, but the shortest and most efficient way was apparently by canal boat.

"Uncle Edwards hired one, leaving tomorrow," Izzy said. "I hope we have found the major by then."

So did Rosamund, for she had no desire to stay here alone, and less to go without him. There was no sign of his ship, and no one she spoke to had heard of it, which brought a new fear. What if it had been attacked by Bonapartists? What if it was sunk or crippled, and he was injured or even dead?

For the first time, she recognized the full hardship of a soldier's wife, waiting in fear for news. For the future, she would have plenty to do to distract herself. For now, the wait was a genteel form of torture.

She looked forward eagerly to Mr. Edwards's report at supper. But he had no news either, except that Giles's ship had in fact docked yesterday and was undergoing repairs. While this was a relief, she then wondered why Giles had not come looking for her. Had he already gone to Brussels? This seemed likeliest and, while disappointing, at least gave her reason to look forward to tomorrow's journey.

THE BUSTLING PORT never seemed to sleep, so what with the noise and her own anxiety, Rosamund went to bed convinced she would spend a wakeful night. However, as soon as her head touched the pillow, she fell into dreams.

She woke from a heavy sleep to a sharp cracking sound. Disoriented, she tried to think where she was. The tap came again, more gently, swiftly followed by a louder one. And then silence.

I'm at the inn in Ostend, alone in my bedchamber, she recalled, *and that noise is....* It sounded again, and she realized it came from the window, as if some bird was knocking its beak against the wooden shutter. *Stupid thing*. She sat up, wondering if she should go and flap her arms at it to scare it off. Or tap on her side of the window.

But whatever it was seemed to have gone, for she heard no more taps, only the rushing of the wind off the sea. The breeze had been much softer when she went to bed, but now it seemed to have grown wilder, rustling the leaves on the tree outside her window and blowing the smaller branches against the shutters. Maybe that was what had been tapping all along.

She lay down again, just as something much more solid struck the shutter, and the wind seemed to swear beneath its breath. She would have smiled at the idea, except yet another sound distracted her. The shutters rattled, first gently, then harder, and it didn't sound like the wind at all. Something metallic slid between them, surely, like sawing.

Rosamund's heart seemed to jump into her throat. Was someone breaking into her bedchamber? With a jolt, she remembered that she had left the window open a crack for fresh air and the smell of the sea which she had grown used to.

Alarmed now, she shot off the bed and reached for the bed-side candle. But she misjudged and sent candle and holder clattering onto the floor and rolling into the darkness. Now, there was only silence.

Had her imagination been playing tricks all along? No, for the shutters slowly opened and a shadow appeared at the window. Rosamund gasped, threw herself to her knees, and reached under the bed for the chamber pot—thankfully empty and clean—before jumping to her feet. Even as she flew toward the window, she doubted it was the right thing to do. She should have fled to Izzy's chamber next door and screamed for help. But she didn't have so much money with her that she could afford to lose it to some robber with the cheek to break into the very room she slept in! And if he stole her mourning gowns, her respectability would be completely gone…

All thought, however ludicrous or pointless, stopped as the black figure of a man pushed open the window and eased his way through. In the darkness, she didn't even know which way round he was facing, but as soon as one foot hit the floor, she raised the chamber pot high to crash it onto his head.

In a flash, something clamped her hands hard to the bowl, preventing it from moving. His hands were terrifyingly strong.

And then he spoke, low and humorous and shatteringly dear. "A chamber pot? Really? I hope it's empty."

She gasped, overwhelmed by emotion. "So do I," she managed shakily. She could not even put the pot down and throw her arms around him as she wanted, for he held her still grasping the pot above her head. Only now she relished the strength in his hands, remembered the unbearable sweetness of their caresses.

Silent laughter shook him. Deliberately, he stepped closer, breast to breast, hip to hip. She couldn't even make out his features and yet desire sparked and ignited.

"I admit I expected a warmer welcome," he murmured in her ear, his lips almost touching her skin. She could feel his breath, warm and exciting.

"You might have got one, if you hadn't tried to climb in my window like a thief."

"I *did* climb in your window like a thief."

"Then what do you expect? No wonder your men call you insane. How did you even know which window was mine?"

"I asked a chamber maid. I never imagined you were such a scold. Do I not get a kiss for my heroism?"

His chest shifted against her breasts, caressing, weakening her knees to jelly. Somehow, she said, "With a chamber pot poised above our heads?"

His knee slid between her legs, and she moaned. Then his smiling mouth came down on hers, and she forgot all about the wretched pot. His hands must have loosened, for hers flopped around his neck as he lowered the pot in one hand and slid it onto a table she had forgotten was there. Other things on the table clattered as they were pushed aside, but she didn't care, for both his arms were around her, pressing her even closer into his body. His mouth, devouring hers, never left it for an instant, even when he lifted her in his arms and strode to the bed—how could he even see it?—and all but fell with her on top of the covers.

She arched into him, hot and desperate. Even after the wonder of their night in Dover, she had never imagined such quick, urgent lust. There was one moment when he tried to draw back. Rising above her, he ground out, "Make me stop. Make me be good like I intended…"

For answer, she merely hooked her arms and legs around him and latched her mouth to his. "Later," she whispered incoherently against his lips. "Later, we'll be good."

They came together in swift, clamorous need. At some point,

her night rail was cast to the floor, but there was no time to divest him of everything before he was inside her, and by then, it was too late for everything except wild pleasure. Care and tenderness remained, but only just as he drove her to the ultimate, shattering joy they both sought.

GILES, DESCENDING SLOWLY from his ecstasy, wondered if he should be ashamed of himself for subjecting her to such urgent demands. Perhaps he would have been had she not cooperated so fully or found her pleasure with such triumph. That alone made him smile and wrap her closer in his arms. He was still wearing his shirt, mostly, and his pantaloons were around his ankles, but he didn't yet have the energy to remove them.

"I love you, you know," he said sleepily, "my wonderful, wanton wife."

She moved, laying her hand on his chest and her chin on her hand while she regarded him. "Wonderful? I thought wanton was bad."

"Not with me. I want you to adore everything we do together. As I do."

She smiled. "You're not like my idea of a husband at all."

"You have an understandably low opinion of husbands. I hope to spend my life changing that."

"If the world will let us."

He touched her cheek. "Losing heart already?"

She shook her head vehemently. "I just don't want our marriage to ruin your career."

"It won't," he said. "I'm pretty sure Wellington is on our side."

Her expressive eyes widened. "You've seen him already?"

"No. But Colonel Davidson—his staff officer who saved my hide in Dover—obviously had instructions concerning both of us.

The duke obviously wants me here."

"Perhaps he told Colonel Davidson to warn me off," she said in a small voice.

"But he didn't, did he? He made sure you got to the Edwardses' yacht, unmolested. Which reminds me," he added with a frown, "what is this Cousin Anthony's problem with you?"

"I don't know. I would say he didn't want me to damage the family honor, except he sent the vile Nimmot after me and threw him in my way again after the funeral. Perhaps he just doesn't like me."

"Is Nimmot his creature?" Giles asked, frowning.

"I suspect they do each other favors, none of which I want to know about." She shivered. "He didn't just want me not to leave the country. He wanted to take me home to Cuttyngs, and I don't understand why. At least, not beyond the 'behavior unsuited to a recent widow' argument. I suppose it must be that. But the thing is, Victor, the new duke, doesn't care what I do."

"Would Victor do Anthony's bidding?"

"God, no." She smiled at the memory. "He doesn't like him. In fact, after the funeral, he threw out all the hangers-on, including Anthony."

Giles sat bolt upright, dragging her with him. "Sophia! I forgot about Sophia again! If she isn't with you—"

"She's acting as Hera's chaperone, with Victor's acceptance if not approval. Not that one really needs a chaperone in mourning, since you don't go anywhere, and no one very much comes to see you."

"Will they be kind to her?" he asked uneasily.

"They won't be *un*kind. They're just a little…distant. But I suspect, if they give her a chance, they will rather like her. She is down to earth and witty. And I was thinking that I would write to her and say that if Hera goes back to her aunt, she should follow me here, at least for a little. If she has not found a more agreeable position by then, of course."

"You have adopted her," Giles said, a warm smile in his eyes.

"You collect charges, don't you?"

"I tried quite hard to adopt my stepchildren, but they were having none of it. I think I didn't really understand them, and they had no idea how to deal with me. Or anyone, in fact. But they are already better without their father. I might even like to visit them. One day."

She seemed to throw her stepfamily off with a shrug as she changed position to sit beside him against the pillows, her head on his shoulder and one arm across his chest. Her lightest hold gave him a sense of intimacy he had known with no other woman. He loved that about her.

"I didn't think you were still here," she told him a little dreamily. Her eyelids looked heavy, arousing his tenderness. "We heard your ship had come in late yesterday, and there was no sign of you in the town. We thought you had gone to Brussels already."

"No, I've been sending everyone else to Brussels! On boats and horses and carriages and carts and any other vehicles I can get hold of. Corny's just left. I should try and get the rest of us out of here by tomorrow before the next ship-full arrives from England."

Her closed eyes flew open again. "Mr. Edwards has hired a canal boat. You could come with us, I'm sure."

He grinned. "Would Mr. Edwards tolerate twenty or so soldiers as well?"

MR. EDWARDS WOULD. Mrs. Edwards was less keen, on account of her niece, but since most of her worries were taken up with the horror of being back on water, she did not quarrel, only begged Rosamund to keep an eye on Izzy.

"Of course I will," Rosamund promised. After a moment's hesitation, she added, "I really don't believe you have cause for anxiety. Miss Merton is lively, but she is wholly devoted to Tom Yates."

Mrs. Edwards eyed her obliquely. "The soldiers don't know that."

As it turned out, the canal boat crew were quite used to ferrying troops. The soldiers were settled at one end, and the family, with Rosamund, Giles, and another officer called Lieutenant Hall, at the other. And, remarkably, the journey turned out to be delightful.

The slow glide of the canal boat, drawn by horses on either side of the bank, caused Mrs. Edwards no trouble at all, and the surprise made her almost as ebullient as Izzy. Lieutenant Hall had perfect manners and seemed content to divide his attentions between everyone. In fact, overall, Rosamund thought he preferred the company of Giles. It was pleasant to stroll the deck and watch the flat, picturesque countryside drift by, along with various villages and the historic town of Bruges. Rosamund enjoyed meals with her companions and amusing conversation. They played cards and charades and, Rosamund thought, everyone enjoyed becoming better acquainted.

For Rosamund, it was almost idyllic, for Giles's mere presence brought her a simple contentment in company or in solitude. They did manage to steal a few moments alone on deck, holding hands in the moonlight and stealing a few delicious kisses, though in the cramped conditions of the boat, there was no question of spending the night together. So, they parted with intimate smiles, Giles to the cabin he shared with Lieutenant Hall, Rosamund to the one she shared with Izzy.

In fact, because of her rank, the Edwardses had tried to give her the main cabin, but she would not hear of it, being quite content to share with Izzy, Perry, and Mrs. Edwards's maid. The journey felt a little unreal, almost like an interlude between one act of an unknown play and the next.

She was under no illusion about the difficulties ahead in Brussels. For all she knew, Wellington might decide to court-martial

Giles, for his views on the practice of dueling were clear. Nor did she underestimate the stigma she would face for traveling here, however quietly, so soon after widowhood. And as for marrying Giles…! Well, she fully expected to be a social pariah and no doubt shunned by the officers' wives. She hadn't come for entertainment.

All the same, as the dwellings they passed grew closer together and the spread of the town of Brussels came nearer, she was conscious of sadness. While part of her looked forward to the next stage and the excitement of life with Giles, another part regretted the loss of the simple, uncomplicated closeness of the journey.

CHAPTER EIGHTEEN

IN GHENT, SHE had to part from Giles again. He would march with the other soldiers to find his own men, while Rosamund traveled with Izzy and the Edwardses in a hired coach that had already been arranged.

She had been in Brussels two days when Rosamund was introduced to the Duke of Wellington.

In those two days, she had seen nothing of Giles who had, presumably, been kept busy with his duties. Or placed under arrest, she supposed uneasily, although she couldn't imagine Wellington demanding his presence in Brussels only to incarcerate him.

The "small house" the Edwardses had taken in the town turned out to be large enough to give Rosamund not only her own bedchamber but a sitting room, too.

"Join us for meals whenever you wish," Mrs. Edwards had said hospitably, "or take some or all in your own rooms. The servants will be happy to accommodate your wishes, as shall we."

"Thank you. You're very good." Rosamund was touched by her kindness, uncaring that there might be some calculation of status in it.

Mr. Merton's sister had married beneath her, taking a husband of no birth but considerable wealth. As such, she hovered between two worlds and would be well aware of the difficulties of carrying out her brother's wishes. Which included, of course, introducing Izzy into the best society, where she could be swept off her feet by an honorable man of birth and fortune, thus eclipsing Tom Yates in her heart forever.

Inevitably, Rosamund had found herself unable to confine herself to her rooms in those two days. Once, she and Izzy had taken the carriage and been driven around the pleasant town, admiring the fine architecture, the Grand Place, and the Royal Park. Rosamund had recognized a few faces among the fashionable British who had thronged there, though she couldn't always put names to them. On the second day, with the inevitable troop of servants behind, they had walked around on foot to examine some shops in more detail. And at the door of one such emporium, she had come face to face with the Duchess of Richmond.

The duchess was sailing out of the shop with a companion just as Rosamund and Izzy were passing by. Rosamund had paused civilly to let the older lady pass. For a moment, she had thought the duchess would not even glance at her, but the sharp eyes had flicked in her direction and away. Then the duchess had halted and looked again.

"Your Grace," Rosamund had said steadily, dipping a curtsey.

"Your Grace," returned the duchess, perhaps with the barest flicker of humor. At any rate, it was not the cut direct. Yet. The duchess had passed on to her carriage, and Rosamund and Izzy had walked on.

On the third day, during the morning, Rosamund poked around in the herb garden at the back of the house with the intention of concocting a tisane that would help Mrs. Edwards with the discomfort of seasickness on her return journey. However, she had not gathered much before Perry came bolting out of the kitchen door toward her.

Rosamund straightened, trying to account for the awe in her handmaiden's excited expression.

"Major Butler is here," she blurted, "with the duke himself!"

"Victor?" Rosamund said, staring in astonishment.

Perry's jaw dropped. "The Duke of Wellington, Your Grace, and he's asking for you."

Rosamund's heart leapt into her throat. This was the moment, surely, when uncertainty ended. Yet if the duke's judgment went against Giles, the uncertainty would surely be preferable.

Drawing a much-needed breath, she brushed her gloves against her skirt. "Where is he?"

"The duke asked for privacy, so Mrs. Edwards showed them both into Your Grace's sitting room."

Is that good or bad? she wondered as she hurried across the garden and back into the house. Either way, she refused to hide from it any longer, even to change her dress. Why bother when everything was black?

Mr. and Mrs. Edwards lurked at the foot of the stairs with Izzy bobbing behind them.

"Did I do the right thing?" Mrs. Edwards asked nervously.

"Of course. Thank you." Rosamund smiled at them all, as if her heart wasn't beating so fast it made her hands shake. As she started up the stairs, Izzy hissed, "Good luck!"

Stupidly, she almost knocked at her own door, then, trying to laugh at herself, she walked quietly in.

The Duke of Wellington sat by the fire, one leg stretched out elegantly before him, while Giles paced the room.

"Rosamund," Giles said in relief as soon as she entered, and strode to take both her hands and kiss them. It seemed rather bold under the gaze of Wellington, who had risen from his chair to greet her.

Without meaning to, Rosamund held on to Giles's hand as she turned to the great man. "Duchess," he said, holding out his hand before she could speak. "A pleasure to see you again."

"And you, sir," Rosamund said, only surprised he remembered their brief meeting at Cuttyngs last year. "Are they bringing tea, or should I send for some?"

"I've already rejected it on my own account," Wellington said. "I can't stay long." His Grace handed her into the chair he had just vacated, forcing her to release Giles's hand at last. "I received your letter. You and Butler here seem to be in a bit of a pickle."

"Major Butler was trying to do the right—"

"Yes, yes," Wellington said testily. "Doesn't change the facts, though, does it? I value Butler. He's a good soldier who will go far in the army, God willing, and I don't want him dragged down by scandal."

"Neither do I, sir."

A smile flickered in the duke's hard eyes and was gone. "Good. Because there's only one thing to be done, as I decided when I first read your letter. You must marry him."

Rosamund felt her jaw sag. Unbidden, her gaze turned on Giles, who shrugged, smiling faintly. She swallowed. "I must marry the man who shot my husband in a duel?" she repeated.

"Take the enemy by surprise," Wellington said sardonically. "What fool marries her lover after he killed her husband? Makes you seem complicit."

"Exactly!" Rosamund exclaimed.

"Do you want to marry him?"

"Yes," she said proudly.

"Good," the duke said again. "There will be gossip and speculation of course, but a nine-day wonder. We can't avoid that, but no one seriously expects you to mourn Cuttyngham."

"They don't?" she asked, startled.

"Not really. The man was a boor and a fool besides. Everyone knows it. As for Butler, he'll have to be an old friend of your family's. Some accident on the journey led to his saving your life at the expense of propriety and so he has offered you marriage. We need provide no details. Keep everything vague. No one will care much once the fighting starts. In the meantime, it will be known that both the Duchess of Richmond and I will attend your wedding. That will offset the worst of it. You can borrow one of my chaplains as soon as you have the special license. Colonel Davidson should have organized that by now."

Rosamund closed her mouth, swallowed, and managed to speak. "I already asked my solicitor to obtain one."

"All the better. We are in accord. Good day, Duchess. I'll see myself out."

He bowed and walked out, not bothering to close the door.

Rosamund blinked and stared at Giles, who gave her a lopsided grin. "This is more, much more than I ever hoped. Did he not even scold you?"

"Oh yes, tore me off a huge strip for dueling and being so idiotic as to be led into a fight with a duke. In the same breath, he said there was reason to doubt my bullet had killed him and issued much the same instructions he has just given you. Then he insisted I bring him to see you while he had half an hour to spare."

Still dazed, she rose and walked into his arms. "He won't let it halt your career," she said in wonder. "That is all I ever wanted."

"Then you'll marry me, Duchess?"

"Don't call me that," she whispered. "I only want to be Mrs. Butler."

THE DUKE'S SHORT, private visit had another unlooked-for advantage. Before the day was done, Mrs. Edwards had received two morning calls, one from a lady who claimed to have known her in her youth, and the other from a complete stranger who wished to welcome her and her family to Brussels.

"Word has got out that the duke was here," Mrs. Edwards said cynically over dinner. "But the upshot is, we have been invited to bring Izzy to the theatre tonight and to a party tomorrow evening."

"Huzzah!" said Izzy. "Will you come, Your Grace?"

"Oh, goodness, no," Rosamund said fervently. "Though I thank you for the kind thought. My reputation really would *not* survive such a public spectacle."

Izzy frowned. "It makes no sense, if you think about it."

"No, it doesn't," Rosamund said. She laid down her fork carefully. "But I will be causing enough of a gossip storm when I marry Major Butler."

Izzy squealed with delight.

Mrs. Edwards exchanged horrified glances with her husband. "So soon?" she said faintly. "Are you sure that is wise?"

"Not entirely," Rosamund admitted, "but it is the advice of the Duke of Wellington and appears to be the only thing to do. I am, of course, quite happy to find lodgings first thing tomorrow—"

"We won't hear of it," Mr. Edwards said emphatically. "Your presence is a pleasure to us, and a boon to my wife and niece! I don't think any of us are blind to the way you and Butler look at each other, and quite frankly, I would rather you were married, however long it is since your last husband died!"

"At Major Butler's hands," Mrs. Edwards pointed out. She glanced at Rosamund. "Sorry, Your Grace, but it's true. And there is Izzy, my brother…"

"When we live in Bill Merton's house, he can decide which of us stays there," Mr. Edwards declared. "In mine, the duchess is always welcome. And if you're honest and forget your overbearing brother, you'll agree with me."

Mrs. Edwards closed her mouth. Izzy crowed with unfilial delight to hear her father called overbearing, and Mrs. Edwards relaxed with a laugh. "What was I thinking of? Of course, you must stay as long as you wish—at least until you are married."

MRS. EDWARDS AND Izzy attended the theatre that evening, and the following day, they all drove out in the carriage beyond the town to witness one of the many troop reviews. Rosamund wore unrelieved black, though she refused to veil herself as though afraid of criticism. She intercepted several glances, saw a few whispering huddles form as she passed. She didn't recognize any of those faces. The few gentlemen who bowed to her, and the ladies who nodded with distant graciousness, she did recognize vaguely, as people who had come to the Cuttyngs autumn balls over the years. These were largely titled and powerful people, either socially or politically. Her husband had only ever associated with such.

She inclined her head in grave response to each of these silent greetings. She couldn't help remembering Wellington's words, that everyone who mattered knew Cuttyngham for a fool and a boor. But beyond a few duty-dances at Cuttyngs balls, they didn't know her at all.

Izzy, of course, was like a magnet, and more acquaintances were made over casual chatter. Rosamund kept in the background, merely smiling and acknowledging introductions. Mostly, she scoured the officers present for a sight of Giles, even though it was not his regiment being reviewed.

Her reward came after the review when Giles appeared at her elbow with another two officers in tow. She could not help her instant smile of pleasure, or the way her hand flew out to him.

His eyes warmed and darkened in instant response, almost as they did when he made love to her. But before her insides could melt entirely, he released her hand to greet the Edwardses, and introduced everyone to his friends, Captain MacDonald and Captain Elton.

"Your friends seem slightly dazed," she murmured to Giles as they all strolled along together.

"I think they came prepared to dislike you," he said with a quick grin. "They think I've lost my mind imagining you'd have anything to do with me, let alone that you'd be prepared to marry me. I believe meeting you has confounded them utterly."

Perhaps he was right, for when they parted, the officers were much more affable. Captain MacDonald even murmured boldly,

"Will Your Grace dance with me at the wedding?"

"If there is dancing, then I will," she replied gravely, while letting her eyes twinkle. Captain MacDonald grinned in delight before turning to excuse himself to the rest of the party.

"Do you have to go also?" she asked Giles.

"I'm afraid so. I'm on duty until the evening." He wrinkled his nose. "The duke wants me to be known socially without you, so I'm going with Corny to some party this evening. I would rather spend it with you."

"That would not be proper," she said with mock primness. "I shall be alone in the house."

Giles groaned. "God, I wish that license would get here!"

"So do I," she whispered, just to see his eyes darken again.

As he walked away, Izzy took her arm and they strolled on. Which is when her casual gaze fell on a familiar figure sauntering with another gentleman toward her party. Lord Nimmot.

At once, her stomach tightened with distaste. Her instinct was to bolt, for his very presence here felt like a threat. As his party came nearer, she saw the moment he became aware of her. Thankfully, he didn't halt and try to speak to her, but his puffy eyes widened, and he smiled in a way that made her flesh crawl. For a moment, she wondered wildly if she should simply give him the cut direct or pretend she hadn't seen him.

He tipped his hat with perfect courtesy, and she remembered in time that she was in no position to upset anyone. For Giles's sake, she inclined her head with distant acknowledgment, and walked on.

LORD NIMMOT ARRIVED at Lady Hartley's ball in high spirits, ready to learn and to whisper.

He had already known the dowager duchess was in Brussels, thanks to a letter from Anthony Severne, and metaphorically rubbed his hands in glee. Here, she had no protectors, only detractors who would be disgusted and incensed by her gallivanting about Europe with her husband barely cold in his grave.

Nimmot was well aware that Severne had his own agenda. Frankly, so did he, and he was no longer terribly interested in Severne's. What he was interested in was having Rosamund, Duchess of Cuttyngham, for as long as he wanted her.

He had courted her long before Cuttyngham had stuck his oar in the race. Nimmot, like the duke, had needed a new wife, and the lively beauty of Daryll's daughter had excited him more than any debutante he had encountered in years. Not that Rosamund had ever had her Season and given him the chance at her hand.

Much to Nimmot's annoyance, her parents had snapped up a better match for her with a duke. Nimmot knew himself well enough to acknowledge that at least half of his obsession with her today was to do with the fact that Cuttyngham had snatched her from under his nose.

For a while, invited frequently to Cuttyngs, it had amused the duke to let him pursue his wife. Her virtue had only inflamed Nimmot. Her aloofness excited him, making him all the more determined to tear it down. Women were all the same, all sluts at heart, whatever their sniveling denials. And as the duke's interest in his wife had waned with the absence of heirs, so Nimmot's had increased. Yet somehow, the young duchess had always adroitly avoided him. Even at the inn when he should have been the one to bring her home to Cuttyngs. Even at Cuttyngs itself for the funeral, when Severne had lifted his "Don't touch" instruction.

Poor Severne. He still believed Nimmot would obey him. Nimmot had *always* intended to touch, and not to wait a year after the old duke's death to do so, either. But Severne's information was useful. Butler, or Battle, or whatever he called himself, the man who had killed Cuttyngham in the duel, was here in Brussels. And there, if Nimmot was not much mistaken, lay an opportunity to further isolate the duchess. The British community here would tear her apart for taking her husband's killer as her lover. Which suited Nimmot perfectly.

So, when he saw her at the review that afternoon, he took the opportunity to ask around. She was not residing with aristocracy but hiding with some cit and his wife, wearing widow's weeds, and neither visiting nor dancing. The opportunity had never been greater.

Nimmot went to Lady Hartley's tedious party mainly to reconnoiter, as it were. To find out what, if anything, was being said about the duchess and feed the scandal if he could. Sadly, his opportunities were few. As he strolled about, listening and gossiping amiably with different groups, he discovered that her presence was not yet one of the *on-dits* of society. He hesitated to bring it up just yet. He would just have to content himself with a few days of delicious anticipation while the story grew.

That was his plan, anyway, until he saw Butler strolling into the card room as if he had every right to be there. Nimmot did not deign to notice him, but for some reason, the officer's presence riled him. The man was a nobody. Worse, he was wanted for murder—the murder of a duke!—yet here in Brussels, he appeared to be welcomed by the English aristocracy. Did they not know what he had done?

Smiling, Nimmot joined a group of men with the full intention of explaining to them exactly what Major Butler had done. Only then, his eye was caught by a pretty, lively, golden-haired girl, laughing as she waltzed past in the arms of a staff officer.

For an instant, Nimmot struggled to remember where he had seen her before. *Ah!*

"Pretty little thing, isn't she?" his nearest companion observed. "Respectable if unremarkable birth and fortune, but she'll do well."

"Who is she?" Nimmot asked as though he didn't already know.

"A Miss Merton. The family has land in Hertfordshire."

"Is her family here with her?"

"She's with an aunt, I believe." The man nodded. "Over there. The husband's doing the pretty with Mrs. Gault. Edwards is their name."

Nimmot spared them a glance. Yes, definitely the same family who had been with the duchess at the review this afternoon. "Edwards?" he repeated. "Are they not the people who accompanied the Duchess of Cuttyngham to Brussels?"

"I believe there's a connection," his informant said vaguely.

Nimmot gazed exaggeratedly around him. "The duchess is not present?"

"Hardly, my lord, with the duke so recently dead!"

"Of course not," Nimmot soothed. "I am surprised to find she is in Brussels at all, to be honest."

"I suppose everything got too much for her in England."

Do you know that the reason for her widowhood is playing cards in the next room? Swallowing his fury for the moment, Nimmot murmured, "I'm not surprised, poor lady. I should call to leave my respects. I was fond of Cuttyngham, you know. I don't suppose you've heard where the Edwardses reside?"

Those nobodies the duchess lived with were here for at least the next two or three hours. So was Butler. While Rosamund was at home, quite alone.

GILES ENJOYED DANCING. In winter quarters on the Peninsula, he had enthusiastically embraced all the social entertainments, so Lady Hartley's partly should have been a welcome relief. The trouble was the only woman he wanted to dance with was Rosamund. No one else seemed to fit his arms so perfectly or waltz so gracefully, so perfectly attuned to his every movement.

Going to parties seemed an odd way to prove to the world that he was worthy of the Dowager Duchess of Cuttyngham, but he bowed to his commander's greater wisdom. Wellington made his own appearance at the ball, and in between dancing and flirting made the time to acknowledge Giles, and even introduce him to the Duchess of Richmond, who appeared to be the queen of the British visitors in Brussels.

He danced with Izzy Merton and Fanny Edwards and with a few wallflowers Lady Hartley presented him to. And began to look forward to his bed, and the morrow, which might bring the special license that would make Rosamund his.

He decided to go and play cards for half an hour with Corny and his friends. His thoughts were so much on Rosamund that he almost nodded acknowledgment to the familiar face that sailed past him and out of the room. Lord Nimmot, who had once accosted Rosamund in an Essex inn.

His hackles rose as he recalled what Rosamund had told him about the man. More than that, the instincts that had so far kept him and most of his men alive over several years of war were shrieking in alarm.

He threw himself into the vacant chair beside Cornhill. "What do you know of Lord Nimmot?" he asked, low.

Corny shrugged. "Nothing much. Not my set, old boy, or my brother's. Friend of the Regent's. A few of the high sticklers don't receive him, but most do. Why?"

"He's here."

"So is half the *ton*." Corny threw his cards down in disgust. "What's your concern with him?"

"That he's here at all. You know, Corny, I don't believe I'll play after all? Excuse me." Rising abruptly, he strode back into the main room and prowled all the way around it in search of his quarry. Discovering a couple of fellow officers blowing cigarillo smoke on the balcony, he said casually, "Have you seen Lord Nimmot? I need a word with him."

"Gone, old fellow," came the somehow chilling reply. "Saw him leave with his hat and his coat on."

Chapter Nineteen

IT WAS, PERHAPS, a little ironic that Rosamund, who had tried to escape her gilded prison at Cuttyngs, now found herself trapped in a much smaller house in Brussels. The difference was, she had chosen this for just a few days.

Alone in the drawing room, she tried to concentrate on a poetry book lent to her by Mrs. Edwards, but her mind kept drifting off to moments spent with Giles. She remembered every detail of their waltz at the Cornhills' ball. She recalled his kiss on the walk back to the inn.

With a jolt, she remembered days long ago, a lifetime ago, when she had daydreamed of the dignified duke and how lucky she was to have won his love. It was laughable, of course. Love had never had anything to do with her marriage. Even hers had been a mirage based on misinformation and wishful thinking. She doubted Cuttyngham had ever loved anyone in his cold, meaningless life. She could never compare him to Giles.

Still, the juxtaposition of memories unbalanced her, and she was quite unprepared when one of the local servants entered the room with a card on a silver tray.

"Visitor, madame," she said cheerfully, offering the tray. Slightly dazed, Rosamund picked up the card and blinked at it. *Lord Nimmot.*

"No, deny me," she said at once. "I am not at home to him or to anyone this evening."

"Too late, Your Grace," purred a hated voice. "I'm afraid I followed the girl in, being such an old friend."

"Your friendship was with His Grace," she sat flatly, "and no doubt with Anthony. I am not receiving."

"I shall not stay. A mere five minutes to pay my respects." He jerked his head at the maid. "You may go."

The maid, whose grasp of English was tenuous, glanced from one of them to the other. Rosamund considered, hastily. Every instinct shouted against being anywhere near him. But did she really want to make an enemy of him now when things seemed to be going according to Wellington's plan?

"A mere *two* minutes is all that would be proper, my lord," she said at last. "You may go, Marie. And leave the door open."

Marie bobbed a curtsey and left.

"How gracious." Lord Nimmot followed in the girl's footsteps toward the door, and Rosamund began to heave a sigh of relief. Then, quite deliberately, he closed the door and turned the key in the lock.

For the first time, her revulsion prickled with fear, and she had to fight it down with sheer fury. "How dare you?" she cried, leaping to her feet. "This is not proper under *any* circumstances. Open the door at once before I ring for the footmen to eject you."

Nimmot smiled with what appeared to be genuine amusement as he strolled back toward her. "Oh, I don't think you'll do that." With a sudden burst of speed, he placed himself between her and the bell pull, and kept coming.

She pretended not to notice and glared at him down her nose. "Then you are wrong."

"Am I? Do you want the world to know you are further compromised?"

Her every instinct was to back away from him, but she refused to behave like a cornered animal, so remained where she was, her fingers clenching as he came right up to her and stopped, almost touching.

"I am not," she said firmly.

"Not what, Your Grace?" he mocked. His breath came in short, excited pants, as though he could smell her fear and that fed his own lust. Beads of shiny sweat gleamed on his forehead and his upper lip. The overpowering Cologne water he used revolted her.

"I am not compromised," she replied and, abandoning dignity, whisked around him to bolt for the bell pull.

But as soon as she moved, so did he, and in a quite unexpected way. His hand lashed out, seizing hold of the shoulder of her gown. With the violence of his tug, and her own forward dash, the silk ripped and flapped.

"You are now," he said with satisfaction.

Gasping with shock, she fled for the bell.

"Really?" he drawled, his voice dripping with the amusement of the bully and a triumph that was even more chilling. "You want the servants to see you in your shame?"

She grasped the fabric of the bell pull. "The shame is not mine, my lord!"

"Tell that to the society who already condemns you for whoring even during the first weeks of your widowhood."

She paused, staring at him, one hand on the bell pull, the other trying to hold up the torn fabric of her gown. Her fingers trembled, and she hated that almost more than anything. She tried desperately to think and was aware only of his bulk prowling toward her, and the dry, sickening taste of fear in her mouth.

Blood seemed to pound in her ears. "Why?" she said hoarsely. "Why are you doing this? Why do you hate me?"

For some reason, the last question seemed to give him pause. He stilled, and his sweaty brow twitched. "Of course, I don't hate you. I have wanted you since you were a girl. This, finally, is our opportunity. There is nothing to stop us."

"Oh yes there is," she whispered, though she didn't know what. She already knew his strength and her own vulnerability, the guilt of her torn gown. She would not give in to the old sense of inevitability crawling over her skin, for this man was not her husband, and had no *right* to touch her, to threaten her.

Her hand tightened on the bell pull and at once his hot fingers clamped around her wrist, stilling it.

"You wouldn't," he said confidently.

He's done this before, the disgusting, vile…

The door rattled so suddenly that both their heads jerked toward it. He laughed softly, because the door was locked, but Rosamund seized her opportunity and screamed with fury. At the same time, advice from Sophia sprang into her mind: *"a knee brought up sharply between his legs should incapacitate him and give his thoughts a different turn."*

The shock on Nimmot's face was almost ludicrous. He even fell back, releasing her and avoiding her jerking knee, just as the door crashed open with a splintering of wood, bouncing off the wall with its force. Giles plunged into the room with Marie and a footman behind him.

With a soundless cry, Rosamund ran to Giles. His arms closed around her, a haven of strength and safety and goodness, even as he spoke harshly over her head.

"Get him out of here now. He is not to be admitted over the door again. Ever."

"She locked the door, not I," Nimmot began, his voice still drawling and amused, but the rest was lost in some kind of scuffle and grunting, and a moment later, the door closed.

"He's gone," Giles said, softly, stroking her hair. He eased her away from him a little so that he could look into her face, his eyes anxious. "Are you hurt?"

"He tore…he tore my gown." Her wrist throbbed where he had grasped it, too, but she didn't care as long as Giles held her. "How are you here? How did you know?"

"He was asking questions about you at Lady Hartley's and then he left. I just had a feeling he was coming here, and the servants told me an English gentleman was with you. When you screamed…!"

"He thought I wouldn't do it. He thought I would preserve my reputation over…" She broke off gasping, and his arms tightened.

"The fool underestimated you, but he won't bother you again, I promise."

He kept his voice soft, without even anger, and yet there was something implacable about it that made her frown and grasp his face between her hands.

"Giles? Don't you dare challenge him to a duel! Have we not had enough of those?"

"More than enough," he said fervently. "I shall merely talk to him. Later. For now, come and sit down." He led her to a sofa and handed her into it, then plucked one of Mrs. Edwards's shawls from the back of it and tucked it around Rosamund's shoulders, hiding the torn gown.

She smiled, just a little tremulously, watching him as he went to the decanter and poured two glasses of brandy and brought them back to the sofa. He sat beside her and took her hand, telling her about the Duke of Wellington's presence at the ball, and how His Grace had introduced Giles to the Duchess of Richmond.

As he talked, easily and casually, his voice soothing her recent fright, it entered her head that he did not even doubt her. But then, she had always known he would not. That was why she had been so prepared to ring the bell and shout. Well, that and the fact she would never give in to Nimmot.

She held his hand now, no longer in fear or relief, but in trust and love and friendship. And he made no effort to make it more, merely clasped her fingers lightly, occasionally caressing with his thumb as they talked or just sat in comfortable silence. She didn't know how long he stayed, but eventually, it came to her that she should go to her own rooms before the family came home, not least in case they brought anyone with them who might glimpse her torn gown or slightly disheveled hair.

He made no demur when she suggested it, though he did not hurry her either. That he let her make the decision was unaccountably sweet, as was his smile and his tender kiss on departure. Despite the earlier threat and her undoubted fright, she retired feeling she was the luckiest woman in the world.

GILES LEFT UNHURRIEDLY and merely strolled up the street until he was sure he could not be seen from the Edwardses' house. Then he sped up, his manner changed completely. He supposed, grimly, that his practice in war stood him in good stead, controlling the battle rage once the fighting had stopped, to allow back in the civilized side of his nature in order to keep discipline for himself and his men, avoid atrocities and shame, and maintain self-respect.

When Rosamund had screamed, his rage had been utter, so that one blow with his foot had been enough to break open the locked door. Had he encountered Nimmot in that instant, the man would already be dead. But the sight of Rosamund, brave and frightened and rushing to his arms, had broken his heart. He had held her and comforted her, for she was his greatest priority. And he had guarded his rage, banished it until it merely simmered unseen beneath the surface, while he looked after Rosamund and considered.

There could be no further threat from Nimmot, not with Giles likely to be called away at any moment, possibly for days or weeks at a time. When Wellington invaded France, there were no guarantees that Rosamund could accompany him. And in any case, Nimmot was vile and overdue a mental and physical thrashing.

It wasn't difficult to discover his lodgings, or even to cadge a ride on the back of a fiacre with another young officer *en route* to his own entertainment. Giles jumped off close to his required destination and waved to his new friend before striding up the street to the house he sought.

Nimmot was sharing a house, apparently, with several other English gentlemen. It was possible, of course, that Nimmot had returned to Lady Hartley's ball, but Giles doubted it. The man appeared bent on destroying Rosamund's reputation, so he would not want an alibi should rumors of her "assignation" with him begin to spread.

"Lord Nimmot in?" he asked cheerfully, pushing past the manservant who opened the door.

The manservant didn't answer, but a young gentleman dressed in the height of fashion, who was dusting off his hat in the hallway, said laconically, "Up the stairs, second on your right. If he isn't there, leave a message with his man. Your servant, sir!" The young man swaggered out, and Giles mounted the stairs with an amiable thank you.

In fact, he encountered Nimmot's valet just inside the door of his rooms. From the room beyond, Nimmot's petulant voice could be heard making various demands. Giles didn't hesitate. In one casual movement, he spun the surprised valet outside into the passage, then closed and locked the door.

At that moment, Nimmot appeared in the inner doorway, and his querulous voice stopped abruptly.

"Not very comfortable, is it?" Giles said coldly. "Locked away from your friends, alone with someone stronger and better armed, who clearly means you harm?"

Nimmot's face was white, his eyes bulging. "Get out immediately!" he blustered, his voice high with distress. "Don't you know who I am?"

"Oh yes. Even worse, I know *what* you are." Giles moved quickly and struck him once, hard across the mouth.

Nimmot staggered backward. "How d-dare you?" he gasped, clutching his bleeding lips. "I am a peer of the realm!"

"So was the nobleman I killed last week," Giles said thoughtfully, advancing once more. "Or was it the week before?"

Nimmot's eyes looked ready to pop. "It *was* you who killed…"

"Indeed, it was," Giles agreed. "I didn't mean to, of course. And I've no intention of killing you either. Yet. I trust you'll bear the transgression in mind? Offending the lady."

Nimmot swore. "You are finished in the army! Finished!" he squealed. "My friends will see you cashiered!"

"Try," Giles said. "You might succeed, though I doubt it. Either way, I have friends of my own, not so powerful as yours, perhaps, in most cases at least, but there are *a lot* of them and not just in this town. To be plain, if you go near Her Grace again, approach her in any way, someone will kill you. I hope it will be me."

Nimmot had fallen back before him and come up against the bed post with a bump. His desperately darting eyes were forced to settle on Giles's eyes. "You're mad!" he gasped.

Giles smiled wolfishly. "So I'm told. You'd be advised not to forget it." He switched tactic. "Why are you even in Brussels? Did the new duke send you? Or the cousin?"

"Don't be absurd! No one *sends* me!"

"But you are in alliance with one of them, aren't you?"

Perhaps the deadly certainty in Giles's voice penetrated because words spilled from Nimmot's mouth in a torrent. "No, no, I broke it! Once, yes, we had an agreement, Anthony Severne and me! He cast her in my way to let me fend off other admirers. I agreed not to touch her for a year after Cuttyngham's death and then I'd marry her."

Giles stared at him. "Seriously?"

His utter amazement seemed to throw Nimmot into splutters.

"So, what I just witnessed," Giles said carefully, "was you breaking ranks from the cousin and striking out alone?"

Too late, Nimmot saw his error—he really was a stupid man—and raised his arm as though to ward off another blow.

"What does he want?" Giles demanded. "The cousin? What's

his problem with the duchess?"

"What does he want?" Nimmot repeated, and now the boot was on the other foot. He clearly thought Giles must be stupid. "He wants the dukedom. He doesn't need any more heirs ahead of him, and with duchess whoring around the country with you—"

Giles raised his fist, and Nimmot slid back across the bed, his legs in the air. "No, no, it's what he thinks! It's what Severne thinks! That's why he asked me to bring her home when the duke died."

Giles paused, fist still poised. "And now you're tired of waiting. Christ, but you're a vile, nasty creature."

Nimmot cowered, both hands over his face, and Giles very nearly did what was expected, which happened to coincide with his own wishes—to beat his lordship to a pulp.

He walked around the bed and stood glaring down at him. "No more chances," he said savagely. "Not with her or any other woman. I *will* kill you, Nimmot. And if I'm already dead, someone else will. I swear it."

And then he spun on his heels and walked out, not troubling to close the door behind him.

CHAPTER TWENTY

ROSAMUND WOKE THE following morning with a curious sense of wellbeing. Memories of last night's events did not alter that—perhaps because those nasty moments alone with Nimmot had actually been very few before Giles burst into the room. Perhaps because she couldn't help believing her scream would have repelled Nimmot anyway, bringing the household to her aid. There might have been scandal, but she would have remained unharmed.

Actually, explaining the splintered wood of the drawing room door to Mr. and Mrs. Edwards would be the hardest part of the whole incident. The pleasantest, covering all with a bizarrely rosy glow, was the hour she had spent alone with Giles, not in passion but in a companionable intimacy that was equally sweet.

She rose early, wondering if she could arrange the repair of the door before her confession to Mr. and Mrs. Edwards, who were bound to breakfast late after the ball. She summoned Perry to help lace her stays and fasten the dull black gown, of which she was already excessively tired. It was while she sat at the dressing table to have her hair dressed that there came a sudden disturbance from the sitting room beyond.

The door had seemed to burst open to the outraged cries of one of the French maids. Then came Giles's urgent, yet half-laughing voice. "Rosa, are you in there? Come out and talk. I have news!"

Rosa. He had called her that last night, too, an intimate, private name she could not help liking on his lips. She jumped up, rushing at once to the sitting room door, with her hair only half-brushed and hanging around her shoulders.

"Your Grace!" Perry cried in outrage, but Rosamund didn't care, merely wrenched open the door and found Giles halfway across the sitting room with the upstairs maid tugging at his arm. His eyes found hers, and her breath caught at the blazing excitement she read there.

"Thank you, you may go," she told the maid who, catching sight of Perry, shrugged and departed. "What is it?"

"Colonel Davidson is back at last with, among other things, our special license."

Her hand crept to her throat as though to stop her heart jumping out. "You mean we can be married?"

"If you still wish it."

"With all my heart."

He grinned. "Then it's at midday. Here?"

"I don't believe there is anywhere else, but midday gives us no time to—"

"It's the only time Wellington is available."

She closed her mouth. The duke was necessary to maintain whatever slender thread of respectability they could maintain, and she wanted it for him. "Midday. We'll be ready."

"Your wedding is *today*?" Perry cried, suddenly rushing past Rosamund and flapping her apron at Giles as though he were a particularly naughty goose. "Shoo! Out you go! You should not even *see* her on your wedding day. Be gone, Major, this instant."

Laughing, Giles allowed himself to be herded out. Rosamund heard his quick steps clattering down the stairs, and a moment later, saw him through the window, striding down the road with a jaunty air that made her smile.

Then she took a deep breath, let Perry cram a few pins into her hair, and set to work.

ANTHONY SEVERNE AND Gregson had arrived in Brussels weary and ill-tempered. Hiring decent horses or conveyances of any description had proved well-nigh impossible, since all were taken or spoken for to transport troops. Anthony had been forced to hire two very sorry nags whose lack of speed and stamina had extended their journey beyond what was bearable.

Having collapsed into the first hotel they found—a cheap and quite unsuitable establishment for a Severne—Anthony had slept like the dead. His first thought on waking was that at least the duchess should be easy to find. If she was still in company with Butler, she must be trailing scandal behind her like a comet.

He shuddered to think of the damage she was doing to the name of Severne. He wondered, during an unsatisfying breakfast of bread and cheese and very thinly cut cold meats, what sort of reaction inquiries for her might provoke. He doubted she was incognito.

After breakfast, he sent Gregson to ferret out what he could from servants and merchants and set off himself in search of familiar faces. He knew that half the *ton* was here in Brussels.

It didn't take him long until he ran into a young Englishman weaving his way along the street as if he had not yet been to bed to sleep off last night's excesses. They were hardly close acquaintances—Anthony could not even remember his name—since the reveler was at least a dozen years his junior. But the youth's face lit up at once, as though he had just rediscovered his best friend after a long parting.

"Severne, old fellow! All of London is here now! You staying with Her Grace?"

"Why, no," Anthony said politely. "Though now you mention it, I heard she was in Brussels. I didn't really believe it since the whole family is in mourning."

"Saw her at a review the other day." He nodded sagely and

swayed a little. "Definitely in mourning. Looked like a blackbird. Doesn't go to parties," he mourned, shaking his head.

"I don't suppose you know where she lodges?" Anthony asked hopefully.

"With a cit family. Edwards? That's it. He's a cit, she's a lady, and they have the prettiest daughter. Or niece, is it? Apparently, there's a family connection, and Her Grace is in their house."

"And where is that?" Anthony kept the smile on his lips although he longed for a bucket of cold water to throw over his informant.

The young gentleman looked surprised. "No idea."

"Well, best be..." Anthony began impatiently, when his companion interrupted him.

"Tell you who'd know—Lord Nimmot. Saw him last night, and he was asking the same question." He smiled as though he was very clever. "Expect he found out."

"Expect he did," Anthony said grimly. He didn't like the idea that Nimmot was here without telling him. Had he come looking for Rosamund on his own account? "I don't suppose," he said to the young man, "that you have any idea where I might find Nimmot?"

"That house there, old chap. Third on your left."

Congratulating himself on a piece of luck at last, he gained entry to the house in question. It was a haphazard place that seemed to be full of single gentlemen, all rather younger than either Nimmot or Anthony.

"I'm afraid his lordship is not receiving this morning," Nimmot's valet informed Anthony politely.

"I'm sure he'll receive me. Here, take him my card and tell him I'm looking for my cousin." *That should bring him to his senses...*

"Very good, sir," the valet said in long suffering tones and left Anthony to kick his heels in the hall.

A few moments later, he heard Nimmot's voice high with fury and something else that sounded very like panic, although

Anthony couldn't make out the words. The servant returned almost at once.

"His lordship is unwell," he said, holding out the card, "and sends his regrets."

Irritated, Anthony snatched the card back, only then registering the oddity of returning it. He frowned and flipped the card over to see an address scrawled on the back. He smiled. "Thank his lordship for me."

At the front door, he bumped into yet another acquaintance, this one in uniform. "Morning, Severne!" the officer greeted him. "Come for the wedding?"

Anthony halted, his jaw dropping. *Surely not*... "What wedding?"

"Her Grace of Cuttyngham to Major Butler!"

ROSAMUND, HAVING SENT a slightly desperate message to Mrs. Edwards via her maid, was already consulting with the housekeeper, the cook, and a carpenter, when her hostess joined them. Having heard the menu, Mrs. Edwards pronounced it excellent but doubled the quantities of everything. She approved the carpenter without even a question and arranged for a large potted plant to be set in front of the repaired door to hide the new wet paint. After that, she breezed off with the housekeeper to see about tablecloths and china.

There was nothing left for Rosamund to do except go and bathe and dress for her wedding as everyone bade her. Sprawling in the warm water was pleasantly soothing and managed to calm the nerves that had unaccountably sprung up. Until, as Perry wrapped her in a large towel, the catastrophe came to her.

She stopped in her tracks, causing Perry to bump into her, and stared at her maid in horror. "I have nothing to wear!"

"Your Grace..."

"Everything is black! I refuse to be married as if I were going to my own funeral! This is awful! I could have bought something, had a gown of Izzy's or Mrs. Edwards altered if they were kind enough, but I have let time slip through my fingers! Oh, Perry, why did I not think of this before?"

"Because that's what you pay a lady's maid for," Perry said. "Come."

Blindly, Rosamund followed her to the large wardrobe. Perry dug inside and whisked out a gown of very dark green silk that she had worn only once before.

"I thought you might need something not quite black, while still acknowledging mourning," Perry said apologetically.

"It's better than black," Rosamund agreed. She liked the gown, only… "Only it's not a very *festive* color, is it?"

"Nonsense," Perry argued. "Wear it with white gloves and emeralds, and it will sparkle on you!"

Miraculously, Perry was almost right. The dark silk emphasized the creaminess of her skin, while the white gloves removed any funereal aspect. Rosamund had not even though of bringing jewels on the journey, but the shining emerald necklace against her throat, and the matching earrings dangling above did indeed lift the gown beyond anything funereal. Only her own nervous expression spoiled the image she wished to present to the world. To Giles.

What is the matter with me?

With an unpleasant thud of her heart, she realized her first wedding was trying to intrude on her happiness. And with it came the hard slap of reality.

I am marrying the man who killed my husband. Probably. It must be a sin before God if not man. How in the world did I imagine—did we *imagine—we could do this?*

She stared at herself in the glass and saw only horror in her eyes. "Perry, I can't."

"Of course, you can," Perry said bracingly, already on her way to answer a knock on the door.

Mrs. Edwards and Izzy rustled in wearing their best morning gowns, the former in shades of blue and Izzy in demure white with pink rosebud trimmings.

"Oh, my," Izzy breathed. "How beautiful you are! And regal. I never realized you were so regal!"

"Don't be silly, Izzy," Mrs. Edwards commanded, peering at Rosamund's pale, still face in the glass. Clearly, she sensed something wrong. "Her Grace is a duchess. Of course, she looks regal, not to say lovely and utterly charming. Just the correct note for the occasion."

"It is too much for daytime," Rosamund said. "I cannot wear all this… I cannot *do* this. It is wrong."

The three women stared at her in consternation.

"The chaplain is here," Mrs. Edward blurted. "Major Butler and his supporters are here. I've just had word the Duchess of Richmond has arrived, and the Duke of Wellington himself is expected imminently. Of course, you can do this! You must."

"Mrs. Edwards is right, Your Grace," Perry said earnestly. "You fought tooth and nail for this moment. You can't let it go now."

Some awful sadness swept up from inside her to meet the absolute knowledge of the wrongness of her clothes, of the occasion, of everything.

"It's just wedding nerves," Mrs. Edwards assured her. "But you must not panic."

Vaguely, Rosamund supposed it must be panic, though it felt much heavier, much more paralyzing.

"Oh dear." Mrs. Edwards sounded stricken. "Izzy, what do we do?"

"We go downstairs. You welcome the Duchess of Richmond, and I will come directly back. Perry, stay with Her Grace."

Rosamund barely noticed their departure. With slow deliberation, she reached up and removed each earring, placing them on the dressing table in front of her. She was barely aware of the time passing, only of misery and her complete inability to deal with it. Why, now of all times, should she feel this?

The door opened again, and Izzy came back in, dragging someone by the hand.

Giles.

Their eyes met in the glass, and without warning, some huge tide of emotion seemed to rush through her. A wild sob broke from her lips. Without meaning to, she had stumbled out of the chair and was reaching for him with both arms.

"He can't be here, Miss Izzy!" Perry exclaimed in outrage. "It's bad luck."

No one paid her any attention, for by then, Rosamund was in Giles's arms, clutching him so tightly it hurt. Vaguely, she was aware of Izzy taking Perry by the arm and leading her into the sitting room before firmly closing the door.

"What is it?" he whispered into her hair at last. "Don't you want to marry me anymore?"

"More than anything in the world. In my heart. And yet everywhere else suddenly feels so wrong. So unfair that we met as we did, that you did what you did. Marriage is *Cuttyngham*—awfulness and humiliation, mixed with mind-numbing boredom and utter uselessness, entrapment, and no hope. It is not *you*. And that, everything, makes this all wrong. The dress is wrong, the jewels are wrong. Everything is—"

"Wrong," he said gravely. "I understand. Am I wrong?"

Slowly, she drew back enough to look into his face, and knew hers was stained with tears. She blinked the dampness from her eyes, and her breath caught. "No." She touched his cheeks, his lips with the very tips of her fingers. "Only you are right."

"But I am not enough?" He spoke lightly, and yet he could not hide the fear, the pain, that stood out in his eyes.

"How can you even think that?" she asked in distress.

"Because you are up here crying when you could be downstairs marrying me."

"It is not so simple, Giles!"

"Isn't it? It was earlier this morning. It was when you wanted to run away with me and hang the scandal." He touched his lips to hers, and even now, her mouth quivered in instant response. "I'll wait for you as long as you want me to. There is only you. Is it the future that concerns you?"

She swallowed and shook her head. "Perhaps our immortal souls."

"Because I killed the duke?"

She frowned. "We don't even know that you did."

"Because he has only been dead three weeks?"

Her lips parted and closed again. "No."

A smile tugged at the corners of his mouth. "Then it's the dress."

"It is the dress."

He spared it a glance. "It's beautiful. But if you don't like it, wear the black. Or your traveling cloak. I really don't care.

A choke of laughter broke from her, more than half sob. "You don't, do you? You love me."

"I love you," he agreed.

The tears threatened again. "And I love you," she whispered.

"Then does it not seem to you that *nothing* is wrong?"

She laid her head against his chest. "Now it does," she said, muffled. "Why aren't you running, screaming from the silly goose I've turned out to be?"

He smiled into her hair. "Because you are *my* silly goose. We have reached this point far faster than we should normally, and so much has happened to us both, particularly you. You were so sure and focused, and now you have three weeks' worth of little doubts landing on your head at once. Perhaps cold feet are inevitable."

She lifted her head. "Do you have cold feet?"

"No, but then everyone knows I am mad. Would you like to be mad with me, Rosamund Daryll? Or shall we wait a little longer."

He would do it, too. He would go against Wellington himself, just to please her silly, incomprehensible moods. And suddenly the thought of him leaving today, of not seeing him tonight or tomorrow, of not being his wife with the right to be at his side—those were the most awful things in the world.

She swallowed. "Just for a moment, I panicked. And it all got…skewed. Will you still marry me, Major Butler?"

His lips curved, reflecting the smile in his eyes. "I thought you'd never ask." Softly, he kissed her lips, and the world stood still, cutting them off from everything but each other.

Without a word, he led her to the washstand, then soaked and wrung out the cloth he found there. She caught it from him with a breath of laughter. "I can wash my own face. I suppose my hair is mussed, too, and Perry dressed it so beautifully."

"It's still beautiful," he assured her.

Finally, her face washed and dried, she looked in the glass again. There were no tearstains. No earrings either. And yet her eyes sparkled as they hadn't before. With new certainty and the glow of love for the man at her side.

They walked together into the sitting room.

"Thank God," Perry muttered. "Go!"

Izzy grinned and fled, leaving Giles to escort Rosamund downstairs to the drawing room. At the doorway, the Duke of Wellington awaited her with a sardonic smile. It seemed he intended to give her away.

With an almost imperceptible wink, Giles slid past them and into the room. Rosamund laid her hand on Wellington's arm and walked in to be married.

THE WEDDING TOOK remarkably little time. She made her vows in a clear if quiet voice, with total conviction. It barely even entered her head that she said the same words before to a very different man and regretted them. Now, she had made her own decision, chosen her own husband as he had chosen her. Just seeing him smile made her happy.

And then she was no longer Duchess of Cuttyngham, but Mrs. Giles Butler, and they were surrounded by the congratulations of friends, first among them, the Duke of Wellington. Even his companion, Colonel Davidson, unbent enough to smile. Captain MacDonald and Captain Elton seemed both awed and delighted by the events.

Then she caught sight of the Duchess of Richmond, smiling graciously, yet standing a little apart from the chattering groups. Rosamund excused herself and went up to the duchess, who immediately offered her hand.

Rosamund took it. "Thank you for your presence today. It smooths a difficult journey."

"You have flouted a lot of…conventions, here," the duchess replied.

"I know." She regarded the duchess curiously. They had never been close, never been friends. As far as Rosamund could recall, they had met only once before coming to Brussels. "May I ask you something?"

"Of course."

"You are a great lady, a leader of Society, as I never was and never could have been, whatever my rank. You may well face criticism for countenancing my hasty marriage to the man who dueled with my husband."

"Dueled but did not kill, according to Colonel Davidson."

"He certainly aimed away from him, though I suppose as long as men point guns at each other as a means of solving their differences, people will die. The point is, we barely know each other, and yet you chose to help me. I am grateful—and curious."

"Oh well, we duchesses must stick together," she said vaguely.

Rosamund caught her eye. "Seriously?"

The duchess laughed. "No, of course not." She hesitated, then said, "Truthfully, I merely return a kindness. We came to your ball at Cuttyngs."

"I remember."

"I… I will not go into vulgar detail, but I was feeling very low."

"You showed no sign of it."

"One doesn't, does one?" the duchess replied. Her lips quirked slightly. "The real point is, you were kind to me, and I never forgot it. I wish you happiness with your major. You deserve it."

With a flickering smile, the duchess moved away toward Mr. Edwards. Thoughtfully, Rosamund turned in search of her husband, and instead caught sight of an uninvited guest standing in the doorway.

Anthony Severne.

Mrs. Edwards was already rustling toward him, the perfect hostess. Rosamund felt an unreasonable spurt of annoyance at the intrusion of her old life so soon into the new. She remembered, with resentment, his alliance with Cuttyngham, his tricks using Nimmot, his efforts to have Giles arrested. She wondered if he had come to cause trouble or to wave a relieved farewell. Or to give her bad news of her stepchildren.

With a sudden twist of her stomach, she went quickly toward him. "Anthony, an unexpected pleasure," she greeted him as he turned from Mrs. Edwards to bow to her. He looked somber rather than angry, so she galloped through the expected civilities. "Ma'am, this is Mr. Severne, my first husband's cousin. Anthony, Mrs. Edwards, my kind friend and hostess. What brings you to Brussels? Are Hera and Victor well?"

"Perfectly, so far as I know," he replied. "But the rest of the world appears to be in Brussels. I called to see if it was true you had thrown off your widowhood completely before it was properly begun. And I see that it is."

"I am no longer a widow," she said evenly. "I have just married Major Butler."

"Please excuse me," Mrs. Edwards said hastily, no doubt unwilling to be party to a family argument.

"Do I need to tell you how unseemly that is?" he asked without heat.

"In the eyes of the world, perhaps. I had no bearing on Cuttyngham's life, and I shall not pretend to miss him."

"Clearly."

"Perhaps a formal introduction, Rosamund," Giles said at her side. His fingers brushed hers, and she knew a moment of pleasure and relief.

"Giles, my late husband's cousin, Mr. Severne. Anthony, my husband, Major Butler."

"Do you think this…charade somehow absolves you of my cousin's death?" Anthony said coldly.

"No, but if you are here to cause a scene, you will be ejected," Giles said pleasantly.

"Dear God, is that Wellington himself, flirting with that blonde chit?" Anthony said, clearly startled.

"Indeed," Rosamund said hastily. "And you may also recognize the Duchess of Richmond."

Anthony glanced at her, not without a hint of admiration. "I take my hat off to you, Rosamund. You have certainly lined up your troops. But to return to your new husband's question, no, I have not come to cause a scene, but to crave a private word with you on a legal matter."

"A legal matter?" Rosamund said with amusement. "Really?"

"Your signature is required."

"Why? As a woman, I have no legal standing."

"Nevertheless," Anthony insisted. "In private, if you please."

"It was borne upon me for many years that I could do nothing on my own account, only with my husband's explicit permission." It was a petty revenge, but she could not resist it.

On the other hand, she had no real intention of denying Anthony his "word." She was even curious. It was Giles who said, "Then I shall sit in on your legal discussions and dispense husbandly advice and—who knows?—possibly even permission. Shall we?"

In the end, Rosamund led the way to her private sitting room, and Anthony immediately produced a document, which he unfolded and presented to her before they had even sat down.

Giles did not read over her shoulder. Instead, he seemed to be watching Anthony, who shifted uncomfortably in his chair while Rosamund read in silence.

A frown of disbelief began to tug at her brow until, slowly, she raised her gaze to Anthony's and wordlessly passed the document to Giles, who was seated on the sofa beside her.

"*That* is what you wish me to sign?" she said carefully. "To swear that Cuttyngham hadn't come to my bed for more than a year before he died and that therefore any children I subsequently bear are not his?"

Anthony flapped on impatient hand. "Why not? We both know it to be true."

"Then there is no point in swearing," she said at once. "That is hardly the point. What is it you fear? That I shall thrust some child under the Severnes' noses, pretending it is the duke's in order to milk Victor's estate? Do you have any idea how insulting that is?"

Anthony waved that aside, too. "I know you for an honorable lady. I do not know your husband at all."

With distaste, Giles pushed the document back across the table toward Rosamund. "Then know this much. There is no way on God's earth that I would give any child of mine into the keeping of the Severne family."

"Then you will sign?" Anthony said with the first sign of eagerness, as though he couldn't quite believe it was that simple.

"I don't understand," Rosamund said to him. "What is it you expect to gain from this? Just to keep my scandalous name out of the succession?"

"Something like that," Anthony said evenly.

Giles leaned forward. "Not good enough. What is this about? What has any of this been about? *What do you want, Severne?*"

Anthony stared into his eyes. "I want to be the duke."

Giles smiled as if he already knew that. Perhaps he did. But to Rosamund, it was something of a revelation.

"I thought you just didn't like me," she said in a rush. "And all the time you were merely afraid I would birth a child that would come before you in the succession. But Anthony, think. Victor is young. He will marry and have children..."

"I am aware," Anthony interrupted. "In fact, I have a perfect bride in mind for him. So, will you sign? Both of you, if you wish!"

Rosamund didn't need to look at her husband. She said, "If I am blessed with children, they will not be Cuttyngham's, and I thank God for it. I am no threat to you and neither is Giles. But no, I will not sign any such vulgar, intrusive document for you or anyone else. Goodbye, Anthony. We have guests."

Giles rose with her, inclined his head to Anthony, and offered Rosamund his arm.

There was no time even to talk about it, for the Duke of Wellington was taking his leave at the front door, Davidson impatiently by his side.

"Thank you, sir," Rosamund said sincerely.

"No need for that," Wellington assured her, taking her hand. "Just keep this rogue of mine out of trouble." He kissed her fingers in gallant, continental fashion and smiled in a way that was not purely avuncular. Then he straightened and threw a glance at Giles. "I expect you on duty tomorrow morning, Butler. Congratulations." And with a quick nod, he was gone.

TWO HOURS LATER, they were finally alone in Rosamund's sitting room. Giles poured them a glass of wine each and sat back beside her on the sofa with a sigh of contentment. He had already removed his coat and sword belt and loosened his cravat so that it hung rakishly over one shoulder. Rosamund had kicked off her slippers, and now drew her feet under her body and leaned comfortably against him.

He said idly, "I arranged with Edwards to contribute to household costs for as long as we're here."

"You don't want to find a place of our own?"

"I doubt we would," he said frankly. "The town is heaving as it is. And besides, if I'm called away urgently, I would rather you were with friends."

"Until you can send for me," she said anxiously.

He smiled. "Until I can send for you. It's funny, you know. In my head, I know we could march on Boney at any time. Or that he could march on us. But here, with you, war seems a whole world away."

"Is that good?"

"It's perfect."

She smiled and sipped her wine. Her free hand was held in his, and he idly, delicately stroked the soft skin between her thumb and forefinger, arousing pleasant little butterflies while they sat together in a kind of heavy yet blissful silence.

He said, "At army weddings, there is usually dancing."

"I'm sorry," she said quickly. "Do you miss it? I would have loved to dance but…"

"I only want to dance with you."

"And I with you, but there is no orchestra. I don't even have my music box."

"You can sing."

"So I can!" She sprang delightedly to her feet, and Giles laughed, taking the glass from her hand and setting it on the table beside his.

He rose and bowed elaborately, then led her to the middle of the room, where he took her in his arms and her breath quickened in pleasure and excitement.

"Music, if you please," he said softly.

Obligingly, she began to hum a well-known waltz, the same one they had danced to at the Cornhills' ball. He joined in, making both the music and the dance more exuberant. Soon they were both laughing breathlessly as they whirled about the room in barely retained rhythm.

Quite naturally, their steps gentled once more, and their voices became lost in each other's mouths. By then, they had somehow waltzed into the bedchamber, and there, they continued the dance to a sweet and ecstatic conclusion.

EPILOGUE

August 1819

AS THE HIRED traveling coach approached the gates of Cuttyngs, Rosamund found her stomach tightening with all the old dread. Giles's fingers closed around hers, easing the furious anxiety.

After all, they had visited here before they had left for India in 1816, and the whole atmosphere of the place was completely different. It wasn't so much Cuttyngs that worried her. It was her old feelings, old memories.

Which made no sense considering the cascade of happy and busy new ones. Her year-old son, bouncing and wriggling on Giles's knee, for one. Her three-year-old daughter, Lily, on the opposite bench for another. Temporarily, Lily had stopped chattering and asking questions in order to stare eagerly out of the window.

The carriage slowed and turned, sweeping through the gates. Old Dan waved and called greetings from his garden, and a flash of memory did strike Rosamund—her first meeting with Giles, there, avoiding Dan's line of vision, stealing General, the horse.

Smiling, she cast a glance at her husband to see if he remembered, too. The gleam of mischief in his eyes told her he did. The last few years had added a certain distinction to his countenance and his manner, for he was a Colonel now, responsible for an entire regiment, and he wore it well. Not that he had lost his sense of fun, but he took his duties seriously. Of course, he always had, though not everyone had realized that.

Now he carried the wounds and losses of Waterloo, and the complicated experiences of India, alongside marriage and fatherhood. In all, despite the whirlwind of activity that often surrounded him, he was a calmer, more contented person.

I have my place in that achievement, she thought with as much smugness as humility. For however much he loved army life, he loved coming home to her more.

Not that she had been idle in India herself, or on the long voyages there and back. She had made friends among the local women and learned from them, helped them when she could. She had treated wounds and sickness among the soldiers and their families with considerable success, so that now they came to her with everything from toothache to infection. On board the ship, the potion she had first developed to help Mrs. Edwards with her seasickness had been much in demand.

And of course, traveling with small children was both risky and difficult. She had known that when they sailed for India with Lily only a few months old. Neither was India's climate kind, but she had read and learned and worked hard to protect them from illness and insects and worse, and on the whole, she had succeeded. They had two healthy, happy children, and she rather suspected there would be a third next spring.

She had found her place in life, the one she seemed to have been born to hold, as Giles's wife and mother to their children. She was useful. She was loved, loving, and happy. The nightmare that had been Cuttyngs could no longer touch her.

She sat forward with unexpected eagerness as the carriage swept around the bend and the house came into view.

"Oh, my, it's a palace," Lily said, awed. "Is the duke like a prince?"

Rosamund laughed. "Yes, I suppose he is in a way. But mostly, he's your stepbrother."

Giles was watching her, even now not quite sure that she would never miss the kind of life she had given up to adventure with him. "Is it like coming home after all?" he asked.

The carriage pulled up at the front door, and she bumped her forehead lightly against his shoulder. "Home is wherever you are," she said softly, and turned to face not the past but the future.

About Mary Lancaster

Mary Lancaster lives in Scotland with her husband, three mostly grown-up kids and a small, crazy dog.

Her first literary love was historical fiction, a genre which she relishes mixing up with romance and adventure in her own writing. Her most recent books are light, fun Regency romances written for Dragonblade Publishing: *The Imperial Season* series set at the Congress of Vienna; and the popular *Blackhaven Brides* series, which is set in a fashionable English spa town frequented by the great and the bad of Regency society.

Connect with Mary on-line – she loves to hear from readers:

Email Mary:
Mary@MaryLancaster.com

Website:
www.MaryLancaster.com

Newsletter sign-up:
http://eepurl.com/b4Xoif

Facebook:
facebook.com/mary.lancaster.1656

Facebook Author Page:
facebook.com/MaryLancasterNovelist

Twitter:
@MaryLancNovels

Amazon Author Page:
amazon.com/Mary-Lancaster/e/B00DJ5IACI

Bookbub:
bookbub.com/profile/mary-lancaster

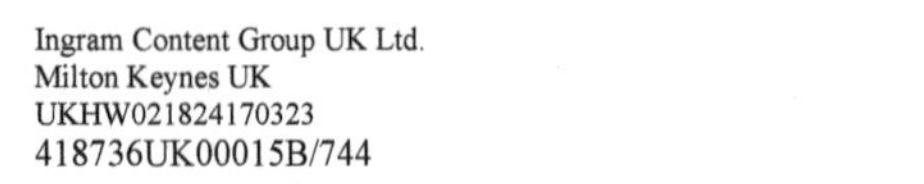
Ingram Content Group UK Ltd.
Milton Keynes UK
UKHW021824170323
418736UK00015B/744